In the time of Herod king of Judea there was a priest named Zechariah, who belonged to the priestly division of Abijah; his wife Elizabeth was also a descendant of Aaron. Both of them were righteous in the sight of God, observing all the Lord's commands and decrees blamelessly. But they were childless because Elizabeth was not able to conceive, and they were both very old.

—Luke 1:5-7 (NIV)

Extraordinary Women OF THE BIBLE

Extraordinary Women of the Bible

TENDER MERCIES

ELIZABETH'S STORY

Texie Susan Gregory

Guideposts

TENDER MERCIES

ELIZABETH'S STORY

DEDICATION

To Tim, forever and always, still my love
To Tyler, my inspiration to persevere
To Libby, my prayer warrior

ACKNOWLEDGMENTS

Elizabeth intrigues me, as I, too, was an older mother. (Not *that* old!) For many years, being a mother seemed a distant and improbable dream. When it became a reality, I was thrilled the entire time—until labor. That's when I decided having a baby wasn't a good idea and tried to crawl off the delivery table and go home. (True story.)

Writing a book is similar. It tugs at your heart like an impossible dream. When it becomes a reality, you're delighted—until the "labor" begins. A heartfelt thank-you to those who kept me from "crawling off the table."

Stacie Ciesynski, Sheri Shannon, Linda Vanderhoof, Kay White, prayer team: "I thank my God every time I remember you" (Philippians 1:3).

Donna Holland, Joy Shelton, Texie Soltis, Victoria Warren, beta readers: "I have not stopped giving thanks for you, remembering you in my prayers" (Ephesians 1:16).

Guideposts' editors/shepherds: "I will give you shepherds after my own heart, who will lead you with knowledge and understanding" (Jeremiah 3:15).

Bob Hostetler, agent: "I can no other answer make but thanks, and thanks, and ever thanks" (Shakespeare, *Twelfth Night*).

Cast of
CHARACTERS

BIBLICAL CAST

Elizabeth • mother of John the Baptist

Gabriel • angel

Jesus • the Christ

John • prophet born to Elizabeth and Zechariah

Mary • mother of Jesus

Zechariah • husband of Elizabeth

BIBLICAL REFERENCES

Aaron • first high priest

Abijah • a descendant of Aaron, one of twenty-four divisions
of priests

David • king and psalmist

Elijah • prophet and miracle worker

Hagar • Sarah's handmaid given to Abraham to conceive a child

Isaiah • prophet who prophesied the coming of the Messiah

Sarah and Abraham • patriarch and matriarch of Jewish nation

Shiphrah and Puah • midwives who defied pharaoh

Solomon • king known for his wisdom and wealth

HISTORICAL CAST

Caesar Augustus • Roman emperor

Hillel the Elder • religious leader

Menahem the Essene • false messiah

FICTIONAL CAST

Abba (Joseph) • Elizabeth's father

Anna • Mary's mother

Caleb ben Shimon • friend

Eli ben Ezra • younger brother of Jesse

Imma • Elizabeth's mother

Jesse ben Ezra • Myrah's husband

Joachim ben Asher • Mary's father

Libi • Myrah's daughter

Myrah • Zechariah's sister

Nathan • Anna's father

Nila • Elizabeth's friend

Samuel the Essene • Abba's brother

Tavi • Anna's mother

Glossary of
TERMS

abba • father

Adonai • Lord

Amidah • a prayer

amphora • a jar with two handles and a long neck

Bar'chu • a prayer service

bimah • an altar

Elohim • God

Essene • a Jewish sect

etrog • a fruit used in festival of Sukkot

imma • mother

ketubah • a Jewish marriage contract

lashon hara • listening to or speaking evil of someone

mezuzah • a small scroll inscribed with Deut. 6:4-9 and 11:13-21
and the name Shaddai placed in a case fixed to the doorpost

mikveh • an ancient Jewish ritual practice of water immersion,
traditionally used for cleansing, purification and transformation.

mohar • bride price

mohel • a person who performs the Jewish rite of circumcision

Nazarite • an Israelite consecrated to the service of God

Pesach • Passover

quern • a hand mill for grinding grain

Sanhedrin • supreme council of the Jews

schuckeling • swaying during prayer

Shabbat • Sabbath

shamor • the Shabbat candle of observance

Shema • a Jewish prayer in Deuteronomy 6:4

shiva • seven days of formal mourning

shofar • a ram's horn trumpet

Sukkot • a harvest festival also commemorating the Exodus

tallit • a prayer shawl

Torah • the first five books of the Bible

zahor • the Shabbat candle of remembrance

CHAPTER ONE

Elizabeth raced into the courtyard. Whirling around a corner, she nearly knocked a small woman to the ground. She reached to steady her as they teetered. "Oh, *Imma*, I'm so sorry."

Imma regained her balance, pulled her into a hug, then gently pushed her away and frowned. "You've been outside. Have you finished your morning duties?"

Elizabeth winced. "I was—"

"And we've told you repeatedly to walk, yet you nearly toppled me over."

"But—"

"I'd never guess you're turning fifteen today."

The playful glint in Imma's eyes and the corner of her mouth inching up gave her away.

"I thought I was really in trouble and that you forgot my birthday."

"Abba is not the only one who can play. Besides, I'll never forget all the work I did fifteen years ago to bring you into the world. Someday, you'll know your own child pains and understand."

Elizabeth gave her a quick kiss, then spun in a circle. "Maybe. But I'm not even betrothed yet." She grinned, snatched a fig, and bit into it. "And today, I'm eating only figs and pomegranates." Sticky juice smeared her chin.

Imma's silence surprised her. "Is all well, Imma? You're so serious."

"Elizabeth, dear one, your abba has decided that today is—"

"Have you told her?" Abba stood in the doorway, his feet apart—a soldier's stance despite his priesthood. His voice was gruff, its heaviness further dimming the morning's joy. Where was Abba's usual smile? Had Imma's illness returned?

Elizabeth shivered. Icy chills like winter rain slid between her shoulders and down her spine. The last time she'd known this shiver was when Imma almost died of a wasting sickness.

"You tell her." Imma's eyes flashed at him with rare anger. "You chose. You did this."

Elizabeth's fingers tightened around the fig. Pulp oozed through her fingers. "Tell me what? Chose what?"

"Bethy." He tilted his bearded chin down and locked his green-eyed gaze on her. "Today is not only your birthday. It's also your betrothal day. We rejoice with you!"

She choked on a laugh. "Dearest Abba, I haven't chosen anyone."

A seldom-seen frown appeared on his face. "It is not for you to choose." He pointed to his chest. "I am the abba. I decide what is best for you."

Imma bustled to her side. "He will be here soon. Come, let's prepare you to be a lovely bride."

A lovely *bride*? Her laughter fled as her eyes narrowed and her insides knotted. "He who, Imma? Do I know him?"

Abba cleared his throat. "He's a priest. It's fitting for the daughter of a priest to marry a priest since we are descendants of Aaron and you carry the same name as Aaron's wife. Remember, too, your imma is of the line of David. You must marry a man equal in worth to you."

Those were familiar words, but the others—*groom, bride, marry*—were for next year or the next. Heart racing, she began to tremble. Surely it was not Zechariah, the only unmarried priest she knew. "But do I know him? Does he live here?"

"We know you want children. He's never married and wants a young wife able to give him many heirs. He's respected in our community, teaches at the synagogue, quite a scholar—spent the last five years studying with the great rabbi Hillel. He bought the empty house near his abba so he could study in peace. You'll have your own home, no demanding mother-in-law to please. I knew you'd like that." His laugh was forced.

The only person she could think of seemed ancient. It could not be him. She clutched the table in front of her, felt blood drain from her face and her hands turn clammy cold. "No, I—"

Abba held up his hand, warning her not to speak. "It is done. We have agreed on terms, and I have the gold ring he gifted you. Accept it as the obedient daughter you can be." He removed the slender band from the sash around his waist.

A ring—symbol of bondage. Servitude. Subjection.

Iron determination lined his smile. She knew this smile. Rare. Implacable. Abba was law or laughter. Nothing in between. Once he decided, neither tears nor pleading changed his mind.

"Yes, you know him and his family. He joined us last Shabbat."

She sorted backward for the blurred memory of last Shabbat. Then she remembered. He was short, with thin hair, delicate as a gazelle.

Zechariah.

His sister, Myrah, her dearest friend—a beauty, always laughing, often mischievous. Her older brother? Unremarkable. Invisible. Nondescript. If Myrah spoke of him it was to boast of his diligence in studying in Jerusalem or when home, at the synagogue. He had nodded to her on the rare occasion their paths crossed but never spoken.

"He's boring." If Myrah knew of this and had not told her, she'd never forgive her. "And ancient!"

"He's only a few years older than you—seven, I think—a suitable age, a fine match. He is a good man." Abba's eyes warmed with tenderness. "I'm trusting him with my greatest joy, Bethy—you.

"I have accepted his *mohar*. His gift for the privilege of marrying you was of the finest craftsmanship." The warmth vanished. "It is settled." He crossed his arms, stone-faced. A sharp nod punctuated his words.

All hope of wheedling him to her way fled. Dazed, she allowed Imma to guide her into the house. A new tunic—shroud of her girlhood—was slipped over her head. Her hair was brushed, rose scented oil rubbed into her hands.

She roused to the inescapable reality as silver bracelets—chains—were secured around her arms and wrists, binding her to a life she did not want, forcing her acquiescence, hurting her pride. She—the acknowledged beauty of the town, educated above the others, only child of indulgent parents—given to a man waif-thin who looked twice her age.

Elizabeth clutched her imma's hands, holding them to her heart. The silver bracelets jangled as they slid down to her elbows. "Imma, please stop Abba. Why is he doing this to me? I don't want to marry that old priest. Can't you say something? Convince him this is wrong? I will be miserable forever. Please, Imma?"

Imma drew her close, nestled her against her soft shoulder. "If I'd been aware of his plans in time…" She sighed. "Now it is done, and child, he's only a bit older than you. It seems hard, but Adonai will bring good from it. I promise you this. Perhaps you will be the one to bear the true messiah."

"But it's happening so fast."

"Zechariah's abba has been ill and wants to see his children settled, in case he does not recover."

"But—"

"Elizabeth, you are becoming a strong woman, stronger than you yet know. Accept that it is done. We will make the best of this—a trip to Jerusalem for the finest cloth and sandals—your abba will not complain. We will even purchase household goods and linens. Your Nazareth cousins, Nathan and Tavi, will attend the wedding next year. I'm sure they'll bring their daughter. Would you like Anna to be one of your attendants? Isn't she eleven? A little young to be a bridesmaid, but she's certainly still a virgin."

This must be how a rabbit felt beneath a hawk's wings. Nowhere to hide, no escape, no defense, only the darkening shadow, wings thrumming death as it circled, lowered, talons outstretched to snatch an innocent's life.

If she was as strong as Imma said, she'd refuse to agree to this marriage. If Adonai wanted good from this, He'd stop it now.

Make the best of it? New clothes and fire tongs mattered little.

She wrapped her arms around her middle and, sobbing, doubled over. Abba had always doted on her even if she was a girl. Had she angered him that he would do this?

Finally spent, she calmed as Imma pressed a cool cloth to the back of her neck, washed her face, and dried her eyes. A growing discomfort warned that the day would worsen.

"Imma, my cycle will start soon." She grimaced as a cramp clutched her belly.

"Sit. I will bring you a tea of chamomile to ease your cramps."

"Abba?"

"The men will have to wait. You cannot faint during the ceremony, but we need to hurry before you are unclean."

She waited until she was alone before she stood. Would jumping and twisting cause the blood to flow sooner? She sat. It would only postpone the inevitable.

Too soon she joined her unwanted groom and their parents before a few neighbors.

Zechariah fidgeted, as nervous as she was reluctant. Maybe he did not want this either. Hope rose. Fell. His voice sounded strong and sure as he recited Hosea's words inviting Elohim into their covenant.

"I will betroth you to me forever; I will betroth you in righteousness and justice, in love and compassion. I will betroth you in faithfulness, and you will acknowledge the Lord."

Forever sounded…endless. Elizabeth swallowed the bile rising in her throat.

Too soon wine was poured into Abba's favorite goblet and placed before the groom's father, who handed it to his son. Too soon Zechariah wrapped both his thin hands around the goblet's bowl and held it out in front of her.

Her stomach cramped. She did not want the cup. She did not want him. She did not want to be here. She wanted to curl up under a blanket with a warmed sheepskin. She clamped her jaws together until they ached—imprisoning her sobs.

"This cup I offer to you." Uncertainty tinged his voice. He must have guessed that she did not want this.

She stared at his offering, her girlish dreams fading. Accepting the drink, she'd place her life and those of her children in his delicate hands. Rejecting it, she insulted everyone.

By Hebrew law, the choice was hers. And hers, as well, the choice to displease and humiliate the two people she loved most, the two she never doubted loved her. Refusing this groom exacted a price she'd not pay. Her beloved abba would be dishonored. Zechariah too would be shamed, and Myrah, furious on behalf of her brother, would no longer be her friend.

She allowed him to press the goblet in her trembling hands with his icy fingers. Hypnotized by the rippling redness inside the cup, she hesitated. If she drank, her life was over, consigned to this man she did not know, who did not know her.

Abba's words rang in her mind. "I'm trusting him with my greatest joy—you." Abba's love was a treasure more precious than Hebrew law.

She sipped from the cup.

Her husband's warm, full voice intoned the traditional words. "You are set apart for me according to the law of Moses and Israel." Joy and relief, evident in his tone.

Now betrothed, she fumbled with the required veil to cover her hair, wishing she could pull it all the way over her face. Did the others realize she did not want this? Could they read resignation in her face? Were her eyes red, her face grief-pale?

Amid the well-wishers, she added her name to the *ketubah*. She watched the ink darken as it dried. The signed contract could not be broken. She was betrothed, a bond as inescapable as marriage.

Abba cleared his throat—a sure tell that what followed would be unwelcome. This time he did not meet her eyes. Suspicious, she tensed. What could be worse than the commitment she'd made? She looked toward Imma, who watched with alarm.

"Zechariah has already fulfilled the ketubah contract. The house is prepared, and his abba and I have agreed the wedding will be in six weeks—"

Imma's gasp may have been heard in the next town. "*Six weeks*? Not a year?" She grasped her head as if in agony. "For my daughter's wedding? It's unheard of! How can I—"

Abba silenced her with a single sideways glance and continued.

"…as soon as his sister, Myrah, returns home. Daughter, your husband wishes to marry immediately."

"Your husband wishes…" What of my wishes? I do not wish to be married or spend my life with this old man or leave my imma's house. She bowed her head in outward submission, her clenched fists hidden in the folds of her clothes. Fifteen years old, bound to this man, her wishes mattered naught.

The shofar's deep cry startled Elizabeth awake, the long, loud blast announcing to the town that Zechariah's abba had chosen this night for his son to claim her as his wife.

Too soon. Adonai spare me for one more day. Her heart raced— from the shofar's blast or that the inescapable had come?

"Wake up." Myrah shook her shoulder. "He's on his way! Tonight! Finally! You're almost my sister."

Elizabeth scooted to the edge of the bed where she and Anna had fallen asleep.

"I can't do this."

If anyone heard, they ignored her. Imma rushed into the room.

"Stand up. Let me see my little girl as a beautiful bride." Imma brushed a tear from her eye. "May you give your husband many sons."

She stood. Accepted the hugs. Did not move as her hair was rebrushed, her clothes straightened, scented oils reapplied on her arms and hands. Sandals were slipped on her feet, a cloak tied around her shoulders, the veil's folds arranged.

Anna stroked a corner of the veil's silkiness, in such awe that Elizabeth decided she'd give it to her for her own wedding in a few years.

Myrah, Nila, and a giggling Anna lit their lamps and scurried out the front door and into the courtyard, lifting their light so Zechariah and his friends, Caleb and Jesse, could see the way to the door. Elizabeth clung to Imma's strong, warm hands and tamped down suffocating fear.

"Imma, if you loved me, you'd not make me do this."

"Hush, child. You are a woman now, not a foolish girl who refuses to control her words."

Choking back a sob, she heard Zechariah's strong voice answering her abba. "I come to your house for you to give me your daughter, Elizabeth, to wife. She is my wife and I am her husband from this day forward and forever."

Imma tugged her forward until she stood before her groom. Abba kissed her forehead and placed her clammy hand into Zechariah's hand.

"Go with Adonai, Bethy. I do this believing it is best." He canted his head. "Bethy, heed these words. The great rabbi, Hillel the Elder said, 'Take care of yourself—you never know when the world will need you.'" A tear sparkled in his eye. He reached for Imma, wrapped her in his embrace, and looked down to wink at her.

Was it possible that she and Zechariah would ever smile at each other, happy just to be in the same room, winking with shared secrets?

Family, friends, and neighbors cheered, clapped, sang, and danced as they escorted the newlywed couple out of the courtyard and along the streets to her new home. Lamplight and flaming torches lit their way. Candles glowed in the arched windows. White flower petals, symbolizing purity, covered the path to the house.

The revelers pushed the couple through the entrance and then closed the door behind them. Laughter rang from outside, gradually fading as their loved ones returned to their beds. In seven days, they'd return for a feast to celebrate the union.

Crickets serenaded the night—the only other sound the breathing of two married strangers. Zechariah and Elizabeth faced each other. Solemn. Uncertain. Awkward. He removed his cloak. She loosened the ties of her mantle. Kneeling, he untied the laces of his sandals. She sat on a low bench, slid her feet free, and placed both their sandals by the door. Her wedding veil drooped around her shoulders.

She trembled. Cold. Frightened. Exhausted.

"Did your imma prepare you for what is next?" His whisper boomed in the room's silence.

She said words I didn't understand, words I don't remember. No, I don't know how to be married. I don't know how to be a wife. I don't even know you. I can't do this. I don't want to do this. Adonai, do You hear me?

Her head began to ache, but she nodded. "She told me what to expect."

Zechariah stepped forward, took her cold hands in his and raised them to his lips. Her feet were bare against his—an odd intimacy—her skin against a man's skin.

***

So that was it and it was over. She was a wife in full and understood what before had been a mystery despite Imma's words. Elizabeth rolled to her side away from her husband, his snoring a soft rumble like distant thunder. Imma had blushed when telling her what to expect, but her eyes had twinkled as if "it" was a good thing. Elizabeth sighed. Although Zechariah seemed happy, she wasn't. She must be doing something wrong.

Zechariah had avoided touching her any more than necessary. Her skin was soft. She sniffed. Her body and clothes were clean, and mint freshened her breath. He'd chosen to marry her, so he didn't find her repulsive. She refused tears, refused defeat, refused to wonder "what if."

Seven more days of seclusion with Zechariah. This man was her husband for all of life. Together they'd have to work through any challenges, even intimate ones. Confused, sore, and weary, she curled into a ball and sought the escape of sleep.

Seven days later, nothing had changed.

***

Elizabeth's face had been sunset red once before. Childishly, she'd sneaked out of the house one afternoon and fallen asleep face up under the scorching Judean sun. The memory of blisters and peeling skin kept her from repeating that defiance. Even lavender oil had not eased the sun's sting.

Thankful for the dark since she was red enough to glow, she cringed as Zechariah handed the bloodied "proof of virginity" cloth to witnesses her parents had chosen. It would be wrapped in a leather pouch and returned to her abba to keep it safe. Another wave of crimson flushed her face.

Ceremony and consummation complete, she had only to endure the final feast. Thankfully, Zechariah had agreed to break with the tradition of the feast being at the groom's house since his imma was deceased and Myrah too young to manage it alone.

Neighbors and family gathered to escort them to the feast, the unmarried girls glancing at her sideways and giggling, the single men studiously avoiding her eyes. She forced a smile as Myrah wriggled her way to the front of the crowd and threw both arms around her in an exuberant hug.

"Sisters. We are true sisters now. It's perfect! My best friend married to the most wonderful brother in the world. Imagine! Now nothing will ever come between us."

"Nothing."

The girls linked arms with Anna between them as Zechariah swaggered forward to walk with the other men. Soon, two men straggled behind—Jesse and his little tagalong brother, Matthias.

"Join us." Myrah wheedled, beaming up at Jesse. "Isn't Elizabeth a beautiful bride?"

"I guess so. Sure." Matthias tried for the deep voice of a man.

"Beautiful as a fresh turnip." Jesse winked, and Elizabeth resisted the urge to stick out her tongue.

Myrah's smile faded. "Oh, I left the amphora gift from your imma at your house, and I promised I'd bring it. I'll hurry and catch up with you in just a bit. Anna, come with me. We'll see who walks faster."

"Thank you, Myrah. Jesse, you and Matthias should walk with the other men. I'm a married woman now." She looked straight ahead and concentrated on balancing, lifting one tired foot in front of the other. Matthias rushed forward as if glad to escape the company of a woman.

Jesse elbowed her. "So proper? No one will see or care. Everyone understands we've been friends for years. Besides, it's dark."

She looked at the flaring torches that lit their way. "Not very dark."

"I want to talk to you. I'll catch up with the others before they reach the feast." He looked down at her. "You're not happy. If I'd known in time, I'd have married you, Turnip. Even if you're more my sister than a real girl. I hate to see you so sad."

She slanted her eyes up at her childhood friend. "Abba."

"Ah. And you had to obey." Jesse nodded, understanding. "Once he decides, there's no turning back. Did he give you any choice?"

"About Zechariah? Do you think an old, skinny man is who I'd choose? At least he has nice teeth." She bit her lip. "Forgive me. It's wrong to speak so of my husband. I'm not used to being married."

"He's not really old, Turnip. He just looks…"

Their gaze met as they settled on the same word. "Ancient."

"Jesse, I had no choice, no chance to choose for myself, not even a warning."

"You did have a choice, Turnip."

"Why do you call me that? Stop it! Yes, I had a choice to thwart Abba, to hurt Zechariah, and to appear fickle before our people, but there's no one else—"

"Not even me?"

She snorted. "I know which girl you've been watching for years, and it isn't me." She smoothed her hand over the beautiful veil. "But Abba has been generous with clothes and comforts. He'd never admit it, but I think he feels guilty for ruining my life and forcing me to marry when I did not want to."

"Guilty for marrying you to Zechariah?"

Elizabeth jumped at the strangled words from Myrah. She whipped around to see Myrah standing behind her, face stricken with hurt and betrayal.

"You did not choose my brother—the ancient man? You were forced?"

She froze. "It's not like it sounded, Myrah."

"My hearing is fine. Your life is ruined."

"Please, will you listen to me?" Elizabeth reached for her friend. Myrah glared, jerked her arm out of reach, thrust the fragile amphora at Anna, and stomped away.

"Myrah!"

Jesse patted Elizabeth's shoulder. "I'll talk to her, Turnip. Enjoy your wedding feast." With his long, muscular legs, he easily caught up with Myrah.

If anyone could calm her friend, it was Jesse.

Zechariah walked back and smiled at her. "Hurry, Elizabeth. We have guests waiting."

Aching in places she'd never known could ache, exhausted from the sleepless nights of hurried wedding preparations and the demands of the seven-day wedding week, Elizabeth summoned the strength Imma promised lay within. She was the daughter of a priest of the line of Aaron. Not only the daughter but the wife of a priest, and maybe—*please, Adonai*—in nine months, she'd be the imma of a priest or even King Messiah. She raised her chin, forced a smile, and quickened her step. Abba was iron. She was steel.

Anna's hand slipped into hers and squeezed it. In young wisdom, she walked silently beside her newly married cousin.

CHAPTER TWO

Six months later

T urnip?"

Elizabeth smiled. Someday she'd make him tell her why he called her the one vegetable she detested. Leaving her spindle on the table, she breezed into the courtyard. "Shalom, Jesse." Her smile faded. Jesse avoided her eyes and his face remained solemn. He swallowed and swallowed again.

"I asked Myrah's abba to marry me. Tomorrow."

"Really?" She smirked. "That's rather unusual."

Jesse swallowed. "I mean I asked her abba if Myrah can be his wife, uh, my wife. I wanted you to hear it from me since we'll be in the same family and there's still strain between you two."

"And because Zechariah will forget to mention it and Myrah will intentionally not tell me and enjoy seeing me look a fool. Thank you."

"She'll come around, Turnip."

"It's been six months." Six months without her friend. Six months without a sign of a child. Six months of almost nightly meeting Zechariah's needs.

"I'm not sure anymore. She forgave you, Jesse. Why not me?"

"I didn't say anything against her brilliant brother. I only agreed with you. Besides, I'm charming."

Elizabeth pretended to cough and choke. "At least one of us thinks that."

He laughed. "The betrothal is tomorrow. Try to be there—for me, Turnip. Myrah's stubborn, but she's always been the one for me."

A tight smile was her answer.

"Jesse." Zechariah, returning from teaching at the synagogue, stopped their guest at the courtyard's entrance. As he peered up into Jesse's eyes, his smile was gentle. "I have heard the news and could not wish a better husband for my sweet little sister. Almighty has blessed us to become one family. Together we will celebrate the holy days, and our children will grow up among their cousins. It is as it should be."

"You will attend my betrothal on the morrow?"

"Of course we will, won't we, Elizabeth?"

She did not answer. It had not been a question.

The day of the betrothal dawned cool enough for Elizabeth to wear a thick, woolen scarf dyed blue, a wedding gift from Nila. Hopefully, Myrah would not remember the gift or be too enthralled with the ceremony to notice her presence.

When she and Zechariah drew near Myrah's home, the crowd parted for him to move to the front near his sister and their abba. She pretended not to see her parents beckoning her closer. They'd insist she stand near the front with them since their families would be joined.

Jesse caught her eye and gave an almost imperceptible smile and nod. He'd understand that she lingered in back because she loved Myrah and him too much to spoil their big day.

More neighbors gathered. Elizabeth edged backward, staying on the fringes of the group. Myrah and Jesse's betrothal had been planned amid joyous agreement—so different from her own betrothal. Alone amid the cheers and laughter, the questions and rituals, a singular tone caused her to turn. Matthias—why was he not with his parents?—stood talking with a man she'd never seen in the town.

No words reached her ears, only tones. Matthias listened intently to the long-haired, bearded stranger dressed in white robes. The man's hands rested open and relaxed by his side, his body wiry with a leanness that bespoke hunger and fasting. An Essene. This man had taken a vow to keep himself pure and obedient to Adonai. It was unusual for an Essene to leave his own community of prayer and Torah study.

Uneasy with a stranger in their midst, even one of a group regarded as godly, she sidled closer and heard a single word, "niece," just as Matthias swiveled to point in her direction. The stranger turned and looked at her with the same slanted green eyes she'd seen every day before she married. This man must be the beloved brother Abba often spoke of, her uncle Samuel.

He walked closer. Unafraid, she remained where she was. He would not touch her in case she was impure.

"I have not seen you since you were an infant and spit up on me."

His eyes twinkled with the same kindness as Abba's. "Forgive me, Uncle. I will try not to repeat that." They shared a smile. "Have you come to visit my abba?"

The light in his eyes dimmed, his voice dropped. "The Lord has allowed me to come and see him once more."

Surprised by his demeanor, she hastened to reassure him. "He will be so pleased. He speaks of you often. If you'd like, I'll walk with you to our home, and you can rest from your travels. Imma has fresh bread, and she makes the best goat cheese and—"

Samuel shook his head. "I am passing through and can only see him for a moment."

Elizabeth ignored his protest. She turned to Matthias. "Please hurry and find my abba and imma. Tell them they have a reluctant guest." She grinned at her uncle. This time he did not return it.

The child darted away and soon returned with her abba.

"Your imma is busy helping with the celebration, directing anyone who will listen. Who is our—" His eyes widened. "Samuel?"

"Brother."

Abba's arms opened to embrace his brother, but Samuel smiled and stepped back

"Remember, as an Essene, I am forbidden physical contact. Do not encourage me to break my vow."

Abba nodded. Elizabeth guessed he barely restrained himself from wrapping his arms around Samuel and lifting him off the ground in a huge Abba hug. His grin shone as wide and bright as she'd ever seen it.

"It has been too long. Welcome. You remember my daughter. Come to our home. Stay with us. Tell us of your life. I have missed you, Samuel."

"And I, you. But, my brother, I cannot stay. I have come only to tell you our relatives, Nathan and Tavi, will travel to Jerusalem with their daughter, Anna, for Hannukah." Samuel closed his eyes and drew in a deep breath as if pained. "I am here to bid you farewell as I promised."

Abba stared at his bother. His face grayed. His eyes lost their joy. "Farewell?"

Stunned, Elizabeth rounded on her uncle. "You have only just arrived, and now you leave us again? Where are you going in such a hurry that you cannot visit?"

"Where He leads me."

"Why bother stopping here if you will not stay and visit?"

"My niece still spits."

Annoyed at his reproof, she turned to her abba. "Talk to him."

Abba ignored her.

The two men shared a solemn look.

Abba looked away first. "Then the time is near." His shoulders slumped as if in resignation. "Thank you, my brother. You are a virtuous man. I knew you were worthy of my trust. Shalom. Shalom."

"The soul is immortal and imperishable, my brother. We part in peace forever and ever." Samuel turned and walked away, his sandals scattering fine dirt behind him.

Elizabeth jammed her hands on her hips. "What does that mean? Hello, goodbye. Time for what, Abba?"

Wordlessly, he shook his head. He turned, suddenly an old man. Leaving the festivities, he wandered away.

Troubled, she watched until he was out of sight, then strode toward home. Tomorrow, she'd visit and ask Imma what distressed him.

"Elizabeth, wait."

Matthias caught up with her and rested grimy hands on his knees until he stopped panting.

"You walk fast for a girl." He flicked sweaty edges of hair from his eyes. "The man I was talking to, that's your uncle? He's an Essene? A real one?"

"Yes, and yes, a real one. Why?"

"I'm going to be an Essene." Matthias stuck out his thin ten-year-old chest.

Elizabeth hid her smile. "You will be a fine Essene, Matthias."

He grinned. "Really? You think so?"

"No doubt. Would you tell me why you choose this path? Did Adonai call you to it? It's a hard life."

"They live in the desert with no immas, no sisters, and no girls, and they grow their own food and study Torah."

"I see. A wonderful life. You love to study Adonai's law?"

"Zechariah said I'm his best student."

Elizabeth inclined her head. "That's quite a compliment from my husband."

He stepped closer and whispered. "I heard the Messiah will be an Essene and will deliver us from evil."

"Matthias! Matthias ben Ezra!"

They turned at the frantic call.

"There you are! I was afraid you left with that Essene. Why did he come to our town? What did he say to you?" His imma shook her head at Elizabeth. "Essenes! That's all he talks about since he heard of Menahem and his prophecies. You didn't encourage him, did you?"

"Heard of who?"

Without waiting for a reply, she pushed her son toward the town center and called back to Elizabeth. "I decide what's best for him. If you'd have your own child, you'd understand and leave mine alone."

Bewildered, Elizabeth had no words. Married a little over six months and already criticized for not conceiving? She was still becoming accustomed to being a wife.

***

Zechariah watched Elizabeth leave the betrothal ceremony that had been so different from theirs. The droop of her shoulders tugged at his heart.

Maybe he'd been wrong to approach her abba before she knew of his interest and had a chance to persuade her to marry him. His plan had seemed quicker, more efficient.

He liked plans. Betrothed. Married. A child in nine months. Another child each year. He'd continue teaching at the synagogue. She'd manage the house, marketing, laundering, and raising the children. She'd need to grow herbs to season the meals she cooked each day. He'd allow her to grow flowers—anything to please her.

His plan had run smoothly until she was late conceiving a child. He'd been patient, but ignoring a plan displeased him—so did not respecting and observing traditional customs.

She'd stayed at the back instead of standing beside him during the ceremony as a wife should have—Myrah would never be so thoughtless. Then she'd wandered off to talk to little Matthias and a stranger, an Essene.

She must not understand that he needed her respect. If she behaved disrespectfully, rumors would spread and threaten his position as a teacher in the synagogue. He'd speak with her in private and not embarrass her. She'd appreciate his consideration. He'd gently correct her. She'd be remorseful, and he'd be forgiving.

Elizabeth's eyes narrowed in a face red with fury. "You know nothing and understand less. Your precious sister would have been livid if I'd stood by her side. Ask Jesse. Maybe he can explain it to you in words you can grasp."

"Jesse is not my wife and does not answer to me."

"Blessed is he."

"Blessed...," Zechariah sputtered. "You have disgraced yourself and me by ignoring the betrothal, leaving the ceremony to talk to a stranger and not congratulating the bride—your sister-in-law—and the groom you claim is a friend."

"The groom understands, and your sweet little sister, the bride, is delighted I said nothing to her. Ask her."

He hadn't realized her eyebrows could go so high. "You are nothing like Myrah. I do not understand you, Elizabeth."

"That's the first true thing you've said." She pursed her lips. "You don't and you never will."

"Only King Solomon could understand you."

She snorted. "Solomon never understood any of his seven hundred wives. And you'll never be close to being as wise as a Solomon."

"Why did I ever want to marry you?"

She drooped, her defiance fleeing. "I don't know, Zechariah. I wish you hadn't."

He walked out the door without closing it. She wished she dared slam it behind him.

"Imma, my mouth! Again! I should sew it closed and never speak another word." Elizabeth propped her elbows on the well-worn table and her chin on her hands. "I apologized. He said he forgave me, but in some ways, I'm glad it happened. I think it's the first time we've been completely honest with each other."

Imma tsked. "That kind of 'honesty' doesn't heal. It scabs over."

"Did you and Abba ever argue like that?"

"Once." Imma looked away. "We said cruel words to each other. I don't remember why we fought or who threw the first word stone. When it was over and we realized the pain we'd inflicted on each other, we vowed it would not happen again. We often disagreed, but we never tried to hurt or demean the other." Shame colored Imma's face. "I still remember how those vicious words wounded my Joseph. It took a long time for us to fully trust each other." She looked up. "It's not worth the pain it causes one you love."

"Imma, I'm sorry I hurt Zechariah, but…" Her voice fell to a whisper. "I don't love him. I'm not sure I ever will. Right now, I don't even like him. I'm a servant, not a wife that he cherishes, not like Abba cherishes you. Never once has he winked at me like Abba winks at you."

Imma reached across the table to take her hand. "Elizabeth, your abba and I spent years building our marriage, learning what caring means to each other. You will not have at six months what Joseph and I have spent a lifetime creating."

"Will I ever?"

"Pray. Keep Adonai at the center of your life. He will teach you how to love your husband and to control your words. You can be vicious, dear daughter. I believe David wrote a psalm just for you. 'Set a guard, O Lord, over my mouth; keep watch over the door of my lips.'"

"That sounds like what I need." She grimaced. "Zechariah and Myrah would advise two or three guards and a door bolted with iron. Did Abba tell you Uncle Samuel would agree with them?"

"They might be right."

"Imma!"

Elizabeth walked home the long way, a back trail that allowed her to avoid seeing anyone. Twice in one day her mouth spewed words she hadn't meant to say, had not realized she was thinking, and was ashamed to remember.

She paused by a eucalyptus tree and broke off a long, narrow leaf. Sharp perfume filled her nostrils, a clean piercing fragrance.

"This is how I want to be—a clean scent to all I meet." She rubbed the leaves between her fingers, releasing the oil. "Someone who eases pain, not causes it."

She looked upward. "Lord, if You still hear me, change me even if You need to send an entire army of angels to guard my mouth. Teach me to speak with kindness. Teach me to love my husband. Make me eucalyptus."

"Turnip, are you talking to a tree?"

She spun and saw Jesse leaning lazily against a boulder. "How dare you sneak up on me?"

He laughed. "Marriage to old Zechariah has not tamed you."

"Did you think it would?" She threw the leaf to the ground.

"Nothing and no one will ever change you, Turnip." He winked and turned to leave. "Be careful walking these back roads. I just saw a snake."

"You did not! Did you? I hate you, Jesse ben Ezra."

"Keep talking to the tree, Turnip."

Elizabeth crept forward placing each foot with nervous caution after scanning the path. It was not until she arrived home that she realized no army of angels had guarded her mouth. Adonai must not have heard or seen her.

But someone else had.

Myrah stood on her doorstep, arms crossed, lips pinched. "Is my ancient brother not enough for you that you meet my Jesse on a back trail? How often do you meet?"

"What?" Elizabeth wiped perspiration from her face. "We didn't 'meet.' We were just on the same trail and spoke."

"He came back laughing. How do you explain that?"

"You were spying on him? How do you explain that?"

Myrah turned on her heel and stomped away.

Elizabeth yanked off her headdress and wadded it into a ball. The gap between them had widened again.

***

"Elizabeth, I received word last week that Nathan and Tavi are coming to visit tomorrow. Their daughter, Anna, will be with them." Zechariah's smile was uncertain, cautious since their fight. "You like them, so I invited them to visit—to please you."

Tomorrow? He'd known since last week and could not have told her sooner? She bit her tongue since the army of angels remained absent from their duty.

"Thank you, Zechariah. You know I love Anna."

And Anna loved sweets. Elizabeth gathered the ingredients for honey date stuffed almonds and began to chop dried raisins and figs for a sweet cake.

She'd plan long walks for them. At night, they'd play Anna's favorite board game, checkers. She'd send a gift home with her too. Something to remind her of their time together. At almost twelve, she was too young for the silk wedding scarf and too old for a toy.

Elizabeth chose the largest water jug. With extra cleaning and cooking, she didn't have time to return for water twice this morning. The sun's height assured her most of the women had returned home by now. This time, she'd avoid their pointed stares to see if her body was swelling.

When she did conceive, she'd cut a huge star out of bright cloth and sew it on her tunic right over her belly, to announce she was with child. She giggled, imagining her husband's face. Zechariah would be mortified.

The spring was deserted. She groaned as she lifted the dripping jug. Lugging it to the speckled shade of a nearby tree, she stole a moment of rest before the uphill walk home. Drowsy, she leaned back against the tree, the spring's gentle gurgle lulling her to the past. Not so many years ago, she'd skipped here alongside Imma. While the women at the spring visited, the children splashed each other, gathered flowers, and, on very hot days, wove crowns and necklaces from water reeds and grasses.

A distant call broke her reverie. She yawned, sat forward, and snapped off a slender reed to wrap around her finger. As a child, she'd woven them together to create bracelets. Perfect! That's what she'd do for Anna. A handful of reeds and in an hour tonight she'd design a delicate bracelet. Myrah once admired her creations. Maybe she'd make Myrah one as an apology.

The sound of a person racing down the path brought her to her feet. No wise person ran in this heat. Someone must be injured and needing water. Alarmed, she waited, ready to offer her filled jug if the need was urgent.

Zechariah rounded the corner. He jerked to a stop, panting. "You're not hurt? You didn't fall?"

Puzzled, she shook her head.

"You were gone a long time, and I feared…" His voice trailed off.

Elizabeth hoisted the water jug. "Thank you, Zechariah."

"It's heavy?" Without waiting for her answer, he took it from her. "Let's hurry. We have guests arriving tomorrow."

Elizabeth smiled. Maybe she could learn to like him.

Elizabeth and Anna sat side by side creating intricate weaves with the reeds they'd gathered. Anna's smaller, nimble fingers tied the knots in Elizabeth's designs.

"Anna, I wish you lived closer. Isn't there someone you'd like to marry here in this town?"

"Yes. Yes. No." Anna's eyes sparkled.

"Hmm. There is someone, but he doesn't live here. Who is it?"

"Joachim ben Asher. He's a vintner near Nazareth. Our parents are friends, and he's everything I've ever dreamed of, not like your—" She dropped the reeds and clapped a hand over her mouth. "I'm sorry."

Elizabeth continued working with steady hands. "Zechariah is the man my abba chose for me. Imma says it will take us years to build a marriage like theirs. We are learning to trust and appreciate each other."

"You're miserable, aren't you?"

Elizabeth groaned in dismay. "Does it show?"

"Only to me. And probably your imma."

Elizabeth dropped the weaving in her lap. "Anna, I'm not carrying a child yet."

"Married for six months. Oh my, you should certainly be worried. Rename yourself Sarah."

"You'd be surprised how people stare at my belly or ask questions that are none of their concern." She pressed her fingers against her mouth and shook her head. "I should not talk to you about this—Anna, my marriage is the opposite of Abba's and Imma's. It's nothing like I expected."

Anna squeezed her hand. "I'm sorry."

"Anna, do you really know Joachim? Have you seen him upset or not feeling well? Does he listen to you? How does he talk to his imma? Do you like him? Does he wink at you when he thinks no one is watching?"

"I could break the ninth commandment and make you feel better."

Elizabeth hmphed. "That's my answer." She tucked her knees to her chest and wrapped her arms around them. "This is what I've learned about marriage. No, don't blush. Your imma must tell you about that part when it's the right time." She rested her chin on her knees. "Adonai has to teach you how to love, and you have to keep asking for wisdom, because sometimes He doesn't answer right away."

CHAPTER THREE

Zechariah grimaced. Elizabeth was the most beautiful woman the Almighty ever created, and she was his wife. Her beauty caused him to sin.

Every time he walked with her, his stride grew bolder, and his chest puffed out with pride—a fault he confessed and repented of daily. He knew others wondered how he'd persuaded her abba to accept his proposal. He wondered himself.

He was confident in his knowledge and smarter than many men, but his looks were, at best, unremarkable. He could discuss Torah all day but struggle to think of a single word in the presence of a woman. His teaching had been praised by the great Hillel, but expressing emotion was as difficult as chanting in Greek.

Elizabeth could read and write, and her voice was musical. Tall and slender, curved and lithe, no one compared to her.

Another sin. Comparison. "Forgive me, El Roi, Adonai, who sees even my thoughts."

He knew her abba had insisted she accept him as groom. He was short and thin, his eyes narrow, his nose large. Of course he'd not been her choice, but who was? Jesse? No. The spark between them spoke of friendship, not desire. Caleb? She found his friend tiresome.

If there had been no one else, he had a chance to convince her to love him as he loved her. More than anything, he wanted to please her, to see her face light up when she saw him, to see her smile when he walked through the door. His sister adored him. His imma—God rest her soul—had loved him. His wife…didn't.

He rubbed the ache from his knuckles. Gazed unseeing at the open scroll before him. Scratched beneath his chin.

How did one tell a woman—a wife—he cared for her?

He belched. She'd prepared a good meal.

"Elizabeth, the lentil stew was good."

She smiled.

One smile from her was not enough.

"It was as good as Myrah's." That would please her and help heal the tension between the two women. He didn't understand why they were no longer friends.

Her smile disappeared. Her lips thinned. Women were hard to fathom. He tried again.

"The house is clean."

No smile.

He returned to his studies, but the words before him made no sense, his thoughts lingering on how to please her.

"Are you happy with me? I've given you everything you could want. And I am glad we are married."

She spun to face him, her dark eyes widening. "Though we have no child?"

Thou shall not bear false witness.

"It is a grave disappointment you have not been blessed like Myrah."

"Myrah? Already?"

"Every day, I pray the Lord will lift your curse and give me a child, a son." This they could agree on, draw closer as they shared the sorrow. He waited in great expectation.

She glared, her mask returning.

What was wrong with her? If she did not want compliments and truth from him, what did she want? Zechariah rolled the scroll tightly and stalked out of the house. He'd study at the synagogue among reasonable men instead of with an ungrateful woman.

Elizabeth watched him stomp out of the house. What was wrong this time? She carried a chipped bowl of water to the courtyard for the stray dog that wandered by their house. Zechariah named it Boy and warned her against touching verminous Boy but had no objection to providing water and food for the animal. He need not know she also scratched behind his lamblike ears.

Kitchen knife in hand, she snipped a sprig of sweet, minty basil for the tomato marinade Zechariah liked. Her cooking was the one thing he usually approved of—until today and his comment about the lentil stew. Disgruntled, she tsked. It'd be a long time before she prepared that stew again. Maybe next time he'd decide it was far superior to Myrah's watery concoction.

She clipped another long sprig of basil. Did he think her a servant to speak of a clean house, as if it wasn't always clean?

Nothing she did pleased him. He said he was glad they married and then spoke of his disappointment in her.

She mimicked his voice. "'Given you everything you could want.'" She severed another stem of basil.

He must resent providing for a childless woman. Fine! She resented all blame being hers. She was disappointed too. She doubted even Adonai noticed her pain. If He did, He didn't care enough to stop it. Month after month after month, without comfort or hope, He let her suffer the disappointment of her husband, the scorn of her neighbors.

The fragrance of basil grew overwhelming, and she realized her hand could hold no more—the plant shorn to the dirt, a parody of her expectations and assumptions of marriage.

***

The tranquility of the synagogue calmed Zechariah's indignation and let truth make itself known. He had failed to grow closer to his wife.

Ignoring the other men, he searched his memory for the Torah's wisdom on contenting a wife. As the Torah instructed, he provided food and clothing and was diligent in marital relations. That was all he could remember. If those were the only instructions, it must be all a woman needed. Adonai had built woman. He'd know what one required.

Something must be wrong with Elizabeth.

"Why, Adonai, did you give me a broken wife?" He frowned. "To bring her to righteousness? Is that why she does not conceive—she is unrighteous?"

Divine silence weighed heavy.

He lifted his arms, entreating the Almighty, denying the wrongness of his request. "Tell me, that I may correct her. Grant me even a sliver of wisdom."

Truth hit hard—like icy water on an empty stomach. He was not to judge her but to love her.

"Lord, how do I convince her I love her?"

Search My Word.

He closed his eyes. Years of study and memorization led him to Adonai's wisdom. "Your unfailing love, O Lord is as vast as the heavens; Your faithfulness reaches beyond the clouds."

Unfailing and faithful. Faithful he could be. Unfailing? No.

"You are the Almighty, ready to forgive, gracious and merciful, slow to anger and abounding in steadfast love." Zechariah opened his eyes. "Lord, I am just a man. I cannot do all Nehemiah proclaims You do.

"Everything I do or say to her seems wrong. She turns her back or looks sad or angry. Is there no pleasing her? Women are a lot of trouble, Lord, especially the one You gave me."

An unfamiliar sound startled him. Zechariah broke off his prayer and surveyed the synagogue. Each person remained immersed in study or prayer. No one looked askance at him or determinedly evaded his eyes.

Still, he knew he'd heard something or Someone. If anyone would have believed it, he'd vow Adonai laughed at him.

Elizabeth gathered the shorn basil into a large bundle and wrapped a damp cloth around it. Nila had mentioned that her basil had gone to seed early this year. She'd welcome fresh basil with extra to dry for the cold months. If Elizabeth walked quickly, she'd return before dark.

Elizabeth hid in the deepening shadows by Nila's door before calling out in a loud whisper, "Nila." Imma and Abba lived close by. If Imma saw her, she'd be hurt Elizabeth did not come to visit her.

"Elizabeth?" Nila opened the door. "Why are you whispering?"

"Shh." She ducked her head. "I don't want my parents to know I'm here. Invite me in. Hurry."

Nila shook her head. "This isn't a good time for a visit." She lowered her voice. "Go away."

"I don't care if your house isn't tidy." Elizabeth pushed past Nila and entered.

"Elizabeth, what a nice surprise." Imma stepped forward and hugged her. "You smell like fresh basil." She pointed to the bundle. "What's this?"

"Oh. Nila, I didn't realize… You have a visitor." Elizabeth smiled weakly. "I brought…uh, basil. I cut too much."

Nila unwrapped the bulky cloth, questions on her face. "Oh my."

"I was thinking of something else and forgot to stop cutting."

"Thinking of Zechariah?" Nila's coy question irked her.

"Yes. In a way, I was."

Imma's face brightened. "Is there something special you came to share?"

"Just the basil." Imma's true question dawned on Elizabeth. "Ohhh. No. Not that. I'm not with child." Heart sinking at the disappointment on Imma's face, she added, "Yet."

"I am." Nila blushed and gestured toward Imma. "I wasn't sure until I talked to your imma, and I haven't told Caleb, so don't tell Zechariah."

Elizabeth squealed and hugged her. "Nila, that's wonderful. Can I hug you this hard? Am I hurting you? No? I'm so happy for you. How do you feel? Can I do anything for you? When will it be born?"

"Fine. Yes. No. That was too many questions. And I'm not sure yet. Your imma and I are talking about that."

"Daughter, you need to start back. It's almost dark."

One final hug and Elizabeth hurried out the door. Nila would be a wonderful imma—Caleb a boring abba—but he adored Nila and would be tender with their children.

Her steps slowed. If she and Zechariah ever had children, what would he be like as an abba? He didn't adore her like Caleb did Nila or Jesse did Myrah. Zechariah might not even like her. If she conceived, would he be indifferent or a loving abba to their children? All he seemed interested in was studying Torah and comparing her to Myrah.

Abba and Imma loved each other, so did the other couples. She and Zechariah… Endured? No, not that bad. Accepted? Not that good. Tolerated? Closer. Loved? Liked? No and rarely.

She ducked beneath a low-hanging branch, remembering her vow to be eucalyptus—not rotting leaves.

Eucalyptus—clean and fresh.

Rotting leaves—slimy old hurts.

It was hard to be eucalyptus when hurts kept coming.

Lord, how do I love someone I don't like and who doesn't like me? No answer came. No voice spoke.

If You're not going to tell me how to love, Lord, I'm lost. I can't like, much less love, Zechariah without some help.

Until Zechariah—and now, Myrah—she'd only known love and approval. Growing up, imagining her future, she'd expected to love her husband, believed she and Myrah would be friends forever. But she didn't and they weren't—and it hurt.

Brooding, she trailed her hand through waist-high grasses, their feathered tops tickling her fingers like Imma's butterfly kisses when she was a child—kisses mingled with scriptures and prayers. From infancy, she'd heard that scripture taught to love others as self, but how did one love oneself?

Loving self must be deeper than caring for herself. Facing her faults, even harder. Her unruly mouth caused trouble, embarrassing her, but despite that, she loved herself. Myrah's words had been harsh, judging, and critical. If she could love herself despite her troublesome mouth, she could love Myrah. Elizabeth felt an inward softening toward Myrah. Was this "loving others" as herself?

Zechariah? She clenched her fist. Every day his deeds dismissed her as less important than his studies. She'd never disregarded him…. Truth flashed an image of his face when she'd spat out she wished he hadn't married her.

She too had inflicted pain. Honesty melted her resentment toward him. Did this mean she'd need to forgive him?

She tugged her veil lower, wishing she could hide. Embracing one's own faults and not judging others galled. It meant she was no better than they were.

***

Over dinner, Elizabeth and Zechariah eyed each other, glancing away when their gazes met. She studied him when he looked down.

Although thin, he was broad shouldered, his carriage straight, his narrow hands clean scrubbed. Other women did not follow him with their eyes, but they did not see the beauty of his rare smile or hear the warmth of his deep voice. They did not know he invited her friends to visit and fed stray dogs and never complained about the courtyard crowded with plants.

He'd asked if she was happy. Maybe she could be.

CHAPTER FOUR

Elizabeth fumed under the silent scolding of the women gathered at the spring. She could not think of a single time she'd acted so judgmentally, but if one more person looked at her belly instead of her face or raised an eyebrow and inquired if she was pregnant *yet*, she'd…do something irrational. Maybe she did judge others.

It didn't help that Myrah and Jesse had welcomed their first child nine months from their wedding week or Nila, married the next month, announced her news with her hand protectively against her belly while Caleb walked around with a foolish grin on his face.

Around her, women clustered in small groups, sharing news and gossip. She nodded and waved but did not join them. Today she had no wish to visit. All she wanted was a cup of warm ginger tea to ease her cramps.

She knelt and filled her water jug, and with a practiced motion she lifted and balanced it on her shoulder. It was heavy and the way home uphill.

"Should you be lifting that, Elizabeth? If you are expecting, I'd advise you to make two trips instead of carrying such a heavy load. I'd know, since I've had a child and you haven't."

She gritted her teeth at Myrah's gooey concern in the company of her new friends.

"No. I'm not."

"Still? It's so sad Adonai has not blessed you like He has me. I've forgotten. How long have you been married?"

"You know how long it's been." Genuine regret prickled tears in her eyes. "Myrah, will we ever talk about what I said? I'm so sorry, and you were right, Zechariah is a wonderful man."

Myrah ignored her entreaty and pretended to ponder her next words. "Maybe you don't really want a child. Maybe you drink olive oil and cedar to keep from carrying the child of that *ancient* man you were forced to marry." Myrah pulled at the tautness of her tunic, revealing the soft jiggles of her body. "Or is it because you are too proud of your flat belly?"

Another woman stepped forward. "Maybe she prays not to have a child."

Elizabeth recoiled as if slapped.

"Maybe she trails after someone else's husband or denies my brother?" Myrah's voice dropped its feigned sweetness. "Is that why there's no child?"

"Never, I—" Elizabeth bit off her words. "It's not your concern."

"Then it is your fault Zechariah has no son." An older woman joined the circle of predators. "Adonai deems you unworthy to raise a child."

"My imma says you're cursed." The girl's voice came from Elizabeth's left. "She says you're not a real woman if you can't have children. My neighbor said you must be barren."

"No, I'm not! A child will come in Adonai's time."

Thunder warned of the approaching storm. The women dispersed, but she heard their murmurs of "Barren" as they hurried up the hill to avoid the rain.

Myrah and Elizabeth stood alone, the wind stirring, whipping their skirts and scarves.

"My friend—"

Myrah crossed her arms. "Friend no longer and never again."

"You are still my sister, Myrah."

"Unfortunately."

"Please." Elizabeth lowered the jug to the ground, extended both hands. "Can we make peace?"

"No."

"Myrah, Adonai teaches us to forgive, to show mercy. He loves mercy."

"Then let Him show mercy. For my brother's honor, I won't." Myrah's smile was wolfish. "When you carry my brother's child, I will forgive you. But you won't because Adonai proclaims you unworthy. Jesse gives thanks he married me and not you."

"I never wanted to marry Jesse. And you speak judgment on me as if you speak for Adonai."

"Perhaps I do. I say you're barren." Myrah flounced away.

Before Myrah had taken two steps, Elizabeth's anger flared. "And perhaps I'll cast the first stone when your words prove untrue. That's what happens to false prophets."

Myrah jerked to a stop. Pivoted. "You would do that to me?"

"It is what you do whenever we meet. Every word you throw at me is a stone, a pebble, a boulder to injure and bruise me. I hurt you, Myrah, and now you hurt me. Will it ever stop?"

The two women stared at each other as rain and tears smeared their faces.

In pelting rain, Elizabeth trudged up the hill, the water jug heavier than ever before. Were the women right? With each step, the words circled her mind—vultures picking at hope, shredding her dreams. Unworthy. Barren. Cursed. Unworthy. Barren. Cursed…

Drenched, she shivered in the bleak cold of her house. She hung her dripping headdress on a peg, dried her face, nudged a low stool close to the hearth, and inched her icy feet close to the glowing embers. A slow warmth crept through her hands and feet, but the chill of Myrah's words remained. She was never to be forgiven for her careless words or a chance meeting with Jesse a year ago.

One decision or a careless word and life spiraled in an unexpected direction like so many before her. If Eve… If Samson… If Jacob… Someday, would it be said, "If Elizabeth…"? She had thrown away a friendship in a pique of frustration and poor judgment.

The fire sputtered. She poked it, adding bits of fuel, letting it grow, needing its warmth to dry out and ease the unseen chill inside her.

If she must live unforgiven, so be it. She could change herself but not Myrah. She shuddered. This time it was not from the cold of the stone house but fear of the Lord for her friend. Former friend. Myrah risked Adonai's displeasure in refusing to show mercy, refusing to forgive, refusing to restore harmony within the family.

Dropping her head onto her knees, she groaned. She'd made it worse. Reacting to Myrah's taunts destroyed any hope of reconciliation. Imma had warned her about her words, and again she'd lost her temper.

A knock sounded at the door. Myrah! She ran to open it, eager to again beg forgiveness and restore their friendship.

"Jesse?"

He stood in the downpour, his cloak dripping. She did not invite him in. He did not expect it. They both knew he dared not risk entering her house while Zechariah was absent.

Without shalom or smile, he blurted his question. "Elizabeth, did you provoke Myrah at the spring? She returned home in tears."

She crossed her arms. "What do you think, Jesse?"

"Of course not. Whatever happened, she started it." He combed his hand through his wet hair. "I know my temperamental wife and I know you, but I promised her I'd speak to Zechariah. I came here instead. She'll never suspect. Turnip, stay away from her. Go early or late to the spring. Avoid her at synagogue and at market. When she's expecting—"

"Again?" She clapped her hand over her mouth.

He colored—the topic inappropriate between them. "Again. She's unpredictable. And Turnip"—he swallowed—"I'm sorry, but it's easier for me if we do not speak for a while. Myrah sees what she chooses to see, and she has this foolish idea that you and I… Never mind."

"Understood. It will be as you say, Jesse. Thank you." Elizabeth closed the door and returned to huddle before the fire. Its glowing warmth did not touch the deep chill inside her.

No child. No Jesse. No Myrah. Thank Adonai she still had Imma and Abba. Oh, and Zechariah.

Elizabeth startled awake. Who was hammering on their door and calling for Zechariah before sunrise? He crawled from their bed, his hair sticking up, his knobby knees visible. Hinges creaked as the outside door opened. Murmurs. A moan. Zechariah cried out and called her name.

She fumbled a shawl around her shoulders, alarmed at Zechariah's urgent bidding. His face was solemn, his eyes reddening. He stood by the door next to Caleb, the neck of his nightshirt torn as if in grief, his words magnified in the morning's stillness.

"Elizabeth, hurry. Dress yourself. Your imma needs you. Your abba, may his memory be a blessing…"

Abba? His memory? Those words were used when someone died. Yesterday, she and Abba laughed over a cricket's sporadic jumps. He could not be dead today. Zechariah was mistaken.

Unwilling to grasp what they were saying, she stopped listening—struggled to awaken, to end this lie.

Caleb's voice droned on. "Blessed is the one true judge. The Lord our Adonai is merciful, bless His holy name. Give thanks, for your abba did not suffer."

Stop talking. She backed into her room to escape the nightmare Caleb's words wedged in her mind. Her tunic hung from a peg. Zechariah had said she was to do something with it.

He entered the room, his voice a distant rumble. "Why do you stand there doing nothing?"

Puzzled, she looked at him. He slid the tunic over her head and gently coaxed her arms through.

"Elizabeth, did you hear Caleb say he did not suffer?"

She nodded. Suffer? Yes, she suffered now, would suffer forever—her heart ripped away.

Sandals appeared on her feet. A headdress covered her hair. Zechariah nudged her forward and took her hand, leading her through a sleepy dawn to a house without her fierce, stubborn, loving abba, a place no longer home.

***

Death—expected or unexpected—a cudgel, a scythe, an impenetrable darkness. Elizabeth stared unblinking at the cloth hiding Abba's lifeless form. Imma clung to her, draining the little strength she held in reserve. Forever after, Elizabeth knew she'd hate myrrh and bitter aloe, the earthy odors emanating from his shroud.

Dead before sunlight. Entombed before moonlight. His life, his light gone in an instant. He hadn't said goodbye.

Elizabeth drew in a breath. Let it escape. The space separating inhaling and exhaling too slight to measure. Life. Blink. Death. No time for farewell. No time to pray for healing as she had when Imma had been so ill.

She shrank from touching the stiff coldness of arms that once held her in warmth and comfort. She closed her eyes like a willful child. If she did not see him, he was not there—he was at market or in the synagogue or anywhere but here, dead.

Imma squeezed her arm. "The men wait to carry him out."

Elizabeth shook her head in refusal. Locked her jaw. Clenched her teeth. Wrapped her arms around her waist holding herself still, quiet. If she did not, she'd scream anguish until her voice gave way to silent howling.

His friends, men of the community, had vied for the honor of washing him, preparing him for burial. They had wrapped a cloth around his beloved face and bound his body in linen strips with myrrh and aloe tucked between each layer. The blue and white *tallit* he'd used all his life was reverently draped over him—a final prayer.

One white fringe had been removed to render it ritually unfit for use. Imma touched two fingers to her lips and surreptitiously caressed a remaining tassel of his prayer shawl—a private farewell.

Imma's voice rasped hoarse with unshed tears. "I think he knew it would happen soon, that he had a warning, a premonition."

No one warned me. Elizabeth looked away from the desolation in Imma's eyes, unable to carry a double burden of grief.

"Less than a week after he spoke to Samuel, your abba showed me where he'd hidden certain papers and the coins he'd saved. He moved the stone I've been fussing about for years and repaired the table leg. Some nights, I woke to find him wrapped in his prayer shawl, staring out the window at the heavens.

"I should have known. He didn't prepare me with words, and I didn't see it then. But now, I wonder, did his brother, Samuel, say something, tell him it was his time? I've heard that some Essenes prophesy."

Samuel. *"I have come to bid you farewell."* The forever farewell. That is why Abba's eyes lost their joy. *"The soul is immortal."* She'd heard the warning but not understood.

"These last months—maybe a year—he didn't laugh as often, but he held me longer. I should have recognized that something troubled him—we've been together so many years that I should have known. Last night, he was fine. This morning, gone—no goodbye—just gone. He never woke, Bethy."

Elizabeth cringed. No one else said her name like Abba did. She didn't ever want to hear it again if he was not the one to say it. And he wouldn't. Ever.

* * *

Gravel crunched beneath her feet as she and Imma led the funeral procession to the family cave where Abba's body would be laid. The community followed, lamenting his passing. Seven times they stopped and recited the psalm of David.

"Whoever dwells in the shelter of the Almighty will rest in the shadow of His wings…my Adonai in whom I trust…

Abba had loved the Almighty, trusted Him. Surely he rested beneath His wings.

"…He will call on me and I will answer him."

I love You too, Lord. Will You answer when I call on You?

The pallet bearers placed the body in the tomb as the crowd who'd gathered blessed him. "May he come to his place in peace."

The tomb sealed. The entreaty spoken, "Remember Adonai, we are of dust."

Two lines formed. Imma grasped her hand and tugged her between them. Two lines of familiar and unknown voices, blurred faces, whispered words, tender hands, warm hugs, countless echoes of the traditional words meant to ease the pain of loss. Even Myrah, her eyes rimmed red, patted Elizabeth's shoulder as she too repeated the ancient words of comfort. "May the Almighty comfort you among the other mourners for Zion and Jerusalem." Abba had been like an uncle to Myrah.

Elizabeth had recited the same words at every funeral procession she'd attended, had wondered how they possibly soothed the rawness of loss. And the words did comfort, soaking into her being, assuring her that she and Imma walked among friends and neighbors who stood with them to acknowledge the loss. The shadowed valley of death remained dark, but they did not walk through it alone.

Zechariah, Jesse, Caleb, Nila, and Myrah returned to Imma's house for the seven days of mourning. She and Imma slipped off their shoes—a sign of being humbled by their loss. She sank onto pillows placed on the floor, grateful for the symbolic tradition of being struck down by grief. It would be impossible to sit upright in a chair when her insides had melted into a muddy puddle. Guests sat on the bench or in chairs grieving with them, ready to do whatever might bring comfort.

"Solomon's proverb teaches that the soul is the lamp of Adonai." Zechariah lit the candle that would burn throughout shiva.

The door opened and closed. Neighbors brought platters of food—entire meals, baskets of fruit, bowls of nuts—reminders that even when it's too hard, life goes on. Myrah directed the placement and storage. She'd spent many hours in this house and knew where things belonged.

For a long time, no one spoke, as was proper. Family and neighbors, wishing to help them, waited to see what most comforted Elizabeth and her imma. Did they need silence or to share memories?

Imma gave a deep sigh and broke the silence. "My Joseph was a good man, a man who knew how to love me, our daughter, and above all, his Lord." She wiped her eyes and took a deep breath.

"I must speak this, and you must listen. It is to fulfill a promise, a vow."

She hid her face behind her hands then lowered them to her lap and straightened her shoulders. She looked at each face and gave a determined nod.

"This will be hard to say, hard to hear. All of you knew the three of us moved here from Galilee, but none of you, not even our daughter, knew that we carried a secret of loss."

The words penetrated Elizabeth's grief. Her mouth opened, and she twisted to stare. Secret loss? Grief weakened Imma's mind.

"Joseph and I agreed that when only one of us remained, our true story would be shared at shiva with those we loved." She coughed. Myrah hurried forward to offer a cup of water.

"Since settling here, we have ignored the rumors and the criticism of why we had only one child. It is not the way of our people, but it was the way we chose without regrets."

Outside a bird warbled, oblivious to the raw grief pulsing inside the house.

Imma smiled through tears streaming down her face and dripping from her chin. "When we met, I loved his laughter and the way his eyes crinkled when he tried not to laugh. I loved how he explained the scriptures. I loved his huge hands and how he was always first to offer help to anyone in need." Her voice wavered between a sob and a broken laugh. "I was young and beautiful, irresistible, or so he said."

"Imma, you're still beau—"

"Hush, child, only to those who love me. My chins sag and wrinkles mark my face. I have the beauty of one who has lived and loved deeply, one who has suffered and survived, but not the flawlessness of youth." She patted Elizabeth's hand. "Your abba always saw beauty inside me. That's all that matters."

She coughed again and took another sip of water. "Joseph's beloved imma died in childbirth, and he admitted he often prayed I'd not conceive.

"But I did, ten glorious, terrible times. We named our little lost ones and grieved every life that never drew breath. With each one, the loss came earlier, and I grew weaker, less likely to survive."

Soft groans echoed in the room. All knew someone who'd suffered the death of a sister or wife while birthing a child. Many of the women had buried at least one child.

She reached for Elizabeth's hand. "That is why we never had another child, never gave you the sibling you begged to have. You were enough for both of us, and he refused to risk my life again. You brought unspeakable joy. He loved you with all the love he'd have given ten children. You, beloved daughter, are the result of my relentlessly beseeching Adonai for a child and His gracious answer."

When the murmurs of disbelief quieted, she continued. "After the death of his imma, Joseph vowed that if he was ever blessed with a wife, he would treasure his family above all others except the Lord Himself. He did. I knew every moment of our life together that I was loved and cherished."

Tearfully, she looked around the room at her neighbors and friends until her gaze lingered on her daughter. "I grieve not only my loss but for those of you who do not know such earthly love."

Elizabeth bowed her head, more alone, more broken, her grief heavier than before Imma spoke. Imma grieved for her.

CHAPTER FIVE

Three years later

Zechariah gave a loud snore-snort. Startled, sleep fleeing, Elizabeth groaned when the familiar ache of her cycle seeped through her stomach and back. Not pregnant. Again.

Zechariah exercised his marital rights as if they brought joy, not pain. With his wholehearted dedication, how could she not have conceived?

She curled onto her side.

Marital relations were an expectation she'd known were her duty to accept, and she did—willingly if not eagerly. Cradling her own infant was worth any amount of discomfort.

What am I doing wrong? She stared at the wall, trying to remember everything she'd heard about conceiving a child. Already she drank so much milk, Zechariah had asked if she wished to buy a goat.

Myrah had married Jesse less than a year after she and Zechariah wed and had borne two children in two years. Was there a secret about conceiving she didn't grasp?

She sat up and flicked her curtain of hair over one shoulder.

Elohim, I ask You, as I have asked You every night. Please open my womb—as You have for everyone else in town—and bless us with a child. Years ago, You heard my prayer and healed Imma. Hear me again.

Lying down, she sought sleep. Maybe by next month, she'd be expecting a baby.

Eight months had passed—more than enough time for Adonai to have answered.

If He heard her. Or saw her. Or cared about her.

She strolled through the market, her belly flat as it had been almost four years ago. Feeling a nudge from behind, she stepped aside. A woman she did not know had run into her.

"Did I bump you?" The woman spread her hands across her belly. "I'm so sorry. I forget I'm no longer as slender as I was." She patted her bulge. "This is our first child, and I'm not used to being as big as an ox."

Elizabeth smiled. "It must be wonderful."

"Do you have children?"

Elizabeth shook her head.

"No? You're young. You have time. Maybe you should ask Adonai to give you a child—if you want a child, and you should. It's your sacred duty. The psalmist says children are a gift from the Lord, they are a reward from Him."

She stepped forward, her belly almost touching Elizabeth. "It took me such a long time to conceive—almost a year—then we prayed for a child, and the next month, Elohim blessed us."

She leaned closer and whispered, "Since I'm of David's line, my child could be King Messiah."

"Praise be to the Almighty." Elizabeth's tight smile stayed in place until the woman waddled away.

The joy of marketing lost, she plodded forward. If she could not give Zechariah a child, she could at least feed him well—especially today when again she must confess no child grew within her womb.

Elizabeth waited until her husband had eaten his fill and pushed away from the table. "Zechariah, I must tell you…"

He looked at her with such hope shining on his face that she could not force out the words. Eyes downcast, unwilling to see his disappointment, she stood before him and shook her head.

Silence. A loud sigh as hope waned.

"Elizabeth, look at me."

She darted a glance at his kind face. "I'm so sorry."

"There must be a reason the Lord has chosen to close your womb. We will pray and not stop asking Him for a child. You are young. There will be a child, and he will be the more cherished because we've waited so long. Maybe you should pray more."

"I pray every day, but Zechariah, some nights I lie awake in fear that—"

"Not now, Elizabeth. I need to leave for a meeting with the other men. I must not be late."

The oil lamp flickered as the door opened and closed. "—we will never be blessed with a child."

Motionless, she waited. If he'd heard her, he might return and she'd confide in him her worry, her fear, maybe even what the other women said about her.

The door did not open.

He had grabbed his cloak and hurried out as if he was late. He wasn't. She knew when the men met. He'd left early.

She cleared the table, cleaned the dishes, and set out bowls of almonds and figs for his return. For such a thin man, he was always hungry. Determined to wait up for him so they could talk, she lifted the Shabbat candlesticks from the mantel and carried them to the table to work.

She scooped up a bowl of ashes and sprinkled them through a sifter until the cinders and grit were removed. She dampened a cloth, dipped it in the sifted ashes, and rubbed the paste onto the silver. Slowly, a warm luster returned to the candlesticks.

"If only it was so easy to make me right—a little water, a handful of ashes, and a cloth."

She studied her warped reflection in the silver's shine. "Adonai, make me shine. Will You fix me? Give us a child? What do You want from me? Do You even hear me?"

Silence. The kind that permeates the soul.

Hours later, the door creaked open. "I thought you'd have gone to bed, Elizabeth"—his irritation evident. "You should not have stayed up."

"I wanted to talk to you, Zechariah. I need to talk to you and tell you I'm afraid—"

"Can it wait? I've had a long day." He yawned. "Good night." He closed the door to their room, the click of the latch loud in her stunned silence.

Daylight coaxed her eyes open. She tiptoed from the bed to begin the morning chores of grinding and baking. Last night, Zechariah must have been too tired to give his full attention. Today, he'd be willing to listen. She laid out extra breakfast for him, adding honey for the warm bread and large slices of melons.

After he ate and before he left to teach the boys at the synagogue, she'd confide her shame in being childless and her ever-increasing fear it was forever. Maybe he could allay her concerns, pray with her, or share a scripture she'd forgotten.

He emerged from their room, snatched a piece of fresh bread, and started for the door.

"Zechariah, I'd like to talk to you about—"

"Not now. I am needed at the synagogue. Could you talk with your imma?"

"Please?"

He paused, his hand on the door handle. Turned to face her, his eyes impatient with no trace of the earlier kindness.

"Elizabeth, you want to whine about not conceiving, but I do not want to foul my day thinking of your failure."

Aghast, she stared at him wide-eyed. Motionless. Dumbfounded.

"I'm sorry, it's not what I meant to say." He rubbed a hand over the wisps of his hair until they stood on end. "I meant… I'm disappointed too. It's been almost four years, and not once have you conceived." His face brightened. "You must be like Hannah. If you will pray to the Almighty—"

She glared at him, through gritted teeth ground out, "I do."

"Do not fret, Elizabeth. You have six more years before Abba and Myrah will insist that I div…" He clamped his lips together. The unspoken word hung between them.

Divorce.

Ice swirled through her veins.

Elizabeth burrowed her damp face in her imma's shoulder and wished she could crawl on her soft lap and cry herself to sleep. "No, he didn't say the whole word, but it was in his thoughts, in his eyes. How could I live with that shame, to have the whole world hear I was not worth keeping without a child? And it's not my fault. I want a child more than anything."

"That might be the problem."

Sobs turned to hiccups. "Nila is expecting again, Myrah is expecting again. Everyone I know, everyone I see is with child. Even stray dogs. Why not me?"

Imma hugged her closer. "Not all women are given a child."

She drew back. "That's not what you're supposed to say!"

"I've always spoken truth to you, Bethy. Speak truth to yourself. If a child never comes, what then?"

"I will die of shame and be an outcast."

"Or?"

Elizabeth sniffled and shrugged her shoulders.

"Or you can turn your eyes to Adonai instead of keeping them on yourself."

"I do! I pray, Imma, and attend synagogue and follow the commandments and try to treat others as I want to be treated."

"Even Zechariah?" Imma's look was skeptical. "Only you know the truth of that." She stroked a strand of hair from her daughter's face. "Do you obey the commandments to receive what you want or because of your love and awe of Him?"

"I'm not sure anymore."

"Adonai never promised you a child. He promised you something more important."

Elizabeth's face crumpled. "You're just saying that. There's nothing more important."

"Ah, yes there is. It is what your abba and I learned and held on to during the years of heartbreak. It's what I cling to with my Joseph gone. Shall I tell you? The Almighty promised He would never leave you nor forsake you."

"But He has forsaken me. I'm as invisible to Him as He is to me." She covered her eyes with both hands. Her voice dropped to a whisper. "I'm so afraid Adonai has forgotten me."

Imma pried her hands from her face. "Hardly! He sees you and hears you and knows your every thought." She winked. "Even more than I did when you were a little girl."

"Once, I didn't doubt Adonai heard me. I could almost hear His voice." She glanced at her imma. "Nothing is how I thought it would be. Not marriage or friendships, and with no child of my own, I'm lost."

"Nila's imma said you help with her little ones."

"And with Myrah's when she's tired enough to let me." She rolled her eyes. "And if Jesse is away. She still believes we meet in secret."

"Jesse's abba just remarried. His new wife might welcome help when—if—little ones come."

"I love helping with the children, but it's not the same as having my own babies."

"No. It isn't." Imma's eyes softened. "Search your heart before the Lord, child. Be honest with Him and with yourself. When you know beyond a doubt who you are to Adonai, you can look beyond what you think you're missing in life and trust His plan for you. Keep your eyes on Him."

<hr />

Elizabeth, mulling her imma's words, wandered to the synagogue instead of returning home. *Adonai, I know what I'm missing in life—a child, a true marriage—but who am I to You?*

She tucked that question away for another day and considered if, in truth, she did worship Adonai to receive blessings, to coerce Him into giving her a child, a marriage of love.

"If so, I'm one foolish woman." She chuckled. Adonai could not be managed, nor did she want to worship a God who could be coerced.

The synagogue's stillness beckoned—a good place to think. She slipped inside to sit in a dark corner of the women's section behind the separating curtain. She scooted as far back as possible, drew her knees up and wrapped her arms around them. Bowing her head, she searched her heart.

If Adonai denies me my desires, does He love me? She delved deeper, daring questions she'd never braved. *First, do I believe there is a God?* She searched for an excuse not to believe and found reasons to believe. *Yes. There is a God. I know that much.*

She probed further. "Even if He is distant and cold and doesn't seem to hear or see me?" She propped her chin on her knees. "Yes. Who am I to demand my Creator behave in a way that pleases me?"

She closed her eyes. "And if there is never a child—Lord, have mercy—if I am scorned before everyone, even if Zechariah forces me to leave, will I still worship Him? Is He enough?"

She imagined living without thinking of Adonai or without His guiding precepts of kindness and mercy. Life without God would be lonelier than life without a child or Zechariah. Hollow.

"Yes." Warmth flooded through her. "Yes. I will still worship You. You are my God. I will never stop asking for Your favor, but if You refuse, You are still my God. You may not see or hear me. You may have forgotten my name, but You are my God."

They belonged together. Joy radiated from Anna and Joachim as their wedding celebration rang with laughter. Bride and groom, dressed in white to symbolize their purity, wore crowns as king and queen of the day.

Anna glowed with happiness. Elizabeth, as a married woman, could not be one of Anna's attendants, but during the final feast Anna motioned her aside.

"Elizabeth, now that we are both married women…" She blushed with the beauty of a fifteen-year-old. "I'm not used to saying that. I want to tell you a secret. I've been having the strangest dream."

"About marriage?"

"About our children."

Elizabeth's gaze slid away. "I'm still not—"

"Maybe not yet, but in my dream, there was something special between you and my child and your child. Maybe it's just a silly dream." Anna's hand fluttered. "It sounds odd when I say it aloud, but I wanted to share it with you."

Elizabeth hugged her. "It's not silly to believe our children will know each other and be close friends."

Joachim hustled his wife away, leaving Elizabeth to think of Anna's confidences. The dream had been sweet. It was natural that Anna, newly married, thought of children.

Elizabeth drifted alone among the throng of guests. Anna's parents, busy with hosting, waved. She blew kisses to them before stopping at a table and scooping up a handful of pomegranate seeds. Pomegranates always tasted better if someone else removed the seeds from each section.

She didn't know anyone in Nazareth except her husband, who stood debating with other priests in a tight circle. Curious, she strolled closer and heard the names Hillel and Menahem, spoken with deference. She sidled closer, eating the pomegranate seeds one by one, until Zechariah saw her and shook his head. She wandered away, coughing as two whispering girls brushed by, leaving a trail of heavy scent. At least one had liberally applied her imma's perfume.

"Come sit with us." A young woman motioned her over.

Elizabeth popped the last few seeds in her mouth. Grateful to be included, she smiled as she scooted between the two women who'd made room for her.

"I'm Malka, and this sweet infant is my youngest, Daniel. You're Anna's cousin from near Jerusalem, aren't you? Did you see that beautiful veil she wore?"

"It was my wedding veil, but it suits her better. She and Joachim look so happy."

Beside her, a woman yawned. "Wait until the babies arrive. They'll just look tired."

"That's my sister, Maya. She had her third daughter nine months ago and is expecting again. We pray this time it will be a boy." Malka peered into the crowd. "How many children do you have? Are they here?"

Elizabeth's heart sank. Could women talk of nothing but children? "None. Yet."

The women around her glanced at each other, busied themselves with rearranging a headdress, patting a child, or chewing a nail—anything to avoid her eyes.

Malka patted her hand. "You're still young. You've been married how long? Maybe it's too soon."

Mouth dry, she moistened her lips and swallowed. "Almost four years." Did she imagine that they leaned away from her?

She'd never been so glad to have Zechariah appear and beckon her to join him. After excusing herself, she hurried to his side. She'd gone only a few steps when a whisper of the hated word reached her ears. "Barren."

Elizabeth, weary from the trip back from Nazareth, was not the only one late to synagogue. Jesse hurried past, avoiding her as if she was leprous. Since she and Myrah argued at the spring, she'd spoken to Jesse once—after his imma's funeral two years ago, when she'd reached for his hand to comfort him. Myrah's glare had nearly blinded her.

One seat remained in the crowded women's section of the synagogue—in the back beside Myrah and her brood of little ones. Elizabeth knew she'd be welcomed by the children. Not her sister-in-law. She squeezed past the other women, ignoring the familiar looks of pity or disdain.

Myrah's youngest held out her arms. "Pick me up, Aunt Elithabef."

Elizabeth scooped her up and settled her on her lap. "Shalom, Myrah. Shalom, my Libi, my heart." Libi beamed at the reminder that her name meant "heart."

Myrah's gaze skimmed over her. "Elizabeth, you look good. Today."

She ignored her, choosing to hear Libi's little secrets and chatter. The three-year-old removed her thumb from her mouth and stroked Elizabeth's face. "Mama say you not wrinkled like her cause you not have baby. You not want baby?"

"I'd rather have the wrinkles. Especially if I had a child as wonderful as you, Libi-girl." Elizabeth slid a finger over her niece's nose and tapped her pointed chin.

Libi giggled until Myrah poked her. "Hush. It is time for the *Bar'chu.*"

They stood for the call to prayer and sat when the Amidah prayer concluded. The Torah was brought from the protection of the ark. Again, they stood. Elizabeth grunted. Libi was a well-fed child. The sacred scroll was placed on the altar near the room's center, the silver guard removed, and the parchment unrolled to the day's Torah portion.

She joined her voice to the others. "Praised are You, Lord our Adonai, ruler of the universe, who has chosen us from among all peoples by giving us the Torah."

The man invited forward read from Psalms.

My Adonai, my Adonai, why hast thou forsaken me?

Grief welled, and Elizabeth bowed her head under its weight. *Lord, I am like David. You are my Lord and You have forsaken me. You do not hear me. You do not see me. Still I cling to You in faith through it seems I am alone.*

"…I cry out by day, but You do not answer…."

I have begged You for a child, and yet Your face is turned from me. This is my prayer, my thought, my sorrow every moment of every day and when I lie sleepless at night. Will You not hear me, do You not care? Here I am, Lord. Will You give me a child I may raise to serve you?

…scorned by everyone…

Even those women at Anna's wedding. Did You hear what they said about me? Yet I live to please You. What more do You require of me? I cannot pray any harder, do not know how to humble myself more. I am scorned, judged, by everyone I meet. Mercy, mercy, my Adonai.

She did not notice the tears covering her face until Libi's tiny finger dabbed them away.

"Aunt Elithabef sad?"

Myrah lifted Libi from Elizabeth's arms. "Of course she's sad. She's not been blessed with children like your abba and I have."

"Imma has a baby inside her."

Elizabeth looked at Myrah for confirmation. "You and Jesse are blessed again. I am happy for you. Children are a gift from the Lord."

Myrah had the grace to nod and look away.

Elizabeth heard nothing of the remaining service. *Lord, keep me from jealousy. Forgive me for questioning, but couldn't You have given one of Myrah's children to me?*

The service ended. Without a word, Myrah gathered her children and left the synagogue with the others. Nila waved but motioned she could not stay to visit.

Elizabeth stood alone. The tears returned. She lifted an edge of the curtain separating the women's section from the men's section. After peering into each corner to assure no one watched, she crept to the front of the synagogue. Maybe Adonai could hear her better here. She placed both hands on the bimah where the Torah had been unfurled and lifted her eyes to the ark protecting it. Her words came broken, jumbled.

"My God. You are my God. Deny me a child"—a sob wrenched from her depths as she surrendered her heart's desire—"but not the belief in You. You are my Adonai. Don't, I beg You, don't let me turn from You in despair." She lifted her arms, a child hungry for comfort and assurance from a beloved parent.

"Hold me, cradle me as I would a beloved baby. Even more than a child, I long to trust You as my forefathers did, whether they slaved in Egypt or hid in the hills with David." She sniffled. "At least they didn't have to endure Myrah and her friends." She wiped her eyes. "Lord, do You remember years ago, when I was a child and You—"

Sandals slapped on the synagogue's stone floor. She backed away from the table to scramble behind the curtain.

"Elizabeth, are you still here? Why do you linger?"

"I am praying for—"

"I'm hungry and wanting more of the bread you made yesterday. Come along now."

She parted the curtain and glanced at the bimah where'd she'd beseeched the Lord. Did the Lord turn from her as well? Did her prayers lie flat, gathering dust on the empty table, doomed to be swept away before the next Torah reading?

Three months later

Elizabeth pressed her hand against her flat stomach. Did a baby grow there? Surreptitiously she touched her breast. Definitely fuller. Hope spiked with joy swirled through her mind. Every fiber in her body tingled with anticipation. A baby! At last! She covered her mouth with both hands and giggled. This! This is how it felt.

It must be true. Her cycle—never, ever late, not since she'd begun at age twelve—was late. Three weeks late. Three! The Lord had heard her prayer. He saw her, remembered her as He had Sarah. After all these years she could give Zechariah what he most wanted, what she prayed for every waking moment. *Thank You, Adonai! You have redeemed me before my kinsmen and the people of my town. I am blessed beyond measure!*

She swung the water jug to her shoulder and set off to the spring determined to appear sedate and not indulge in wild dancing and skipping like David before the Ark of the Covenant. This exhilaration must be what bubbled up from his soul and overflowed into every muscle. For the first time, she understood why his love for the Lord burst into physical praise.

"Calm yourself!" Until she was certain, she'd hold this treasure close. Time later to share it and relish the looks of astonishment. "Forgive me, Lord, for wanting to gloat."

Would the other women guess her news just by looking at her? She'd become adept at discerning when a woman was expecting—the better to avoid her. A certain way of moving revealed her secret.

If only Imma and Abba still lived and could know of this child. Imma would set to sewing and Abba would announce the news of the little priest's arrival to everyone he met, friend or stranger.

She'd share with Zechariah first, send word to Anna and ask her to attend the birth. Then she'd tell Nila, and lastly Myrah. *Thank You, Lord. I will never cease praising Your name.*

If it was a boy, they'd name him Zechariah, for he would follow in the steps of his abba and become a priest. If she carried a girl, she'd have someone to inherit her cherished blue amphora. She'd ask to name a girl after her imma. He'd say yes.

"If I give him a child, even a girl child, he'll say yes to anything I ask."

She slipped past a low-hanging olive tree branch, resisting the urge to grab the branch and swing on it. Even if she suffered the morning sickness so many women did, she'd praise Adonai through every inglorious moment of it. Glory, all glorious glory to Adonai.

She'd never noticed how soft the spring water felt or the sparkle of the dove-gray stones surrounding the spring. Today, even Myrah could not cloud her joy. The women at the spring—bathed in the soft glow of morning—chattered among themselves. She nodded and smiled and heard not a word.

Water jug filled, she set it on her shoulder and faced the uphill walk, slower this direction—the jug was full, and already she sensed a heaviness in her body. So many signs of pregnancy, it must be true. Her lips curved upward.

"Lord, let this child bring healing between Myrah and me."

Near the top of the incline came a dampness she ignored—a twinge she dismissed. No. She forbade it. A low ache spread from her back to her stomach—a familiar ache, refusing denial despite her efforts to do so. Not again.

She lowered the jug from her shoulder and clutched it to her chest with both arms—a shield from truth. Suddenly weak, she trembled with the chill of desperation. Heart heavier than all the rocks she tripped over, her steps slowed until it required all her effort to place one foot in front of the other. "Dear Adonai, let me be wrong." But she knew. No gift of a child grew within her unblessed womb. No answered prayer. She remained unseen. Unheard by the Holy One.

Empty arms. Empty heart.

CHAPTER SIX

Ten years after Elizabeth and Zechariah's wedding

Elizabeth raised her chin and bit the inside of her lip to stop its quivering. *I am the daughter of a priest of the line of Aaron. My imma is of David's line.* She refused to weep or plea. Her shoulders tensed, their trembles shaking her entire body.

Today was the reckoning for her failure to become pregnant. Nothing had helped—not prayer, not eating mandrake stew, not drinking jugs of milk until she mooed. Today marked the end of a decade of chances to produce an heir. According to tradition, Zechariah could divorce her. Not all men invoked the right. Not all men had a family who hated the barren wife.

She squinted in the dimness of the setting sun, trying to read her husband's face—the stranger she'd lived with for ten years. Long years. This day, Zechariah either bowed to his family's insistence that he divorce her or accepted that he'd never be an abba and renewed his commitment to her.

A rogue tear escaped. How had it come to this? She'd been fifteen when she obeyed her parents and married their choice for her, turning her back on her dreams. She'd been a faithful wife, a dutiful wife, a praying wife. It had not been enough to thwart that sly thief—time.

Elizabeth knew from the sight of her father-in-law's grim face and Myrah's crossed arms, a decision had been reached. Legs water-weak, she drew a mantle of dignity around herself and stood taller. She, a descendant of the high priest Aaron, who stood with Moses in the presence of Pharaoh, refused to falter before her own people. They would not see her flinch, would never guess the emptiness gaping inside of her—an emptiness deeper than the desire for a child, deeper than the disappointment of her marriage, deeper than the isolation she endured each day.

If Zechariah divorced her, she'd not starve or be forced to sell herself in the streets of Jerusalem. She'd move to Nazareth, close to Anna and Joachim. Her family would take her in, even though she was disgraced.

Surely Zechariah would not turn her out as some did their wives with nothing except the clothes she wore. He'd allow her to take a donkey for the journey home. She shrugged. If not, she'd walk.

She'd carry the blue glass amphora in thick cloth tucked in a basket. Imma had given her the vessel on their wedding day—her family's traditional gift from mother to daughter. It was hers. It was going with her even if nothing else did. If Zechariah remarried—and it would be easy as a priest living a single day's walk from Jerusalem—the new wife would bring her own treasures and…

"Elizabeth."

Zechariah's voice ruptured her thoughts. "Sit down. I have something to say."

She shook her head. Raised her chin. Better to hear the news while standing so she could walk out of his abba's house. She'd shake the dust from her feet, walk home, and gather her things.

Zechariah rubbed his hand over his eyes. When had his knuckles become so swollen?

"According to the precedent set by Sarai when she sent Hagar to Abraham's bed, I can divorce you, since there have been no children—not even a pregnancy in ten years of marriage."

"Zechariah, every day I beseech the Lord for—"

"Let me finish. Ten years ago, I vowed to honor and protect you. I will dishonor neither you nor the vow, though we remain childless."

She blinked, searching his words for the dismissal, the rebuke, the verdict—"divorce."

"You are not divorcing me?"

"No."

Her legs gave way, and she sat.

As they returned to their home, he seemed more tender, more patient after announcing to his family the decision not to divorce her. Or was it her relief at escaping shame that eased the tension between them, allowed a shared smile? She knew it had been uncomfortable for him not to follow his abba's advice or Myrah's wishes. The newfound peace between her and Zechariah did not extend to his family.

Zechariah touched her arm. "Elizabeth, it's best to avoid my sister. She's disgruntled about the decision. She's accepted that you are unlikely to give me a son and heir, but I think it is more than that. Even if you gave me a son, she'd be discontent." He lifted both palms in confusion. "I've never understood why she turned on you as soon as we married. I thought you were good friends—she was often at your house—and that our marriage would please both of you, becoming true sisters."

She closed her eyes seeking courage. Zechariah had been gracious to her. After ten years, they had a new beginning. It should be built on truth. "I know why."

The confusion in his eyes tore at her heart. "The last night of our wedding week, when we walked to the final feast, Myrah overheard me say something I should never have said or even thought. I was tired and angry and scared, but it was inexcusable. It was about you, Zechariah. It was unkind, and during these last ten years, I've learned it was untrue. I'm sorry."

His eyes widened in surprise. "All this time, it's been about me? Myrah never told me what happened."

"Your little sister is very protective of you. I've apologized, but it hasn't been enough to restore peace. I was wrong, very wrong. The discord, the fault is all mine, not hers." She worried her lip, waiting for his reaction.

"There's more. Jesse and I..." She hesitated as his steps faltered. "We are friends, like cousins or siblings." The words tumbled out in a rush. "That is all we've ever been, although Myrah saw us in the woods together and in Jerusalem and believes we are more to each other. Zechariah, we were talking, nothing more."

Truth did not always smell fresh and clean like eucalyptus. He could still change his mind and divorce her.

It seemed more likely when he did not speak. With each step, her legs grew wobblier, her heartbeat more frantic. In the dark, she could not see his face and judge his thoughts. She should have never told him. Abba always said she spoke a bowl full when a spoonful would have been enough. This time, she'd thrown away a chance for a new beginning.

"You wronged both me and her with careless, unkind words."

She bit her lip. "Yes. I did. Can you forgive me even if she won't?"

Again, the stifling silence.

Finally, he spoke. "Now she wrongs you in refusing to forgive, in withholding the mercy Torah teaches us to give."

"What?" She might have to sit down again.

"And you have wronged me—again—by denying my right to protect you—even from my little sister and her possibly erroneous beliefs."

Possibly?

Hope strained to survive. "Are you angry with me?"

"That you continue to dishonor my vows to you, that you refuse to allow me to protect you? Ten years ago, I would have been furious. Now, I have other things to concern me instead of your opinions. We have been married long enough to know it's useless to waste time on what we cannot undo. No. I am not angry. It's of no concern. Do not bother telling me what you said to Jesse."

"I never said it was Jesse I spoke to."

He ignored her protest. "I'm not blind, but it doesn't matter anymore." He sighed. "Let's just try to live in peace. I will show mercy even if Myrah will not."

They walked the rest of the way in a silence throbbing with tension, careful to keep their arms from brushing or their eyes from meeting. Hurt by his indifference, she wondered if divorce was always a severing or if sometimes it lay like a dead thing in a marriage.

Elizabeth wrung out the cloth and wiped it over the table a final time. Their meal had been silent, awkward as the first time they'd sat alone at this table after their wedding. Neither had eaten much ten years ago or tonight.

Zechariah left for the synagogue without a word or glance. This was to be the life she lived for all her days?

Life's emptiness haunted her. Each time she heard a child's laughter, she grieved the ones she'd never had. Every child a reminder that she'd failed her sacred duty. Beyond barrenness—and its grief of losing nothing and everything—beyond a loveless marriage, beyond loneliness, was the sense of deeper loss.

She snapped the wrinkles from the cloth and hung it to dry near the fire.

Flames twisted and darted in mesmerizing abandon. Something tugged the brink of her thoughts, almost out of reach, almost beyond words. Something glowing softly with mystery, its memory inexplicably warming and encompassing her. Something no longer tended, grown cold, quenched. Its scattered gray embers lifeless around the hearth's edges.

Faith—her deepest loss.

She wanted that certainty again, the irresistible joy of a living faith, the absolute, unquestioned knowing that her God saw her and cared for her. Yes, still, always, forever her God. That she held tightly. It was the assurance that He heard her pleas that refused to ignite.

When in the years of Adonai's silence had faith's blaze once again cooled to cinders, become the smoldering of doubt, the dullness of indifference? As hope for a child thinned? When fear of divorce festered? When Imma and Abba died? As loneliness companioned her?

Now, the flicker of faith was seldom visible, reduced to a smoldering remnant. This emptiness deeper than any disappointment, a fear beyond shame or loneliness or divorce—this is what she hid from all others, hid from herself. Once, faith had burned so brightly. Years ago, in the synagogue, she'd surrendered her doubts and fears, believed that never again would she question Adonai's ways and tender care.

I obey every commandment, serve all who allow me near, attend synagogue, and memorize scripture.

She knelt before the hearth and poked at the embers with the etched tongs purchased in the weeks before her wedding.

If You loved me, You'd give me a child.

Could hope again flare inside her? Could faith be rekindled? She jerked away from the promise of the flames. Banked the fire. Left a single oil lamp to break the darkness. Weighted by years of discouragement, she curled up on the bed in the spare room.

Awake, she heard Zechariah close the outside door, shuffle across to their room and return to snuff the lamp. He knew she was not in their bed. If he came to her, extended his hand, she'd welcome the hope he offered. They would start anew, truth between them. He did not call her name. Her door did not open.

Sleepless, she stared into the darkness, loneliness tucked around her like a blanket.

Dry-eyed, she counted back. How long since she talked to one who loved her? Years—five since Imma died. She'd not then realized it was the last time she'd see Imma's eyes soft with love or hear her voice. She closed her eyes, remembering….

"Elizabeth, do not interrupt. Soon I will be gone." Her frail hand had covered Elizabeth's. "Do not bother telling me it isn't true. I have always spoken truth to you. Yes? I will not stop now."

Tears sprang to Elizabeth's eyes. "Imma, don't leave me, not you too. I still need you."

"Child, no tears. I have lived long. Let me die in peace. Now, heed my words, Bethy. You have suffered disappointment and loss. Your marriage is not what your abba and I prayed for…." She mumbled to herself. "My Joseph was so sure the Lord spoke to him, guided him to accept Zechariah for you."

"Imma, we have learned to live in harmony."

Tears puddled in the old eyes. "It is not enough. Learn to love, to cherish him."

"I will. Rest now, Imma."

"When I began to heal after you prayed—yes, your abba told me—faith glowed inside you. Are my eyes too old, my mind too weak, or has your sweet, stubborn faith in Elohim dimmed?"

There was no need to answer the blunt question. Imma both spoke and saw truth.

"Act as though faith already flames within you."

No heat could ease the chill of Imma's hand. Still, Elizabeth cradled it tightly between her own warm hands.

"Do what you did when it burned bright and intense and filled you with warmth. Faith will awaken to warm you again."

She had promised Imma. For five years, she'd tried to keep her promise. Even when Imma, like Abba, left without saying goodbye, she searched for the return to faith. She'd acted as if she believed, prayed as if she did, served as if she did.

Elizabeth rolled to one side and covered her head with a pillow. "I have done this, Almighty, and still I shiver in doubt's coldness."

⁂

Zechariah trudged home. His head ached. His joints ached. His heart ached. If Elizabeth waited up for him, he'd confess he did care somewhat for her regard. He smoothed his thoughts over the admission, felt its splinters. Truthfully, he cared too much. He'd always fallen short of who he wanted to be for her. She'd seen disappointment with himself as disappointment with her. He hadn't corrected her misunderstanding. He'd let her blame herself for the distance in their marriage, let her think his reserve was because she had not conceived a child.

He wronged her today, lied saying he wasn't upset by her confession, when truthfully, he was disappointed he'd failed her again. He'd noticed that something was wrong between his wife and sister. He'd ignored Myrah's jabs at Elizabeth's barrenness and let her fend for herself. He'd seen that his wife was unhappy, and such a man he'd been to hide behind his scrolls. Disgust curved his usually rigidly straight shoulders. What a fool he'd been. He cringed and mimicked his words, "I will show mercy." He knew donkeys more gracious.

He quickened his steps at a flicker of light through the window of the house. If she was not too upset, he'd ask her to rub the balm she'd made into his hands and he'd look at her and if she spoke, he'd listen to her. He'd confess his lie, and, if she allowed it, he'd cradle her in his arms, ask for nothing other than to hold her. They could begin again with truth between them.

He opened the door to emptiness. She had not waited up. Disappointed, he crossed to their room hoping she was still awake. Her scent surrounded him, but she was not there, the room cold and barren—somehow darker without her presence.

Returning to the main room to extinguish the oil lamp, he saw that the guest room door was closed. This was to be his life? In the darkness of the room, a depth of grief he'd never known coursed through him. He'd lost her, the gift entrusted to him by the Almighty.

He had not divorced her as was his right. She had severed ties with him as he deserved.

Two weeks later at the evening meal, Elizabeth placed a platter of sliced meat and roasted vegetables in front of Zechariah. They were his favorites—food, the only way she knew to keep her promise to Imma and move beyond the dusty vows binding her to Zechariah.

He caught her hand, lifted it to his lips. Her eyes blurred when his tears dampened her fingers.

CHAPTER SEVEN

Five years later

Elizabeth scrutinized the house. Everything was in place, every nook tidy, every corner swept. The courtyard was draped with flowers. Pots of herbs warded off bugs and gnats beside low benches inviting guests to sit and rest. The bed in the guest room had new covers and clean woolen coverlets. Thick stew bubbled on the hearth. Sun-bleached linen towels covered crocks of cheese and yogurt. Fresh cinnamon bread scented the air. Dishes of pomegranate seeds and olives circled a vase of purple flowers. She'd prepared Anna's and Joachim's favorite foods.

Everything seemed perfect. Almost. She thumped her forehead. "I forgot the roasted-almond and raisin mix."

"Zechariah! Elizabeth! We're here. Are you home?"

Amid the flurry of arrival, hugs, assurances of well-being and an uneventful journey, and settling their belongings in the spare room, there was little time to spare before finishing dinner preparations. Anna toasted almonds while Elizabeth set out dishes for their food.

Zechariah returned from teaching. After another round of greetings and assurances, they gathered for the evening meal.

Halfway through, Elizabeth saw Anna's head begin to nod. The trip had been harder than she'd told.

"Anna, dear, if you need to sleep more than eat, go to bed. We understand. We'll talk tomorrow."

Anna covered a yawn then looked uneasily at Joachim.

"Elizabeth, there's something I need to t—"

Her husband interrupted her. "Elizabeth is right. We traveled a long way today. Rest, Anna. Tomorrow is soon enough for you women to talk."

The couple exchanged a look, and Anna nodded. "Tomorrow, then."

Elizabeth hummed softly as she cleared the table from the evening meal and prepared for the morning's breaking of fast. Anna being here meant someone to talk with who loved her, someone who understood the secret shame of being childless.

Each morning, they'd grind wheat into flour, set out a breakfast, and try new ways of braiding their hair, before walking to the well. They could talk of flowers and herbs, sit in the courtyard spinning as they watched doves alight on the wall to peck at the crumbs and seeds she scattered each day. The increasingly shaggy Boy might limp by for a crust of dry bread, and they could laugh over his antics for more food.

In a few days, the four of them and Jesse's half brother, Eli, would walk to Jerusalem for the Sukkot festival. Anna and Joachim's pilgrimages to the city of David in obedience of Torah had become her favorite three times of the year. Zechariah stayed home and laughed more when they visited.

The solitude of barrenness was less painful since she and Anna had borne the same struggle and together had released it to the Lord. Since then she'd—mostly—left it to His will and not snatched it back into her understanding.

The surrender had happened during Hannukah several years ago. Joachim and Zechariah had left early for Shabbat worship. She and Anna had lingered at the table, both dreading the nips and jabs of others' words, knowing they were both guilty of *lashon hara,* listening to the unkind words directed at them. She remembered Anna's question.

"Elizabeth, is it your choice to be without child?"

"No more than it is your will to be the same, little cousin."

"Then it is the Lord who holds this, not us."

Elizabeth sat straighter. "You're right. And if it is His will, we are wrong to walk in the shame others heap on us."

They'd stared at each other as the new thought spread its veracity through their understanding.

She'd spoken slowly, testing her words for truth. "Anna, it's a tangle of sorrow and relief. I grieve to relinquish my hope for a child, but I'm relieved to accept His will instead of pleading for my own." She'd searched Anna's eyes for judgment. "Does that make sense?"

Anna had raised brimming eyes to meet her gaze. "I feel the same way. It's a strange peace, isn't it?"

Together they'd walked to worship. It was the first time in many seasons that Elizabeth ignored people and focused on her Lord.

As sleep hovered, contentment surrounded Elizabeth. Tomorrow morning, she and Anna could visit uninterrupted.

Early the next morning, Elizabeth sat at the quern, disappointed and alone, turning the handstone to grind wheat into flour for their daily bread. Anna's exhaustion was unusual for one of such high energy. Last night, her color had not been good, and she'd pecked at her food like the sick bird that had sheltered against her courtyard wall....

A sick bird. Dear Lord, no! Realization turned her hands slick with sweat as they gripped the quern's handle. Sick. Anna was sick like Imma had been.

Rivers of pain she'd believed dry as a summer's wadi flooded her memories. She'd been young—not quite a woman but more than a child—when Imma sickened.

Imma's relentless need to sleep had been the harbinger of a wasting sickness. She'd slept long hours at night and again during the day, yet awakened exhausted. Food held no interest. She'd picked at it, pushed it aside claiming nausea. Her skin grayed, her shiny hair grew dull. Imma, once softly rounded, shrank into sharpness and angles, her arms too weak to work the quern or carry water from the well. Or hug the child who watched in terror.

Abba had prayed and fasted, fasted and prayed, seldom leaving his wife's side even when she slept. He too became gaunt and pale, the circles beneath his eyes black and swollen.

Terrified of losing both her beloved parents, she'd badgered the Lord with her petition for Imma's healing. Adonai did the impossible for old shepherds and slaves and kings. They'd been imperfect. She did not have to be perfect either.

Praying with the fervor of desperation, praying with the faith of one who believed because Adonai listened to Abraham's petition for a son, and Jochebed's cry to save Moses, and David's plea for forgiveness, He'd listen to her too.

And He had. She'd tried to tell Abba but for once he had not believed her, so she held it tightly to herself, certain of both its truth and that it could not be shared.

One day, Imma ate cheese with her bread. Soon she slept less during the day. She smiled and the dimple reappeared. She sneezed and did not cringe in pain. It had taken more than a year for Imma to become soft and round again, but she had. Anna could too.

She began again to turn the quern. Grain did not turn to flour without effort.

When Anna awoke, she'd remind her of Imma's sickness and recovery. Again, she stopped the grinding. Imma had hidden her sickness until it was no longer possible to excuse it away.

She'd refused to acknowledge it. Anna too might not be ready to speak of it. She'd wait until Anna confided in her and not rush her into sharing before she was ready.

⁂

The musty scent of frankincense perfumed the air. Elizabeth counted fifteen drops of the precious oil into melted tallow for

Zechariah's joint-pain balm. Last month, she'd tried oil infused with cumin, but it had not worked well. Eucalyptus oil diluted in almond oil helped, and with so many eucalyptus trees, the oil was less expensive than frankincense from Yemen, but if this was more effective, well, they could afford it.

As she blended the mixture, she watched Anna. One elbow propped on the table, she arranged and rearranged the bit of food before her. Finally, Anna spoke.

"Elizabeth, you might have noticed I'm still tired from the trip and not very hungry."

"It was a long walk. We're not as young as we were." Elizabeth laughed. "No one is as young as they once were, so it's a foolish thing to say. Did I mention that Jesse's stepbrother, Eli, is walking with us to Jerusalem? He's young, maybe he'll carry us." Talking might distract Anna. Coaxing her to laugh would be better.

"That's nice. Elizabeth, you need to hear me. It's more than that." Anna pushed the food to one side and twisted so it was out of her sight. "I'm often queasy."

"Is the frankincense bothering you? It's a strong scent." Elizabeth poured the balm into a wide-mouth clay jar and covered it with cloth to cool. "Some people don't like it."

"Yes, but I need to tell you something."

So soon? Elizabeth's heart raced. She wrung a towel with both hands to keep from covering her ears or having her fears confirmed. "I could make you a tea. Three types of mint are growing in the courtyard. Which would you prefer?"

"Please. Elizabeth, sit down. This is hard for me to share with you. Let me finish while I have the courage and before it's too late." Anna's eyes softened with tears. "You need to hear this from me, not as gossip."

Elizabeth swallowed past the lump in her throat.

"I have dreaded telling you because it will remind you of what you'd like to forget."

Elizabeth nodded. Anna had been too young to remember Imma's wasting sickness, but Anna's imma must have told her and warned her that Elizabeth refused to talk about that year.

Anna dabbed at her eyes and nose. "It seems I cry all the time, and now I'm afraid I'm going to hurt you so I'm crying more." She drew in a deep breath. "Better to have it said so we can go forward. Elizabeth, I'm—"

"I already know, Anna. I noticed as soon as I saw you that something was different."

"You guessed?"

Elizabeth smiled at Anna's incredulity. "Yes, dear. I recognize the signs. Remember, I've known you since you were an infant. How could I not know?"

Anna tumbled into Elizabeth's arms. "You won't make me go through this alone? I was so afraid with what you've been through that it would be asking too much." She drew back and sniffled. "Joachim said you'd understand. I should have trusted him and you."

"Of course."

"You're not hurt?"

"Only that you thought I would be, that you hesitated to share your life with me."

Anna wiped her eyes. "Will you be with me when the time comes?"

Elizabeth could not speak. She nodded. She would not leave Anna's side. She would pray and fast as Abba had for Imma.

Elizabeth jumped. "Ouch! Careful! Those palm fronds have sharp tips." She narrowed her eyes at Anna's mischievous look. "That was not an accident."

"Maybe, maybe not." Anna grinned. "I was thinking of all the times you yanked knots out of my hair when I was little. My hand might have slipped." She tied the tip of the date frond closed.

"The Torah teaches forgiveness and mercy."

Anna yawned. "I missed that lesson."

"Tired? Let's go back to the house. We have palm, willow, and myrtle, and we'll buy the fruit, a perfect *etrog*, in the city."

"Would Adonai notice if we just used a lemon? They look and smell almost the same."

"Anna!"

They gathered their cuttings into a basket. The men would bind the boughs and branches before tomorrow's journey.

"Anna, have you shared your uh…condition with anyone else?"

"Joachim, of course. No one else. I needed to tell you first, and I'm not ready to share with others. It's a lot to think about and prepare for."

Elizabeth circled Anna's shoulders with one arm and hugged her. "Thank you for trusting me with this."

———

Zechariah and Joachim walked ahead of the women, clearing a path through the mass of people going to Jerusalem. This festival of the last harvest and celebration of Adonai's provision for forty years in the desert was not as well attended as Pesach's celebration of the Exodus and Adonai's love for His people, but the press was large enough to leave the women bruised and jostled. Early in the day, Eli had joined with other young men from the town and disappeared into the throng.

Both men carried a long, thin bundle of branches, each one mentioned in the Torah and required for Sukkot, the Festival of Tabernacles. Centering the bundle was a single date-palm frond. Two willow tree branches were bound on the left and on the right, three boughs of myrtle leaves. The fourth part of the offering, an unblemished etrog, top intact, would be purchased when they arrived.

Anna elbowed Elizabeth. "The closer we are to Jerusalem, the faster those two walk. They haven't noticed they are far ahead of us."

"We'll walk as slowly as you need and stop as often as you'd like. Save your strength."

"This is a good pace. If we arrive in time, I'd like to shop for cotton for when the time comes. If I start now and wash it every week, it will be soft enough."

Elizabeth caught her breath at the reminder. Imma's skin had become so sensitive that she tolerated only worn cotton touching her.

Linking arms helped the women stay together as the road grew busier, the crowds louder. This was a joyous festival, a time for gathering and giving thanks.

Anna raised her voice to be heard. "Do you know where to go?"

"Same place as last year. Caleb invited all of us to join his family again. He came up earlier to build the booth." Her brow furrowed. "I think I can find it." She shrugged. "I hope Zechariah and Joachim will wait for us near the gate."

Elizabeth cringed, remembering last year. Jesse had waited by the gate. He'd smiled and patted her shoulder as he reached for her traveling pack. Myrah came around the corner, scowled, and, with her eyes if not her voice, accused them of impropriety.

"Joachim is very tender and protective of me these days. He'll wait."

Elizabeth bit her tongue. If she were dying, would Zechariah be tender and protective like Joachim and Abba? That would need a miracle. She changed the subject.

"Zechariah will eat and sleep in the sukkot for the entire seven days. We can stay indoors with Nila's aunt, but I'd like to go to the Temple for one of the waving ceremonies and one night when the offering of water is poured on the Temple altar."

"Agreed. We cut those branches to be offered in love. We love Adonai. We should see them waved." Anna nodded emphatically.

"All six directions!"

"The offering of water, I'll have to miss." Anna's shoulders drooped. "I'm so tired by sunset. You go and then describe it to me, the lights and dancing and music, every performance."

"Of course." She'd remember and make every facet come alive for Anna, but her joy dimmed. This might be the last time they shared a festival.

Elizabeth's foot slipped a little in the mud. With the end of Sukkot, the rainy season had begun. Zechariah walked beside her. Ahead of them walked Anna and Joachim, his arm around her waist. Elizabeth made a face. Zechariah never hugged her in public and as little as possible in private.

Abba had touched Imma whenever he could. He'd rub her shoulders, tap her nose, pull her close in a hug. Abba had loved Imma. Zechariah tolerated her. She released a deep sigh. At least they'd learned to live in comfortable companionship.

Ahead of her, Joachim stopped, released Anna, and bent over to adjust his sandal. In a strong gust of wind, Anna toppled into the mud.

As if in a dream, Elizabeth saw Joachim lift her to her feet and steady her. He bent close to Anna's ear. She smiled up at him and placed a hand on her belly.

A jolt of lightning could not have made it clearer.

Elizabeth staggered past Zechariah and stood between Joachim and Anna.

"You're not dying!"

"No, I'm… You thought I was dying?"

"I—of course, yes! Everything you said matched Imma's time of sickness." Elizabeth grabbed Anna in a fierce hug and rocked back and forth. "You're not dying. You're expecting a baby. Dear Adonai in heaven, thank You. I could not stand to lose you, Anna."

"You're not angry?"

"Angry you have been blessed with a child? Never."

Anna burst into tears. "You'll still come when it is time?"

"I will be there whenever you need me."

Joachim chuckled, but Elizabeth glimpsed her husband's face and knew he too grieved that she'd never carried a child.

Zechariah blessed their guests as they started the journey back to Nazareth and walked with them as far as the synagogue. There, he taught the children without seeing them, listened to their recitations without hearing them, dismissed them without noticing that they left.

Denied a child. The aching loss resurfaced, startling him. How could he miss what he'd never had?

He'd seen the longing etched into lines on Elizabeth's face when she thought no one was watching her. Each year lengthened her list of "nevers." She'd never nurse a child, never hold hope that she carried Messiah, never gift the amphora to a daughter or in-law, never be a grandmother. Worse, she'd never escape the "nevers." Would she always be known as the woman who never had a child instead of for the way she helped others?

Through the years, he'd wanted to shake his fist at Adonai and turn his back. He'd wanted to cajole and demand and bargain. He'd wanted to shrug his shoulders and burrow into his studies.

He'd done none of those things.

Zechariah closed the synagogue. Trudged home. Sat in silence with Elizabeth as she served their meal. When it was time to retire for the night, he lay in bed. He did not sleep. They lived amicably. It was the most he could hope for.

CHAPTER EIGHT

Five months later

Elizabeth folded one last scarf and tucked it into her bag. She tapped her finger against her lips. Did she have everything she'd need for a two- or three-month stay in Nazareth? How long she stayed depended on when Anna's child decided to be born. She ticked off the list on her fingers. Clothes. Food. Coins. Gifts for Anna and the coming child.

The baby gift, at the bottom of the bag, could not be presented until the infant was born. She did not fear evil spirits, nor did Anna, but it would cause unease for others in their community. At her age, she'd learned not to ruffle feathers.

Zechariah had offered to walk with her to Nazareth. She'd expected to travel both ways with a caravan. He was kind—though he did not love her—more protective than in the past.

She jumped as a shadow darkened the doorway.

"Myrah?"

"Zechariah travels with you tomorrow? And then he returns immediately?"

"Shalom. Yes." She nodded, puzzled. Myrah already knew this. "He offered to take me there but does not plan to stay."

Myrah clenched her fists. "Zechariah is the only family I have since Abba died last year. He's my family more than he is yours. This trip will be too much for him. Are you trying to kill my brother to be free of him?"

Kill him? She was serious? Elizabeth chuckled. It was the wrong thing to do.

"Myrah, I know herbs. I could have poisoned him years ago if I'd wanted him dead." It was the wrong thing to say.

"He's not as strong as he looks."

This time she curbed her tongue. Zechariah had never in his life looked strong. Could Myrah be expecting yet again?

"You have Jesse and a handful of children. They are your family."

"But he's the only one never annoyed with me. You don't understand. You never have."

"I guess not. Explain it to me?"

But Myrah had already left. Elizabeth heaved a sigh at the dramatics. If she told Zechariah about the visit, he'd be offended by Myrah's words. She cringed. And maybe offended by her words about poison too. Or grateful. Where were those angels tasked with guarding her tongue?

⊱ ━━━━━━ ⊰

They left early, before the sun rose to blister the land and anyone foolish enough to venture outside. Remembering the pain of her childhood burn, Elizabeth kept her headdress well over her face.

Red dirt soon covered their feet. As she skirted rocks that had tumbled into the road, Zechariah kicked them aside.

Others walked the same road, calling out greetings in the morning's freshness, forsaking speech as the sun's fierceness increased. It was a hard walk, the path twisting over land as rumpled as an unmade bed.

Elizabeth and Zechariah hid under tangled branches near a spring to escape the heat through the hottest hours. Drained from the heat, she drowsed until Zechariah nudged her. It was time to continue. Nights, they sheltered at small inns. By the third day, Elizabeth doubted her clothes would ever be clean again.

Every hot, dusty step proved worth it when Anna squealed in delight at the sight of their dirty, dusty faces. After the two travelers washed themselves and changed clothes, the men settled in the courtyard, the women inside.

Elizabeth eyed her. "Are you certain this is your eighth month? You're not very round, and you don't waddle."

"I'm certain." Anna glanced out at the men. "My imma did not grow large with me either."

"Are you ready?"

Anna covered her mouth and laughed. "Definitely yes and absolutely not."

"As long as you're sure."

"I can hardly wait to hold this little one, but, Elizabeth, I don't know how to be an imma. What do I do if he won't stop crying or if he's fussing for hours? How do I tell if he's hungry or hurting? I've heard a new imma doesn't sleep through the night for months."

Anna chattered on, unaware of the pain surfacing. Elizabeth thought she'd accepted the Lord's will for her life, but hearing Anna, she ached for these worries more than all the gold in Caesar's treasury. Years of sleepless nights? No comparison to the joy of holding her own child. Hungry or hurting? She'd welcome the challenge, and not rest until her babe rested quiet and content.

She stretched a smile across her face. "I believe you will be a wonderful imma, Anna. Show me what you've done to prepare for the birth."

Anna returned with a basket and lifted out each item. "Salt. A knife. Oil. Cloths to wrap him in. Clean clothes for me and a stack of thick cloth." She unwound a cloth-covered packet. "This is the sash I've sewn for the Torah scroll he'll use at his bar mitzvah and his wedding. Can you think of anything I forgot?" She repacked the basket, unaware of Elizabeth's struggle.

Salt. Oil. Knife. Every day Elizabeth used them to prepare food. She'd helped deliver many infants, but never had she been so acutely aware that salt, oil, and a knife were part of birth. Now, she'd never forget.

She coiled her fingers deep into her tunic, twisting the material into a wad. No matter how much she loved Anna, being here, seeing her glow with a new life inside, chafed more than she'd expected. She released a long breath. She'd promised to be here, and she'd not let her disappointment gnaw away Anna's joy.

Elohim had not blessed her with a child, but He'd blessed her with Anna. She would love Anna's little one as if he were her own.

The pangs began three weeks later. By noon, Anna's writhing had loosened her hair until it straggled around her shoulders. Elizabeth combed her fingers through its sweaty dampness and worked it into a loose braid. She wiped Anna's face. Held her hand when she groaned. Childbirth was harder when the first-time mother was older. A first-time mother in her late forties was almost unheard of.

A long day. During the second night, Anna's faint whisper drew Elizabeth closer. "Promise me. If…" She stopped as another pain wracked her small frame. "…you will raise my son."

Elizabeth had watched Death creep forward many times. She did not offer false hope. "If Joachim allows it, I will love him as my own." She forced herself to breathe slowly, speak calmly. "He will hear all about you, his incredible imma."

Was this how Adonai answered her prayers, giving her Anna's son, taking away Anna? Anna, more sister than cousin, the faithful friend who knew her heart, who'd shared the grief of childlessness.

An indefinable urgency surged inside her, and with all the fervor she'd possessed as a child pummeling Adonai with prayers for Imma's life, she prayed for Anna's life, calling out with faith to the Healer.

As from a distance she heard the midwife gasp the words, "Push. Again. Once more."

A small, bluish bundle streaked with red appeared. Coughed. Breathed.

Elizabeth squeezed Anna's hand, stroked her face, willed her to live. "Anna, Anna, stay with me. Don't leave us. He's here. Your son is alive."

"No."

The midwife's words jarred her. The smile shook her. And then the words…

"It's a girl. Your Anna has a daughter."

***

Mary's tiny head fit in Joachim's palm. Straight dark hair stuck out like porcupine quills. She hiccupped, her eyes alert—darting back and forth, her mouth pooching. She was the funniest, most beautiful being Elizabeth had ever seen.

Anna reached for her daughter. "I would not have survived without you here, Elizabeth." She studied the small person in her arms. "Neither of us would have lived."

Elizabeth bent down to kiss her forehead. "You are stronger than you realize, my Anna, and you will raise a strong daughter." Elizabeth gathered another pile of fouled cloths into a basket. "I'll set these to soak."

Outside, she shuddered and released the tears she'd denied for two days. Tears of fear that she'd lose Anna to unspeakable suffering, tears of renewed grief that she'd never hold her own infant, tears of joy seeing Joachim's awe as he first met his daughter.

Cleansed and spent, she lifted her praise to the heavens. Even the miracle of witnessing an entirely new person enter the world dimmed before another new birth. Hers. Adonai again heard her prayers, inclined His ear to rescue three lives Death had marked as its own. Anna and Mary from physical death, and herself—tottering between a life of living and a life of deadness.

Anna called for her. She wiped the wetness from her face with a sleeve and returned. She need not explain her tears. Her red-rimmed eyes would go unnoticed. Joachim and Anna looked only at little Mary.

Elizabeth kissed Mary's tiny hand. The baby looked at her with solemn brown eyes. "Come see me, little one, as soon as your imma is well enough to travel."

"We will visit so often you will add a room onto your house."

"I'll warn Zechariah as soon as I'm home."

The women hugged. Elizabeth nodded to Joachim. One last look at the miracle named Mary, and Elizabeth joined the caravan headed south, headed home. Once, she turned to wave, but Anna and Joachim had already started back. She walked alone, the others in family groups or accompanied by servants.

Each step forward carried her closer to resuming a life of loneliness. Those she counted as friends were few. Nila sought her out at synagogue so they could sit together. Myrah's children were grown and no longer raced to her side at market, although—likely unbeknownst to Myrah—Libi came by the house every week to visit. The oldest women at the spring chatted amicably with her, and often she found a pretense to carry their water jugs uphill for them.

Life had changed for Anna and Joachim. And for her too.

Outwardly, everything might look the same. The herbs in the courtyard required daily tending and taming. She'd set out water in case a stray dog wandered by and scatter crumbs on the wall for the doves. She'd still clean and wrap the town's deceased, still nestle newborns in new mothers' eager arms, still scrub the synagogue floor, still be generous at market.

Nothing might seem different, but Adonai had birthed new life for her as well as Anna.

Almighty, You heard my plea! I cannot be lonely with You by my side. You hold me in Your arms as tenderly, as joyfully, as willingly as Anna holds Mary and Joachim holds Anna. I will search for Your blessings, carve a path in my heart to seek You each day.

I am as needy as little Mary. It is not my cloths that need changing but my thoughts. It is not the comfort of cradling arms I long for but the knowing of Your will. It is not warm milk I crave but the fire of Your holy scripture.

Zechariah was not home when she returned just before sunset. If not at Myrah's, he'd be in the synagogue studying and had probably forgotten to eat. She gathered a bit of food—there wasn't much. Either he'd been eating with Myrah and Jesse or not eating. Tomorrow she'd market and restock their food supply. After adding a flask of water to her food basket, she walked to the synagogue.

She peered inside the darkening building. Empty. He must be with his sister. Elizabeth left the food and water outside before entering. Habit propelled her to the back behind the curtain separating women from men.

Bowing her head, she praised and prayed, worshiping the One who healed, who rescued her from faith's death, Anna and Mary from death, and Joachim from loneliness and grief. Harsh whispers broke through her prayers. Jesse? Who was he angry with?

"Eli, listen to me. This Menahem the Essene is a heretic."

"He is a prophet. Had you heard that he met Herod and told him he'd be a king? Herod was not even the heir—he was second born."

Jesse scoffed. "He calls himself Messiah."

"Maybe he is. Maybe he's the one to deliver us from Rome."

Eli's defiance was so unexpected from his usual deference to Jesse that Elizabeth gasped. The brothers stilled. Unmoving, she waited.

"You say exactly what he told us people would say."

"Us? Who is 'us'? You have met with the Essenes?"

"I have. In the Essene quarter of Jerusalem where Messiah teaches."

Elizabeth crept to where the curtain's edges met. With one eye, she peered through the scant opening. Part of the men's profiles were visible.

She knew Jesse was glowering at his brother when Eli raised his chin a notch.

"Messiah Menahem is the suffering servant described in Isaiah."

Jesse snorted. "He suffers as he drapes himself in his silk robes in Jerusalem. Let me suffer like that."

"It is a hardship for him. I'm sure he'd rather be in one of the desert communities studying Torah than living in the Essene quarter of the city."

"Then you are more fool than I thought."

Eli turned to go. Jesse grabbed his arm. "Forgive me, little brother. You have never been a fool. I spoke in anger."

The brothers sat facing each other on the front bench. Elizabeth leaned forward to catch their lowered whispers.

"Eli, I question Menahem as the Anointed One, not the Essenes. The Essenes live an honorable life that demands total dedication to Adonai. Has He called you to set yourself apart to pray and study the scriptures?" He glanced sideways at his brother. "To live in celibacy? What of the beauty I saw you with last week?"

"I wish to be free of Rome, and Messiah says the time is now, that following him will assure it."

"Promise me two things."

In the dim light she saw Eli stiffen.

"Promise me you will learn more of the Essene way before you join them, and you will inwardly question what your Menahem says. Pray about it, little brother."

"That's three things."

"I was never good at numbers." Jesse clapped him on the shoulder, and the two left.

Legs cramped, Elizabeth dared not move until all was silent, but her mind sorted through all she'd heard. Could Menahem be the long-awaited Messiah? Had Messiah come in her lifetime?

Remembering her new commitment to carve a path and seek His will, she bowed her head. "Lord, when You send Messiah, make it clear to all."

CHAPTER NINE

Fifteen years later

A strong west wind curled around Elizabeth and Zechariah, whipping the hems of their clothes, shoving red dirt between feet and sandals as they pushed open the door to Myrah's house. She turned from setting the Shabbat candles on the table.

"Elizabeth, is there any more dirt and debris you can allow into the house? Why not just hold the door open all night?" She snatched a broom and began to sweep away the leaves and dirt that dared trespass. "I just finished cleaning and you've ruined my work, not that you'd care or notice. Married to my brother, you pay someone to do your work."

"No. I—"

Zechariah moved between them. "Blessed Shabbat, sister. Jesse."

"Shalom, brother." She watched Myrah's narrow face gentle. Zechariah did no wrong in his sister's eyes. Elizabeth did the wrong for both and half the town too.

"Shalom, sister." Elizabeth knew better than to wait for a cordial response. She inhaled the sharp scent of cumin and onions. "Something smells so good. Thank you for sharing your Shabbat meal with us."

Myrah pursed her lips. "I felt obligated. Zechariah is looking so thin. He needs a decent meal. I'm sure you do the best you can, but..." She shook her head. "It's not good enough—never has been."

"Myrah!" Zechariah frowned at her.

Elizabeth had heard this too many times to take offence. "Sometimes I see Libi at the spring. Are your other children and grandchildren well? It's so quiet with all of them grown and gone. You arranged a lovely wedding for Libi."

"Libi is expecting her first child, our tenth grandchild. I suppose Zechariah will never experience the joy of a grandchild that Jesse does."

Zechariah escaped to join Jesse, by the fire.

"Shalom, Jesse."

"Shalom, Zechariah. Please, sit. When you were last in the city, what did you hear of Caesar Augustus? Has he returned from Germania?"

"No, but I have news closer to our hearts. You remember when Rabbi Menahem declared himself Messiah?"

Jesse nodded. "My brother—remember Eli? He was in the room when Menahem proclaimed himself the Anointed One. Eli returned home for a week and then left. We haven't heard from him in years."

When Jesse paused, Zechariah continued. "A priest returning from Jerusalem shared the missing facts. I knew Menahem resigned from the Sanhedrin and left Jerusalem with eighty disciples, all dressed in silk robes. Was Eli with him?"

Jesse shrugged.

"The Sanhedrin did not support Menahem's claim, and he was killed at the hands of our people. Another false messiah, Jesse. When will the true one appear?"

The men's backs to them and Jesse's big voice blocking out her words, Myrah squinted at Elizabeth's belly. "Have you gained weight? Are you finally pregnant after all these years?"

Another familiar jab. She smoothed a hand over her taut belly. "No, Myrah, I'm not expecting. It's been almost a year since my cycle. I am unlikely to ever conceive."

"Your cycle ended so soon?" Myrah tsked. "Barren, then. Maybe my husband is safe from you now."

Weary, Elizabeth nodded. "It must be as you say."

Flickering light softened the wrinkles marring Myrah's forehead. Elizabeth stared at her, glimpsing the young woman whose smile and quick wit once filled a room with laughter, the girl who had been her dearest friend, her confidante.

Myrah stared back as if she too saw the young Elizabeth.

Hope lifted its fragile head then drooped when Myrah crossed her arms. "It's been too many years to go back."

"We were friends."

"Were." She pivoted and returned to finish setting the table.

Elizabeth followed her and placed a hand on her bony wrist. "Myrah. We remain family even if we are not friends. Can we make peace after all these years?"

Myrah jerked away. "Not after what you said. Not after years of you chasing Jesse. Be glad I never told Zechariah."

"Myrah, years ago, I told him…"

"You want peace? Then leave me alone. It's too late. I'll never understand why he didn't divorce you."

As Myrah's voice rose, Zechariah turned. "Elizabeth? Remember we are guests."

Jesse started to speak, but a look from Myrah stopped him. He swallowed and busied himself with straightening his chair.

Elizabeth's face flamed at her husband's public rebuke. Did he hear how often Myrah's words cut her? She had sought to restore harmony, but instead, she stood shamed before his family. Again.

The meal was silent after the Shabbat blessing. The walk home long. Inside their home, the door bolted for the night and the fire banked, Zechariah turned to her, his face stern.

"Myrah is not without fault. She refuses to offer mercy for what happened so long ago, but it saddens me to see you provoke her. Is it jealousy? That is not a godly attitude."

Elizabeth did not reply. It would be useless. Zechariah—like Myrah—saw what he wanted to see and heard what he chose to hear.

He bent over to unlace his sandals. "I do not mean it unkindly, but I've long believed you resent her being blessed with five children and you have none. Elizabeth, your imma taught you better than this and would be so disappointed in you."

She flinched, his words a stinging slap.

"It is the Lord's doing that my sister and Jesse have been blessed and you remain cursed. Anna and Joachim are blessed as are Caleb and Nila, but you are not spiteful to them. Why my sister? Do not blame Myrah for the Almighty's will." He stretched his hands to the fire. "Have you prayed for a child?"

Had she…? "Night and day, Zechariah. Year after year. You know this."

"Perhaps if you rid yourself of bitterness, you would conceive." He looked around the room. "You still have time to bear a child, don't you? Where did you leave the balm for my hands?"

"On the mantel. Beside Imma's amphora."

"I cannot open the lid tonight. My fingers are so stiff."

She opened the clay jar and massaged ointment on his hands. "Zechariah, I have prayed every day of our marriage that the Lord would look on us with favor and grant us a child."

"Perhaps you should pray more."

Baffled, she stared at him. Did he not hear her? She replaced the lid and set the jar on the mantel. "Good night, Zechariah."

Sleep refused its blessed escape. She lay awake rethinking Myrah's words, Zechariah's words, Jesse's lack of words, her words, and the Lord's long silence. Tonight, the truest ones spoken were "It's too late."

Too late for everything: a deep relationship with her husband—she'd accepted that long ago. For her friend Jesse to stand up for her, for Myrah to make peace—how much longer would she cling to that absurd hope? Too late for a child—her body had extinguished all hope—too late to be accepted as an equal among the women. Faith drooped tattered and thread-bare—no longer the warp and weft forming her life.

Dry-eyed, she wished she could weep, let tears wash their healing balm over the "too late" that most grieved her. Instead, she felt her heart harden, another chunk of faith crumble to the ground.

It was too late for faith to awaken. The admission brought an unspeakable ache in the core of her being, too deep for tears, too tender to endure hope. Once, long ago, she'd believed Adonai heard her, saw her, knew her, loved her. Twice He'd heard her pleas, saved Imma and Anna and Mary. Then fifteen years of silence. Fifteen years had chipped away the assurance that He cared. Such a tiny bit remained. A memory, an answered prayer. The dregs of faith, the remnant of hope, a grain of sand.

If she'd had a child, she'd listen for his voice, recognize his needs, be quick to hold his hand or offer comfort. If she had a child, she'd give him or her or—blessed thought—both, all that was good and protect them from harm. Why didn't Adonai treat her like this?

She rolled over to her side. *His ways are not our ways.* Obviously not.

In the past she'd believed her faith was solid, secure. Now? She felt like a child on a wooden swing. One minute flying into the sky like a bird and the next plummeting to the ground. She was too old for that game. If God wanted her to have faith, He'd need to create a miracle.

Having tossed the responsibility to Him like a child playing catch, she curled into a ball and sought sleep. When it came, it brought dreams of a little boy—his eyes the color of Abba's—laughing, swinging, jumping into her arms, confident she'd catch him, sure he was loved and safe.

The next morning, her eyes were red, swollen with tears. Zechariah either did not notice or did not comment. He left the house. She no longer asked when he'd return.

The tranquil coolness of the courtyard beckoned. She had taken a blanket against the chill, and now she wrapped it around herself. A tiny bird huddled on one leg against the side of the wall. She scraped a few crumbs into her hand and tossed them closer to him. He watched her, ignoring the crumbs.

"Fine. I'll leave. Eat while I go for water."

Inside, she covered her head and lifted a large jug to her shoulder. She did not mind the walk, only the sight of new mothers with their precious bundles.

Myrah stood near the spring. Elizabeth paused beneath the shade of a tree and watched her sister-in-law. When they'd been young and friends, they would sneak out at night to meet at the spring. Stripping to their shifts, they'd soak their feet in the water, splashing each other until they were soaked and shivering. Nila had never dared join their escapades.

Once, Jesse had followed them and threatened to tell their parents. For months they'd bribed him with sweet cakes to keep their secret. When they spied him tasting forbidden food, the bribes had stopped. He knew he'd be in trouble if they told on him.

The three of them had been such good friends even though he was older and not supposed to be with them. After last night, if Adonai healed the fractured relationships, it would be a miracle. Again, she felt like a child tossing a ball to someone.

She skirted Myrah and her friends, filled the jug, and began the uphill trek home. When she and Myrah had been children, they'd raced up the hill. Whoever won proclaimed herself queen for the day.

Everywhere she looked held a memory of childhood, a memory of Myrah.

CHAPTER TEN

Six months later

"E lizabeth."

She startled at the sound of her name and noticed once again that Zechariah did not look at her. Not that she expected it. It had been many years since he looked at her with interest, but it hurt to be almost invisible. It had not always been that way. When they first married, his eyes frequently flared with desire. Over the years, the disappointment of each month dulled his beautiful eyes a bit more.

"After the funeral, shiva for Libi's baby will be held at her imma's house. You are to mourn with them in my place."

"I'll go…if your sister does not object."

"Myrah will welcome you. It's an honor to have the priest's wife as one of those who offer comfort."

Myrah would welcome her like a snake in the grain sack.

Zechariah continued to trim his fingernails. "I leave for Jerusalem and cannot serve at the Temple if I go into the house where someone has died."

She resisted the urge to roll her eyes. She knew—had known since childhood when her abba listed the rules of Temple service—knew as every priest's wife and most Hebrew women did the laws that must be followed before Temple service. She and Imma had often stifled a giggle when Abba began yet another recital of don'ts. No contact with a dead body, no contact with a woman on her cycle, no fruit that had fallen into unclean water.

In a streak of mischief and thinking he would not notice, she fluttered her lashes. "Oh! I shouldn't have roasted a hare for dinner."

Zechariah's shoulders stiffened. "You are not amusing, Elizabeth."

She sighed. Humor had never been part of her husband's life. Devout, faithful, loyal, knowledgeable in scriptures, yes. Humorous? Not a fingernail's depth of it. It had been childish for her to tease him.

"I'm sorry, Zechariah."

"No matter."

His words stung. Even knowing he referred to her tease, it reminded her that she was of no matter. Many men would have meant that. Zechariah didn't. He was a good man, a law-abiding man. If he'd followed the tradition of Sarah...

She thought back to their tenth wedding anniversary and his refusal to divorce her. After all these years, Zechariah remained a loyal provider to a woman he no longer saw and had never understood.

Elizabeth coaxed the seven-spot ladybug onto a stick. She crossed the room, opened the door, and tapped the stick, setting the bug free. "Fly away, little one. Find seven joys instead of seven sorrows."

Bug rescued, floor swept, dishes scoured and put away, she wiped the dampness from her forehead. She secured the scarf over her head and gathered coin and a market basket. Zechariah would be away for two weeks. She wouldn't need much food. Fish for tonight, eggplant, goat cheese, and as always, olives and bread. Tomorrow she'd pack freshly baked bread, the last of the goat cheese, and almonds for his journey.

As she strolled to the edge of town, the tie of her sandal loosened. She saw a boulder nearby and knelt behind the higher side. Some days she felt her age. This was one of those days when she'd need something to hold on to as she stood up. She set aside her basket and tightened the straps. Once home, she'd rub Zechariah's hand balm on her knees.

Before she stood, a flower bobbed its red head at her. The tiny plant had fought its way through cracked rock. She cupped it between two fingers to admire petals as soft and delicate as an infant's skin.

A swish of skirts alerted her to the presence of others, but before she could stand and make herself known, their words stung her ears.

"Such a pity about Elizabeth. She seems like such a nice woman." Elizabeth recognized the voice of a local woman who lived on the other side of the town.

"She must have d-displeased Adonai to never have been b-blessed with a child—not even a girl. I think her 'nice' is f-false."

Elizabeth searched her memory for someone in the town who stuttered.

"For all these years? No, I've known her since I was eight. Myrah doesn't like her, but I think she's jealous. Everyone knows Myrah is a gossip and Elizabeth is godly."

That third voice—Hannah? Little Hannah with the curliest hair Elizabeth had ever seen, who'd knocked on her door every day for years asking for and receiving a handful of dates and almonds.

"The prophet Samuel said Adonai sees the heart," the first woman said. "If she's godly, she'd have had a baby."

"Myrah says Elizabeth is always praying, acting like she's b-better than us." The woman with the stutter snorted. "And her being childless, I'd say she's less. M-Myrah says she wants J-Jesse as husband. Poor Zechariah, to be stuck with her."

"And Myrah too."

"Well, I did hear that when Elizabeth was younger she..."

The women's voices faded as they moved away. Elizabeth remained unmoving, the red petals crumpled, her fingers stained bloodred.

Still? After all these years, her sister-in-law continued to attack her?

⁕

Elizabeth's steps slowed—snails moved faster—as she approached Myrah's house. She paused at the top of the path to Myrah's house. A path so smooth it seemed her sister-in-law had run out of household chores and swept the dirt between her door and the street.

Dirt must be braver—or more foolish—than dust, Elizabeth mused. Dust knew better than to cross Myrah's threshold. She knew better too, yet here she was about to brave her Goliath, her Jericho, her Red Sea. Was this how the midwives of ancient times, Shiphrah and Puah, felt when approaching Pharaoh? Had they dragged their feet, wished to be turtles hiding inside their shells?

Once, she and Myrah had been the closest of friends, confiding secrets and hopes and childhood hurts. If Myrah had married first and not been with her during the walk to the feast, if she'd not overheard words not meant for her ears, if she'd allowed Elizabeth to explain, to apologize, if Myrah understood that Jesse was only and always just a friend… If, if, if—a useless word, a hopeless word.

Elizabeth roused herself and ordered her feet to advance. Voices sounded from the house.

Fortifying herself with a deep breath, she hailed the house. "Myrah?" No answer. She entered the courtyard. "Hello?" No answer. She knocked on the inner door and then shifted the basket of bread and cheese she'd brought to share. "Myrah!" Silence—the silence of held breath and shadows. She knew they were home. She'd heard talking as she approached.

"It is I, Elizabeth, come to mourn and sit shiva with you."

The door opened just enough to show Myrah's face framed with gray frizzles. "You are not needed. You don't understand what it means to lose a child. Didn't think you'd bother to come since Jesse is in Jerusalem."

Hoped I wouldn't. Elizabeth heard the unspoken truth.

"There's no room for you, so many have come to mourn with *my* daughter."

Elizabeth ignored the emphasis. "Zechariah told me to come."

The door opened another handsbreadth. Myrah would never go against her brother's wishes. Defeated, she jutted her chin. "I knew you wouldn't be here otherwise. I'll tell him you were here. Go away."

"She is my niece. I am family. It is an honor to grieve with her."

"She's not your niece. She's Zechariah's niece."

"And I'm his wife."

"Unfortunately." Myrah leaned forward, garlic breath hot on Elizabeth's face. "If you insist—but leave her alone." She blocked the open door, her spider arms akimbo. "She doesn't need you and your fancy ways. Don't upset her. She has spoken to no one. She's fragile and she's—"

"Aunt Elizabeth!" Libi looked up, wiped her sleeve across her nose and eyes and rushed into her aunt's open arms. Elizabeth gathered her close and smoothed Libi's unkempt hair as the girl clung to her. She murmured words of love. Libi was not ready to hear the traditional words of comfort—*May the Lord comfort you with all mourners of Zion and Jerusalem*—only to express her grief.

"I didn't get to bathe him or dress him or show how perfect he was."

"Of course he was perfect, Libi-girl."

"He wouldn't move. Babies are supposed to cry, but mine didn't." Libi's voice tightened. "Just cold and blue and still and… so cold."

"Your heart aches because you loved him."

Libi nodded. "And I lost him. I'm useless like you, Aunt Elizabeth."

She absorbed the cruelty. It was unintentional—words wrenched from the icy grip of grief.

"Help me, Aunt Elizabeth."

Beside her, she felt Myrah bristle. "I'm the one to help you, daughter. Come to Imma. Enough tears. There will be other babies."

She held Libi tighter, taking in her pain. "Myrah, that doesn't help. This infant's life was precious to your daughter. Let her mourn this loss."

Libi sobbed harder.

"See what you've done, Elizabeth? You intrude. Leave. You've upset her." Myrah pulled her daughter away. "You're young. There's time."

Elizabeth clamped her lips together. *You're young. There's time.* How often had she been battered with those same words? And now she was old, and the thief named Time had long since stolen her heart's desire. *Almighty One, let it not be so for Libi.*

Giving a curt nod, she turned and left the room. Intentionally, she closed the door softly.

Serenely, she walked—her pace measured and determined—until she was out of sight of the house. If she glanced back, she might turn to a pillar of salt like Lot's wife and forever be facing Myrah—a miserable fate.

Away from the house, she quickened her steps. Her hands curled into fists. "That woman is the most bitter, angry, revengeful person Adonai ever created. Doesn't care who she hurts if it also hurts me. If she listened to the Torah about forgiveness, she would not be so unbearable. How were we ever friends?" At her jagged tones, a squirrel in the path pivoted to face her then scampered away, his tail high. He leaped onto a tree, scrambled to a branch above her, and scolded her thoroughly.

She ached for Libi, subjected to her imma's thoughtless words. If only there was a balm she could concoct for her niece or a reasonable excuse she could make for Myrah.

"Almighty, make Libi deaf to cruel words, and help me to forgive Myrah for being..." Words—mostly unflattering—crowded her mind. At last, she knew the right word. Elizabeth released breath she'd not realized she held. "Help me forgive Myrah for being Myrah." Her shoulders softened and tears tricked down her face. She did not wipe them away. More would follow.

Home. She must get home before sorrow crippled her, blinded her. Was it not enough to lose her best friend, to lose her heart-dream of a child, to lose the attention of her husband? Must she still be seen as useless? Still be the subject of gossip and conjecture?

"Almighty, I try with all that is within me to live a life honoring You. Show me Your higher ways. Let me not fall back into seeking my own will. I no longer ask for a child, only to please you, only for peace."

Tear-blind, she stumbled over a root. Pain shot through her ankle, tumbling her to the ground. She moaned and clasped her hands around her foot.

"Can I help you?"

Elizabeth looked up into the face of a stranger, a young woman whose glow and soft caress of her abdomen announced to all she carried the fullness of life.

Lord, I ask for peace, and You send a reminder of what You denied me?

"I twisted my ankle." She hoped the woman would attribute her teary eyes to physical pain.

"Can you stand? Let me help you to your home."

"Thank you, no. It's just around that corner. I'll sit here for a bit and be fine."

"Then I'll sit with you." The woman lowered herself to the ground. "I'm Kerren. My husband and I and our soon-to-be just moved here from Netanya."

"Elizabeth. Welcome to our town."

Wariness flickered across Kerren's face. "Elizabeth the priest's wife? I've heard of you." She shifted so her tunic no longer touched Elizabeth's foot. "The women at the spring talk, and I listen."

Elizabeth waited, a mouse beneath an owl's watch.

"Most name you as righteous, but others call you cursed. How can both be true?"

"I am childless. That much everyone knows." *And remind me at every turn as if I could forget for a moment.* "Righteous? I do not name myself such. That is for the Almighty to judge."

"If you have no child, you cannot be righteous." Kerren stood and took a step backward. "If you need no help, then I shall be on my way. Shalom."

"Shalom." Kerren left in such a hurry, the hem of her tunic swept dirt puffs to each side.

Elizabeth burrowed her head in her hands. After a few minutes she stood and hobbled home. Zechariah left in the morning. When she knew she'd be alone, she'd pour out her heart to the Lord, surrender her will again and again until only His will filled her.

***

Zechariah left for Jerusalem just as the sun kept the promise of a new day of joy. Elizabeth, ankle bandaged, limped beside him until their ways parted. A murmured farewell and she hobbled down the path to the spring. It would be a long return home lugging the water uphill with her ankle already throbbing. Perhaps someone would offer to help.

In the quiet of dawn, she knelt by the spring's edge. This early, the water was cool, the spring untroubled with children's toes and the demands of lowered jugs.

Elizabeth dipped her fingers in the water's sharp, cold cleanness and splashed her face to wash away the traces of a sleepless night. Nothing was cold enough or sharp enough to cleanse the hurt of yesterday. There existed no thread or leather strip sturdy enough to bind brokenness into wholeness: no prayer left unoffered, no plea unspoken.

Doubt settled in as she feared herself unheard by her Lord, spirit broken, pain festering. Escape into doubt beckoned and she followed.

Shivering in the morning's briskness, Elizabeth swirled her hand in the water. Ripples raced to each side. Raising her cupped hand and spreading her fingers, she watched water drops glint in the brightening sun.

"My tears, Lord—like my prayers—are ceaseless. I no longer feel Your presence when I pray. Do I say the wrong words? Ask the impossible? Hold me tightly, do not let go. Do not let me seek my will as in the past."

She spun her hand in the water and held it up, each finger dripping with clear water tears. "Your will is my will. Pleasing You is my heart's desire, but judgment hasn't stopped. Scorn and rumors haven't stopped. Reproach and dishonor haven't stopped. Make me deaf to what others think of me—that I am not guilty of lashon hara, of listening to hurtful speech. You are my God. I have worshiped no one else and nothing else."

Voices sounded in the distance. Lingering meant she'd face another wave of disdainful and pitying women. But a thought she could not evade paralyzed her.

Motherhood had once been her god, her singular focus. She huffed in frustration and shoved aside that uncomfortable conviction. Some women might not want to be mothers, but they did not live in her town. She brushed the dirt from her clothes and pushed the thought from her mind. Every woman she knew wanted a child and had a child. It was what women *did*. Wasn't it the reason Adonai created woman? What more did Adonai want from her that first He denied her a child and now denied peace?

Unbidden came the prophet Micah's words. *"And what does the Lord require of you? To act justly and to love mercy and to walk humbly with your Adonai."*

The words played through her mind again. Slow realization came as she spoke them aloud.

Babies were not mentioned.

She blinked. Scripture named children a gift from the Lord, but—she struggled forming the thought—not necessary for her worth to Adonai. Was it possible He said no to her as an imma, not no to her as a person? She balked at the strangeness of it.

Familiar voices warned that the women drew closer. The uphill climb loomed before her, the jug of water heavier than yesterday.

Worth not counted by bearing a child? Motherhood not necessary to please Adonai? It was too new a concept, too foreign. Along with the day's water, she carried confusion home.

Elizabeth bolted the door and latched the shutters against the coming night. The two white candles in polished silver candlesticks waited to be lit, their wicks tall and straight. She stood alone as light faded from the sky. It was time. She touched a flame to the candle of remembrance, *zahor*—remember the Shabbat Day—and the candle of observance, *shamor*. As the light flickered, held, grew, she covered her face with her palms and murmured the blessing.

"Baruch Atah Adonai Eloheinu. Blessed are You, Lord our God, King of the universe, who has sanctified us with His commandments and commanded us to kindle the light of the Holy Shabbat."

She folded the light into herself, accepting His light and His Shabbat promise of rest and peace. With a glance at the candles, she whispered her own requests.

"Adonai, blessed are You. In Your mercy, hear my prayer."

Hesitating, she sorted through a litany of requests—shallow, temporal, impossible—some so large they seemed distant and not of her heart, some rote, some tangled in selfishness.

How many Shabbats had she asked for a child, peace with Zechariah, forgiveness from Myrah? Weeks grew to months grew to years until those prayers were empty words, distant hopes, their realization no longer anticipated. What remained? A life narrowed to routine tasks.

Gone was expected joy. She sought peace, mercy, His purpose for the remainder of her days.

"Adonai, this is my heart's true prayer—your purpose for me."

It caught her by surprise. A whiff of sweetness, a quiver of peace, the shimmer of light.

Years ago, each Shabbat as she watched Imma light the candles, Elizabeth had delighted in the moment's holiness, knowing the outer flame was a reminder of God's light within her.

As a child, she'd felt swaddled in peace. Often, after they'd shared the meal, Abba would cup her little face tenderly with his roughened hands and remind her that the flame of God's light sparkling inside her was a shield against darkness—the dark of night and the darkness coiled inside each person. He'd insisted that dwelling in Adonai's light would guide her and must be shared by kindness.

Adonai—her dwelling. Showing kindness—her purpose.

Elizabeth spread her hands. "Shabbat shalom." The empty room filled with peace.

CHAPTER ELEVEN

Zechariah heaved a sigh of relief as he approached Jerusalem. The day's walk neared its end. The city was not far, but each trip took longer, required more times to rest. He could rest, and tomorrow when he woke recite the morning prayer on the Shabbat within the golden walls of the city of Adonai, the city of David, the most beautiful place in the world. Nothing compared to being in Jerusalem, the place God chose to rest His name.

"Oh, beloved." Lovingly, he brushed his hand against the city walls, relishing the white dust of the limestone on his palm. Breathing deeply, he inhaled the scent that was Jerusalem's alone—cinnamon and history, sewage and incense, opportunity and oregano. Eighty thousand feet shuffled through the city's dust as a thousand dialects stirred the air. The boasting of vendors, the bleating and cooing, a mother's frantic call— Jerusalem pulsed with life.

"No wonder the Almighty loves you, Jerusalem. And He has given me eight glorious days here to worship Him."

The Temple shone from the highest hill, a crown worthy of the city. His legs trembled after the long trek to the top.

"Shabbat to Shabbat," he reminded himself. "More than worth the effort to climb the mount." He stopped, breathing hard.

The Temple's Hulda Gate—which only priests could enter—stood wide. Its open arms welcoming him as a father would a precious child. Remembrance surged. The pang of grief as familiar as his heartbeat. Not for him the joy of flinging open a door and welcoming home a son or even a daughter. Would a child have been short like him or tall and slender like his Elizabeth? Would their child… "Stop." He scolded himself. "Stop these useless thoughts. It is as Adonai wills."

Forcibly he turned his mind to the task at hand and turned toward the priests' *mikveh*. The law required he purify himself and show that he had no broken bones nor any skin disease before reporting for his time of service. Thankfully, swollen knuckles did not exclude him from serving.

The next morning, inspected and purified, he went to the sacred chamber to don a linen tunic. Fingers stiff, he fumbled to tie the embroidered sash around his waist before setting a linen turban on his head. On warm days like this, the rule against wearing woolen garments was another of Adonai's mercies. Zechariah broke out in a sweat at the thought of scratchy wool against his skin.

Midday, after the morning sacrifices, the shifts of priests changed. Zechariah joined his division, the descendants of Abijah, as they gathered in the hall of priests. He murmured greetings to several until a deep hush signaled the approach of the High Priest to select five men by lot, the priests who would offer the sacrifices, who would give the priestly blessing to the people, and the greatest honor of a lifetime, who would burn incense before the Holy of Holies.

Forty years he'd served—since he was twenty—and never once been selected for a special act of service.

The High Priest cast the lots. Called two men to service. "Abel ben Ethan, Jonathan ben Levi. The Lord has chosen you to offer the sacrifices." The men raised their arms, thanking Adonai for allowing them to serve.

"Caleb ben Shimon, Joram ben Reuben. The Lord has selected you to give the priestly blessing." Caleb and Joram bowed their heads in awe of the honor.

"Zechariah ben Levi. The Lord has called you to burn incense at the altar before the Holy of Holies."

The words rang in his head. He did not move. Of course he had conjured them out of his deep wish to so serve. Unable to see over those in front of him, he glanced to one side. Who had been chosen by the Lord for so great an honor? The man beside him nodded. Confused, Zechariah looked to the other side. That man too was staring at him. Someone nudged him from behind.

"Zechariah ben Levi…"

Whatever else the High Priest said disappeared in an implosion of humility. Zechariah fell to his knees. Covered his face. Wept. "I am not worthy to serve the Almighty."

A hand rested on his shoulder. "Nor am I. Nor are any of us, but we have been called and we obey. Stand, Zechariah."

With the help of those around him, he staggered to his feet, tears smeared across his face, and looked into the stern eyes of the High Priest. For a moment, Zechariah forgot he was speaking to the most powerful man of his faith, the only one who could enter the Holy of Holies where Adonai's presence appeared.

"I am a sinful man undeserving of this honor. It is enough for me to be in His Temple. Give this task to another."

"Zechariah, I did not choose you. It is the Lord Himself who called you to this task. Rejoice in this blessing. Prepare yourself. Serve with thanksgiving. Adonai made it clear that you are to be at the altar of incense today for the Shabbat evening."

"But—"

"You, a mere man, a priest of the line of Abijah, defy me? Defy the Almighty?"

Zechariah drew himself to his full height, almost reaching the chin of the man before him. "I will serve with joy and give thanks every day for the rest of my life."

It was time. Zechariah placed two handfuls of incense into a golden bowl. He approached the entrance to the Holy Place.

He knew without looking that a multitude of people gathered behind him. Until today, he had been one of those standing outside, praying as incense was burned. This act of worship could not be performed alone. It required the prayers of the faithful, for the Lord would not accept the incense without prayer. "May the merciful Adonai enter the Holy Place and accept with favor the offering of His people."

As he stepped forward, he released the ridicule of his childhood peers, the pride of his parents when he became a priest, the disbelief of being chosen for this service.

Heart thudding, he heard as if from a great distance the tinkling bell announcing that he had entered the Temple to burn incense. The seven-branched candlestick on his left stood taller than he had ever been. He passed the table of shewbread on his right and stopped before the incense altar.

Scripture named it "most holy to the Lord." Not because of the acacia wood overlaid with gold or the golden horns gracing each corner. It was only as high as the knot in his linen sash, but it lifted the sacrifice of prayer high to the Lord.

Four rings of gold were built into the altar so it could be moved with gold-covered acacia wood poles. *Samson could have lifted it alone.* An odd thought until he remembered that today's portion of the law and of the prophets had been about Samson's conception and the Nazirite law Adonai gave Moses.

On the far side of the altar hung the thick veil of blue, purple, and scarlet stretching wall to wall and reaching to the ceiling—a warning not to enter. Beyond was the Holy of Holies. The mercy seat. The Ark of the Covenant.

To be so close.

Zechariah's hand trembled. He sprinkled the incense on the fire, breathed in the sweetness of the spices, the frankincense. Prayed his heart was pure, that he offered no offense to the Almighty.

And then no thoughts came. No words. Any semblance of expectation disappeared. His only desire—to be vulnerable and known before the Almighty. To worship with every fiber of his being. Unworthy, yes, but the longing overwhelmed him, and he fell to his knees, opened his heart, and prayed with his soul.

A presence, a warmth, a whisper of the unworldly pierced his consciousness. Raising his head to behold a shimmering splendor, he staggered backward, tumbling to the floor, terrified of the powerful man standing to his right. Zechariah's arms and legs refused to obey his desire to hide. Unable to flee, Zechariah could not look away from the compelling visage. Bathed in brilliant light, the man loomed over Zechariah, glowing with a radiant luster as if he'd stood in the presence of Adonai.

"Do not be afraid, Zechariah. Your prayer has been heard."

Zechariah gaped at the Being, astonished that he understood the music of his speech.

"Your wife, Elizabeth, will bear you a son, and you are to call him John."

This living, speaking thing, this man of light, knew his name and Elizabeth's name and—did he say a child—a boy named John? His heart thudded, leaped, quivered. He rose to his knees, the power emanating from the man drawing him closer.

"He will be a joy and delight to you, and many will rejoice because of his birth, for he will be great in the sight of the Lord."

His son, yes, the man's beautiful words referred to the child as "he," great in the sight of—was it possible? Zechariah clutched his heart. Was he dreaming? Had he died?

"He is never to take wine or other fermented drink, and he will be filled with the Holy Spirit even before he is born. He will bring back many of the people of Israel to the Lord their Adonai. And he will go on before the Lord, in the spirit and power of Elijah—"

Elijah? *The* Elijah? Zechariah grasped the neck of his robe, ripping it as he gasped for breath.

"—to turn the hearts of the parents to their children and the disobedient to the wisdom of the righteous—to make ready a people prepared for the Lord."

He scrambled to his feet, wobbled, sought to balance himself. Holding out his arms, he pleaded for assurance. "How can I be sure of this? I am old and my wife is well along in years."

"I am Gabriel." Thunder rumbled his words. "I stand in the presence of Adonai, and I have been sent to speak to you and to tell you this good news."

Light pulsed from Gabriel, the white shock blinding Zechariah, forcing retreat.

"And now you will be silent and not able to speak until the day this happens, because you did not believe my words, which will come true at their appointed time."

The light, luminous and living, disappeared. The warmth faded. But the sense of unworldliness clung to him as a sheen of sweat.

At last, he lurched to the exit, dizzy, still blinded by the angel's radiance. Stepping into the daylight, confronted by those who waited to be dismissed with a blessing in the name of the Lord, he opened his mouth to speak.

Nothing. He tried again. Horrified, he grasped the reality of Gabriel's words. He gestured with both arms. The other priests must understand what—no, *who* he had seen.

Cold eyes condemned him for offending the Almighty and thus endangering their prayers being heard and answered.

He shook his head. *No! No! I have been blessed beyond belief, not condemned. Corrected, not punished.*

Murmurs swelled around him as the others cast their doubts, voicing their confusion, grasping for understanding.

"He still lives."

"But struck mute."

"How did you offend Adonai?"

"What sin do you harbor?"

Words stormed against him until Zechariah gripped his head, knocking his turban to the ground. Wisps of baby-fine gray hair straggled across his head. *No! No! It is right I was chosen for this time.*

And then he heard Caleb. "Zechariah. Look at me."

He sought the familiar voice as a bird seeks its haven.

"My friend, have you seen a vision?"

Yes! Yes! Sobs of relief shook his shoulders. He nodded, locked eyes with Caleb, and spread wide his arms to portray the glory that had surrounded Gabriel.

Caleb elbowed his way to the front of the stunned priests. "You saw a vision. Something happened that left you mute. Right?"

Zechariah nodded once and ducked his head in shame. His doubt in the face of Adonai's gift had caused this.

"Zechariah, did you touch the veil to the Holy of Holies?" The high priest's voice was cool, terse.

He raised his head. Looked him in the eye. Shook his head.

The man studied him through narrowed eyes. "I do not know what happened nor why you were chosen for a vision whereas I was not..." He pursed his lips. "I will inquire of the Lord if you are to continue serving or if you are to return home. Remove these garments and go to your chambers."

Caleb picked up the dirtied turban and slipped his arm around Zechariah's shoulders to lead him from the stares. "You tremble with exhaustion, my friend. Once you have changed clothes, rest, eat. I will bring word to you of your service this week."

Voiceless, Zechariah covered his heart with his hand in a silent thank you to Caleb.

***

Zechariah brushed dust from the linen turban, unwound the sash, and pulled the tunic over his head. He folded them, his hand lingering on the tidy pile. Would he ever wear them again? He knew someday would be the last day, but now, so soon? Was this the final time he'd stand in the priest's changing chamber, this morning the last time he'd don the cool linen of a Temple priest? He smoothed his beard. If he'd not doubted Gabriel, he could have shouted to the world the words the angel spoke.

Perhaps in mercy the angel stilled his voice.

Startled, he knew it for truth.

Had he not been hushed, would he have continued to question and doubt Adonai's gift? Or perhaps he'd have burst from the Temple proclaiming, no *boasting* of the great gift he and Elizabeth were promised—a son, not just a male child, but a

Nazarite, a prophet like Elijah, boldly preaching repentance, like Samuel, chosen for all his days.

A Nazarite! *His* son, chosen to be consecrated to Adonai's service. Oh, the favor Adonai showed him! And each time he spoke his son's name, John, *the Lord is Gracious,* he'd remember to praise Adonai for His graciousness. John's entire life, set apart from anything unclean, his mind and body kept from darkness. His son, a messenger of Adonai to all of Israel.

Zechariah fell to his knees, humbled by such favor. That he should have a son was all he'd ever desired, but to father such a son left him speechless even without Gabriel's decree.

He dragged his mind from praise and prayer when a hand rested on his shoulder and Caleb's voice pierced his mind.

"The High Priest instructs you to continue serving in the Temple. We will walk home together when your time of service is complete."

Home, where he'd share the news with his wife.

He looked up and saw Caleb watching him. For a moment, he considered cupping his hand over his belly to show an expectant woman. No, his wife should hear this first.

Caleb cleared his throat. "I can explain to the townspeople and Elizabeth that you were given a vision."

Elizabeth. Childbirth was difficult for a young woman, but to bear a child at her age could be deadly. Adonai promised him a son—not that Elizabeth would survive the ordeal. Was she the cost, the sacrifice for this child? Would she be willing to give her life for the joy, the honor of carrying a son, the banishment of her disgrace?

Of course she would. She'd do anything to please the Lord, but out of courtesy, he'd ask her. His eyes widened at the irony. A woman announced to her husband they were to have a child. He was the first man to share the news with his wife.

He'd sit down beside her, or maybe they'd walk to the stream near their house, and he'd speak… No, he'd not speak.

He frowned and then his face brightened. As a priest's daughter, Elizabeth could read. He'd write out the story, and she'd understand all that transpired. As if his hands knew his thoughts, they dealt a sharp pang. He glanced downward. With his swollen joints, writing a name was all he could manage. Drawing a picture had always been beyond his ability.

At last, he shrugged. If the Lord could cause a child to bloom in Elizabeth's womb, He could guide this bewildered husband how to convey all that occurred.

Tomorrow, he'd again serve in the Temple, his praise burning so brightly with joy and gratitude that sacred embers might not be needed, and the High Priest might be singed if he moved too close. A small smile curved his lips.

Synagogue without Zechariah felt wrong. Elizabeth arched her back and stretched her neck from side to side to ease the tension of sitting on the cold stone bench. While her ankle swelled and her bones stiffened, he would be standing in the light and beauty of the Temple. Worshiping there, Zechariah wouldn't notice his hands hurting until evening.

She lifted her ankle a handsbreadth from the floor to adjust the bandage. She should have packed some of the ointment for his knuckles. Myrah's bony finger poked her in the back as she hissed for her to sit still. She resisted the childish urge to turn and stick out her tongue. Gracious! Where had that come from? Zechariah would be horrified.

Hands folded, head lowered as if in prayer, Elizabeth let her focus wander to Zechariah's dark eyes and rare smile. Was it beautiful because it was so seldom seen? She did not hear the Torah portion read nor notice when the others stood. Myrah would rightly reprimand her for that too.

Elizabeth squirmed. Swatted at the gnats. Scooted back. Sat tall. Slumped. She crossed her ankles with a moue of distress. Nila elbowed her. "Stop wiggling. You are worse than a child."

With a loud sigh, she stilled herself. Closed her eyes. Clasped her hands. *Adonai. Holy are You.* Gradually, the sounds of the synagogue service receded. Mothers did not hush restless children. Chants and prayers fell silent. Even the hum of gnats quieted.

Fiery light filled Elizabeth, her only thought to pray for Zechariah. Something was happening to her husband. Chills rippled across her shoulders. An odd awareness of her breath moving in and out of her body, of blood pumping through her limbs, a tingling dizziness behind her eyes converged until every fiber of her being compelled her to pray for him. *Mercy, Lord, mercy for Your servant Zecharaiah, who loves You above all else. Mercy, Lord.* Assurance came. He lived—uninjured—but something or someone had interrupted his life, his time at the Temple.

The inward light dimmed. The cacophony of gnats and children and chants resumed. When the service ended, Elizabeth struggled to stand. She could not tell anyone what she'd experienced—the words refused to form. Confused, ankle throbbing, she stood, hearing nothing. Myrah stood before her, hands propped on her hips. She guessed she was being scolded for her restlessness.

Weary, she limped away while Myrah's mouth still moved. Someone caught her arm. Nila. Seeing genuine concern, Elizabeth struggled to hear her friend's words.

"You are pale, Elizabeth. Is your ankle so bad?"

"No."

"Later this week, let's share a meal while both our men are in Jerusalem."

"Yes." It was all she could manage. Nila's bewilderment showed that it had not been enough.

Senses heightened, Elizabeth limped home, grateful to escape people and their sounds and smells and motions.

For three days she stayed inside her house. Shabbat challah bread and days-old water sustained her. She wanted nothing more. No word arrived from Jerusalem summoning her to Zechariah's side or warning her he was ill. She did not think. She did not pray. She sat and breathed.

On the fourth day, as she watched the birds flutter to the wall for seeds and breadcrumbs, Nila's voice called her name.

"You live! Are you well?"

Her voice disrupted the solitude Elizabeth craved. She roused herself to force a reply.

"Yes." Not enough for a dear friend. "I'm better." The lie eased Nila's look of worry.

"I brought fresh water and food. You've not been seen at the market or the spring in several days. I should have come sooner."

Nila carried her gifts inside the house with the easy familiarity of a long friendship. She returned, munching a fig.

"How many more years do you think our men will travel to serve in the Temple? Zechariah's joints and Caleb's stomach problems make it hard for them. They both love serving. They are so alike in their commitment to the Lord. What do you think about…?"

Nila chattered. Elizabeth nodded whenever she paused. While Nila went inside to prepare a tray of foods, Elizabeth leaned her head back against the wall and soaked in the moment of silence. Nila's return disrupted the stillness.

"Your color is not good." Nila set down the platter and sat on the edge of the bench. She squeezed one of Elizabeth's hands. "Your hands are cold too. Has something happened? You were so wiggly at service and then so still I wondered if you died sitting upright." She tilted her head. "That was supposed to be funny. Elizabeth, what's wrong? Are you sick—like your imma—and not telling anyone? You know you can share anything with me. I'm not Myrah to judge you."

"It's Zechariah." Her voice sounded strained in her own ears. "I think… On Shabbat… There was a moment… I sensed…" The words refused to form into a coherent sentence. "I'm just tired, Nila, and that makes me worry more. He's not a young man."

"I understand completely." Nila patted her knee. "Remember, the road is short and well traveled. No robbers. Caleb is with him, and right now they are in Adonai's Temple. What could happen?"

Elizabeth nodded and smiled. "Of course, you're right."

The smile disappeared when Nila left.

CHAPTER TWELVE

More alarming than Myrah's appearance in her doorway was the pallor of her face and the desperation of her frantic words. "Elizabeth, hurry! Zechariah returned and he's… Oh, just hurry."

She'd sensed something was wrong. The strange apprehension and physical sensitivity during the synagogue service was sent to warn her, prepare her.

Elizabeth dropped her pestle into the mortar of basil and followed Myrah through the arched doorway and onto the street. Shocked when Myrah grabbed her hand and yanked her forward, Elizabeth heard her heart pounding so loudly in her ears that she could not hear what else Myrah said. They raced to the town square, tripping over the uneven stones, their sandals slapping the pavement.

Zechariah. Wounded? Arrested? Dead?

The women ducked through the crowd of onlookers and elbowed their way to the front. Zechariah stood in the center, Caleb by his side.

Gasping for breath, she raked her eyes over her husband's figure—a small man, thin, with grayed hair and a nose too big for his narrow face, his shoulders wide, his carriage straight.

Not dead. Not injured. Not arrested. He stood on his own power, no wooden staff helping him balance. His garments were not bloodstained. His face was unbruised. Roman soldiers did not grip his arms to drag him away.

But something—something was different. She looked again. His eyes were different. Slightly dazed but glowing, the light emanating from within.

"Zechariah? Myrah, what—?"

"I'm trying to tell you. He cannot speak. Caleb said he was struck mute while offering incense to the Almighty."

Elizabeth's eyes widened. "He was chosen to offer the incense? Such an honor."

"*He cannot speak!*" Myrah's shrill tore through Elizabeth. "He must have offended Almighty, and this is his punishment."

Elizabeth grasped Myrah's arm to steady herself. "No. It's not possible."

"Elizabeth." Caleb stood in front of her. "There is more. The High Priest requested I escort him home and spread the word that Zechariah was given a vision."

She gasped. "Of what? What was the vision?"

Caleb raised one eyebrow. "We don't know as he can't speak."

"Is it permanent?" Elizabeth blinked at her foolish question. "Oh. We don't know. He can't tell us." She'd miss the warm resonance of his voice.

Zechariah drew closer and shook his head. He raised nine fingers.

"Nine months? Nine years?" Caleb leaned forward. "This is new information. So it is a temporary affliction, and eventually he will share his vision."

Zechariah took her elbow and tugged, his hand trembling.

"I think he wants to return home. Thank you, Caleb." Elizabeth motioned to Myrah, and the three left the crowd but not before they heard scattered mutterings.

"Both cursed. Her barren, him mute."

"Three of them—his sister too—the gossip."

"Cast from Adonai's presence."

"Shame."

"If he's mute, he'll no longer blaspheme."

Elizabeth tensed. Had they not heard Caleb's assurance of a vision? That did not sound like he had been disgraced. And even if he had, did years of service to these people mean nothing? How could the days of sitting shiva, attending births, sharing their sorrows and joys be so quickly forgotten? She longed to cover his ears and spare him the sting of their words. She'd become accustomed to them, but not so her husband.

The women steadied Zechariah as they walked downhill and through the streets. Inside their home they helped him remove his cloak and settled him in his favorite chair. Myrah knelt to untie his sandals and bathe his feet as Elizabeth rubbed ointment into his stiffened fingers.

How could Zechariah have offended Almighty? He was a good man, a godly man even if their marriage was not what she'd hoped for when...

Without lifting her head, Myrah whispered the question for both of them. "Brother, did you offend the Almighty? Is that why you are struck mute?"

At his silence, the women shared a look of fear before realizing Zechariah had fallen asleep.

"He's exhausted." Myrah stood, her shoulders slumped. "Please, will you tell me if you learn more?"

The tenderness of Myrah's tone tugged at Elizabeth's heart. This was the girl she'd known years ago. She nodded, aching for her sister-in-law, who held such pride in her brother, and for Zechariah, who dedicated himself to being right with Adonai yet had been disgraced.

For herself, she felt nothing. Her life would not change no matter what had happened in the Temple.

⋯⋯⋯⋯⋯⋯⋯⋯⋯⋯⋯⋯

Zechariah inhaled the scent of roasting meat and pepper-onion stew. Elizabeth had prepared his favorite foods to welcome him home. He shifted in his chair. So much had happened since last he sat here: chosen to burn incense before the Holy of Holies, receiving the vision, learning he'd have a son. He sat up straighter. A smile tickled his lips. He was going to father a child with Elizabeth.

He watched her through half-open eyes. She was tall for a woman, still slender as a girl. Would she move as gracefully when heavy with child?

He needed to prepare her for what Gabriel foretold. She'd be stunned for more than one reason. When had they last slept cradled in each other's arms? His face warmed with shame. In this he failed his duty as a husband.

If he reached for her tonight, would she submit or pull away? Maybe tomorrow would be soon enough. *Coward,* he named himself.

How would he tell her of the vision, this experience that changed the comfort, the course of their life? He turned his hands over, ruing their stiffness. He could write a word, maybe two—not the entire story.

"Zechariah? Are you hungry?"

He shook his head and patted the seat beside him. She sat on the edge looking at him, her gentle eyes full of questions. He stroked his beard. How to share the most glorious experience of his life with no words?

He curled two stiff fingers and his thumb close to his palm, forming the other two fingers into a person's legs and walked them upward.

She brightened. "You're going to tell me the story!"

Nodding, he made the motion again.

"You went up to Jerusalem."

He nodded, pleased she understood. He templed his fingers.

"And you prayed, of course you did. And Caleb shared you were selected to burn incense before the Holy of Holies. Oh, I'm so happy for you. A once-in-a-lifetime honor from the Lord."

He smiled at her excitement. He pointed to the flaming oil lamp and spread his arms wide.

Horror darkened her face. "You burned the Temple? It caught on fire? No, Caleb would have said that." She clasped her hands at her chin. "Did you knock the altar over, add too many embers?" She gasped. "You burned the curtain separating you from the Holy of Holies? Is it ruined? Are you burned? Was anyone hurt? No wonder—"

Stopping her with a lifted hand, he shook his head emphatically.

"The curtain is intact? Thank Adonai." She slumped in relief.

Zechariah's nod assured her. He pointed to his eyes.

"Oh. Is this the vision?" Elizabeth leaned forward and laced her hands. "I'm listening, er, watching."

Observing her closely, he placed a hand under his chest and curved it over his stomach. She looked at him blankly. "You ate too much? Your stomach hurts?"

He gestured for her to bring a pen and a tablet. Laboriously he wrote *John*.

"John? Who is John? A new high priest, someone you met?"

Again, he curved his hand over his stomach but pointed to her. This time she understood, but instead of the joy he expected, hurt warred with confusion. "Zechariah, I've never known you to be cruel."

He reached for her hand. She yanked it out of his reach. Refused to meet his eyes. He opened his mouth to insist she look at him. No words emerged. How could he get her attention? Standing, he moved in front of her and lifted her chin. The stubborn woman avoided his eyes. If she wouldn't look at him, how could she know his heart?

You do not see her.

The thought stung. It could not be true. He brushed it aside as he would a biting insect.

He released her chin, and ignoring the meal she'd prepared, turned his back and stalked from the room. He was tired. It had been a long journey. Tomorrow he'd try again.

⁕

Elizabeth sat stiffly, arms crossed, jaw locked. If she looked at him, opened her mouth, moved other than to breathe, she'd spill such hurt it would forever taint their marriage—if he listened. He had never heard her before now.

Her nostrils flared as hurt hardened to anger. If he thought to make her laugh, he'd failed. Or did he think her a fool? Obviously, she was well past childbearing time. He'd never been cruel before. As man, priest, and chosen to burn incense—none of it gave him permission to ridicule her in such a way.

He'd never struck her, but his fist could not have hurt more. She wrapped her arms around her middle and doubled over in despair.

Abba never spoke to Imma this way. Jesse would never treat Myrah with such disrespect nor would Caleb do so to Nila. And Joachim would die before causing Anna such hurt.

The kind man she'd unwillingly committed her life to had turned cruel. Their familiar unease had warped into harshness.

She pushed herself upright. This was Adonai's plan for her life? No wonder she'd let the path to Him become snarled with debris and undergrowth.

Abba had not followed Adonai's leading like Imma said. If he'd had chosen someone else, maybe she'd be loved.

Her chin trembled and she thrust it forward. "No tears! I am the daughter of a priest of the line of Aaron and the house of David. I am of value, of worth…" Her mind blanked. "…to no one—a barren old woman invisible to my husband and my Adonai."

Hours later, she curled up on Zechariah's chair and slept.

Relentless light slipped through arched windows, across stone floors, and into the wrinkles of her neck, the slight lines of her face. When the amphora on the mantel reflected its brilliance, she surrendered to the day. She stretched kinks from her neck and back, straightened her clothes, and recited the morning prayer.

"I offer thanks to You, living and eternal King, for You have mercifully restored my soul within me. Your faithfulness is great. Blessed are You, Lord our Adonai."

She flushed in shame at the night memories and bowed her head. "Oh Lord, You are my God. You are faithful though I am not."

Zechariah stood before her, questions in his eyes.

She rose, retreated behind the table, a safe barrier between her and this man she no longer knew. She crossed and uncrossed her arms, gripped her hands. Without looking at him, pain-laced words tumbled from her lips.

"Three things only have I prayed for. More faith, pleasing you, and a child."

Zechariah moved toward the table. She retreated a step.

"No. Listen to me. I failed you. I understand that." She bit her cheek to thwart betraying tears. Blood soured her mouth. "We have no child. Years ago, the shame overwhelmed me. But a child was not the Lord's will, and I accepted that. I hope you realize I'd have given my life to carry and birth a child. Given anything.

"Even Imma's blue amphora." Her wobbly chin destroyed the attempted smile. "I ask you for nothing"—her breath caught on a sob—"but I cannot bear to be ridiculed for what was not my choice. Isn't it enough to feel the pity of other women? I am determined to move forward, to live my final years in peace. Do not pull me backward."

Eyes blurred, she did not see Zechariah step around the table. He drew her close, lowered her head to his shoulder, rocked her as he would a child. They stood locked in a grief only the childless fathom.

A voice boomed from outside the door.

"Zechariah? Elizabeth? Are you home?"

Elizabeth ducked her head. Jesse and Myrah would question her runny nose and red-rimmed eyes.

Jesse stopped on the threshold. "May we enter? Your sister brought home strange news. Is it true? Shalom, Elizabeth."

At Zechariah's nod, Myrah sniffed. "I told you."

"What of the vision? Can you tell us what you saw?"

Zechariah glanced at Elizabeth, pointed to his mouth, and shook his head.

"Mute. Of course not." Jesse wrapped his hand around the back of his neck. "There's talk in town. False, but you should be aware and take caution—"

Myrah interrupted. "It's rumored that Caleb lied to protect you as his friend, and you desecrated the Temple or blasphemed the Almighty. There are angry people who will look for a reason to hurt you. Stay home, brother, until you can speak and clear your name."

Zechariah smiled blandly as if asked if he was well. A twinkle in his eyes, he raised his hands to display nine fingers, shrugged, and included the tenth finger.

"Nine what? Ten?" Confusion crossed Myrah's face. "Did Caleb say if he fell? He must have hit his head. What is he talking about? Did he tell you, Elizabeth?"

Elizabeth stared at him. Surely he would not continue his game when she'd just told him how much it hurt. "Uh, no. He tried, but I'm not sure I grasp it."

"Not surprising. You're slow to understand." Disdain returned to Myrah's voice.

Zechariah frowned and leaned forward. Pointing to his mouth, he shook his head, claiming the blame for himself.

Oh, the healing balm of Jesse and Myrah's shock at his rebuke.

Like a seedling—birthed through stone to the sun's warmth—hope grew in Elizabeth that someday she and Zechariah would have a relationship like Imma and Abba. If what she thought he said was true, someday she'd swell with the fullness of life and know the joy she heard in Anna's voice during each festival visit.

Caught in the loveliness between hope and certainty, she didn't notice Myrah and Jesse leave.

Zechariah gathered her hand in his and led her to a chair. He lifted his hands in the air, then covered his eyes as if blinded. He touched his lips, let his hands flutter away.

"The vision spoke to you."

Approval lit his eyes. Gently he touched her belly, raised nine fingers then curved his arms as if cradling a child.

Elizabeth gulped. Her eyes widened. Slowly she moved her head from side to side in disbelief. He looked at her steadily. Smiled.

Dropping her hands in her lap, she stared at him. Then winced. "It cannot be. I am no longer able have a child. I am well beyond the age… My body… I no longer… It's impossible."

He placed a finger on her lips, stilling her words, and pointed to the heavens.

"Oh. Of course, nothing is too hard for the Lord, but a *baby*? Like Sarah and Abraham? Zechariah, that's a miracle." She looked down at her hands and blushed. "When?"

In answer he stood and urged her toward their room.

"It's daylight!"

***

Zechariah stared at the ceiling. Had it been too many years for them to again join their bodies? Eager for the promise to be fulfilled, he'd gritted his teeth in frustration when Elizabeth tensed and pushed away. The sooner their son was born, the sooner he'd regain his voice.

He rolled to one side and watched Elizabeth stare at the ceiling.

"I'm sorry. I just can't." She turned her back and curled into a ball.

Not even to give him a son? Annoyed, he left the bed, dressed, and stalked from the room. After breaking off a piece of bread from yesterday's loaf, he left the house.

That woman is not cooperating, Lord. How can I have a son if she refuses me?

He strode from town, ignoring the curious stares and pointed fingers. Soon vineyards surrounded him, trellised in the new Roman custom instead of trailing the ground or trained over a pole. His temper cooled and his footsteps slowed. Years of prayer nudged him toward seeking divine guidance.

Guide me, great Jehovah.

As no thoughts came, he studied the vineyards. With the harvest complete, the vines had been severely pruned, leaves stripped in preparation for a spring growth and harvest. Workers hoed around the stems, digging trenches, and planting vine-stems.

He was a scholar, not a farmer nor vintner. The process of preparing vines for a new season disturbed him. How could a plant so harshly pruned live to bear fruit? The barren fields showed no sign of life—like Elizabeth's womb.

He halted. Pivoted. Stared at the branches bereft of life.

What had she said this morning? Three things she'd prayed for: a child, more faith, and pleasing him. He swallowed hard. Faith—granted. A child—promised. Pleasing him—she did. Did she know this?

Cold drizzle prompted him to turn back. He slogged through dirt turned mud, slipping but not falling. He had both slipped and fallen in his duty—no, in his faithfulness to provide for Elizabeth. He had fulfilled his ketubah commitments. Her garments were the finest, their food plentiful, and their home more comfortable than most in the town.

Her words—was it only this morning?—told that he had failed to provide comfort to her, failed to protect her from scorn suffered at the hands of other women. Myrah was probably the worst of those who hurt her. Once her closest friend, Myrah had turned hard-hearted toward Elizabeth.

Shamed, he shook his head. He knew a woman was expected to bear children, but Elizabeth always seemed so quiet, so steady. He hadn't guessed that beneath her serene surface she ached with shame.

Hosea taught about wives, though his Elizabeth was nothing like the unfaithful Gomer. He recalled his vow to her. Compassion, righteousness, justice, love. That was more difficult than the Torah's list. It was the difference between following the commandments and the Shema—loving the Lord with all his heart and soul and mind. It was commitment, attitude, a choice no matter what happened.

Drizzle became downpour, soaking through his cloak and tightening the leather straps of his sandals. His hands throbbed. Plodding through empty, rain-drenched streets, he sighed in relief at the sight of his own courtyard and the promise of warm food and a hot drink.

Elizabeth brushed his stiffened fingers away to remove his cloak then handed him a cloth to dry his face. She knelt at his muddy feet and with strong, sure fingers loosened the leather straps. Had he ever thanked her? He stroked her cheek in gratitude. She shied from his touch.

"Can you hold a bowl of stew? It's lentil."

He stretched his hands to the fire, needing warmth before food. If only he could ask for the balm she'd created that eased his joints. Without a word she took the jar from the mantel and rubbed it on his hands.

The wetness on his face was salty. She did not notice.

Words he could never utter flooded his mouth. *Beloved, I do not need a child to love. You are all I need.* He amended Elkanah's words to Hannah. *Elizabeth, you are worth more to me than ten sons.*

The ache in his fingers eased. The ache in his heart did not.

She dipped water into a basin and knelt before him, lifting first one foot and then the other into the warm water and cleaning his feet of the muck he walked through. He saw the silver glinting in the hair of the head bowed before him. All the silver and gold in Jerusalem could not replace her. *A child is not worth the risk of your life. If I lose you, I lose everything.*

Elizabeth set aside the basin of soiled water and dried his feet with a soft cloth. Eyes downcast, she knew if she'd not failed before, she'd failed this morning, and yet, no matter how she scolded herself, she knew to have responded differently would have been impossible. She trusted Zechariah with her life—as Abba had promised she could—but when he took her in his arms, she'd panicked. Too many failed attempts hovered between them.

If she could talk to him, explain her fears, share her shame, maybe…maybe. This morning she'd tried to explain. If Jesse and Myrah had not interrupted… That useless word "if."

And now? She did not doubt the Lord could open her womb. She doubted she could open her heart. The fear of another debacle shook her to the core. There would be no child.

Zechariah studied the emotions flitting across his wife's face. Emotions were not something he'd invested time in deciphering. His life's devotion had been dedicated to studying and reviewing the commandments, memorizing and reciting them. He understood how saturating himself with Adonai's teachings helped him live, helped him please Adonai.

Emotions? Those things that fluctuated and morphed from one extreme to another with no warning and no logic bewildered him. They were indecipherable and inconsistent.

Adonai's word did not change. The commandments remained the same no matter who ruled Rome or what newest rumor came or if the streets flooded.

Of course, on occasion he experienced emotions: joy at marrying Elizabeth, sorrow for their childlessness, anger if Adonai's name was misused. His heart had raced with fear when Gabriel appeared, and at times he'd heard stories that disgusted him, such as the golden eagle Herod placed over the Temple gate claiming the Temple for Rome.

He counted—five emotions. Enough for anyone. Elizabeth seemed to have more than five. He'd heard her use a dozen to describe one event. She'd been frustrated, annoyed, irritated, outraged, and... He chuckled and gave up. It made him frustrated, annoyed, and irritated to think of it.

He was bewildered by her reaction to the news she was to have a child. She did not throw her arms around him or dance around the table or giggle or do any of the things he'd seen happy women do. Of all the ways he thought she might respond, shaking her head in denial and insisting it was impossible had never occurred to him.

What was wrong with her? No. He clenched his teeth. That way of thinking brought emotions he didn't want to harbor. Forging a new thought demanded he seek Adonai's help.

Why would Elizabeth retreat from her life dream?

Fear. Reasons flooded his thoughts. The greater danger at her age. She'd witnessed Anna's excruciating pain and near death. Who would raise the child if she died? Even if she survived the birth, she'd probably not see him grow to be a man.

The discomfort of carrying a child when already your body protested the burden of a water jug. And the conception itself.

No wonder fear darkened her face.

He pushed the cloth she'd used to dry his feet out of her hands. She looked up at him with uncertainty, her beautiful brown eyes as timid as a fawn's. He could not utter a word to assure her that he saw her fear. Instead, he smiled and squeezed her hands, willing tenderness into his touch.

She did not pull away when he squeezed her hands. Relieved he was not angry, she returned his smile. If they could talk now as they never had before, maybe there would be a healing between them.

He watched her, and she knew if he looked carefully, her thoughts were easily read. Nervous, she ventured a few words, expecting him to lose interest and study his hands—a signal for her to stop talking.

"From the Torah readings, I believe we are to care what Adonai sees in our hearts and not to worry about what others think or say about us." If she'd missaid this, he'd look perturbed.

He dipped his head, acknowledging she was correct.

"I struggle with this."

His shoulders drooped a bit.

"Oh, Zechariah, I was not speaking of you. Of course I care what you think of me, but that is between us. I meant...in town…your si…and there are others who—" Speaking ill of his sister would not ease the tension between them. Muddled, she rubbed her forehead against the ache forming.

He tapped her shoulder. She looked up and saw his bewilderment. He shrugged his shoulders, lifted his hands in confusion.

She blinked. A divine mending of frayed threads—another piece of her made whole. Perhaps Zechariah's indifference was rooted in obliviousness, not callousness.

She dared a bit more. "Some of the women call me cursed."

His jaw worked. His fists clenched. Agitated, he stood and paced. The vein on his forehead bulged.

This too he'd not realized. Another rip in her heart, repaired.

"Zechariah, sit down. You will make yourself ill." She urged him to a chair. "I've heard it so often, it no longer upsets me—much."

He winced as if a rock hit him. Pulling his hands from hers, he covered his face.

She could not see his face to read his feelings, but he began to rock back and forth. Not the beautiful *schuckeling* when he learned Torah truths, his soul alight to worship Adonai with his entire being.

This rough swaying was not the rhythmic schuckeling when he concentrated on reciting scripture or moved in memory of the trembling of the people when they were given the Torah.

This was jarring, unnerving, harsh. It jolted her that he so grieved for her suffering.

Rising to her knees, she rested her head on his lap and wrapped her arms around his legs. Imperceptibly the rough swaying changed to a gentle *schuckel*. Whatever he thought or felt had turned to prayer.

CHAPTER THIRTEEN

Anna braided Mary's hair. Approaching thirteen years of age, Mary was gaining soft curves that filled her tunic. Almost gone was the awkwardness of one adapting to a new height and shape.

Elizabeth reached over Anna's shoulder and tugged on Mary's braid. "It's so long! When you were born, it stuck out like a porcupine's quills."

"You say that every time our family visits you."

Elizabeth grinned. "Because every time it's true, and your hair is longer."

Mary's laughter lit her face and filled the room. "I'll be back from market soon."

"Blessed." Elizabeth and Anna shared a smile as they spoke in unison.

They moved to the courtyard to water the herbs and flowers Elizabeth loved.

"Zechariah watches your every step, and you seem…better. No, that's not the right word. Um…more serene."

"Anna, he's changed since that week in Jerusalem." She flicked a bug from her arm.

"Who wouldn't change? I'd have died of fright." Anna shuddered.

"Yes, that would be a noticeable change."

"Ha." Anna flicked water at Elizabeth. "Did you know word of that day has traveled all the way through Samaria and up to Galilee? Joachim overheard the story from one of his vineyard workers. The worker didn't remember the priest's name, but we knew it was Zechariah when he mentioned it was an older priest from near Jerusalem."

"It could have been Caleb."

"True. Strange, but somehow, I knew it was your Zechariah. How is his sister coping with this? Any friendlier than a snake? Does she still think you wanted to marry Jesse?"

Elizabeth snapped off a sprig of mint and rolled it between her fingers. "Myrah is…Myrah."

"That's profound."

"I mean—oh, this is horrible—she's like a skunk, ready to arch her back, stamp her feet, and spray you if you ignore those first warnings."

Anna cackled. "That's a picture! Myrah as a skunk. I'm sharing that one with Joachim."

"Hush. Zechariah will hear you." Elizabeth laughed. "My mouth is such a problem! I didn't mean it quite that bad."

"Mm-hmm. Of course not."

"Myrah, I meant skunks—stop laughing, Anna—skunks eat mice and wasps and bugs. Anna!" Elizabeth gave up and laughed with her friend until both held their aching bellies.

"Listen to me!" Elizabeth gasped for breath. "Myrah lets no one say a word against Zechariah. If she thinks there is the slightest shadow cast on her precious brother, she homes in and swats it out of existence. No one wants to cross Myrah, so even if they mistakenly believe Zechariah is hiding something, no one is bold enough—foolish enough—to suggest a misdeed where she might hear it."

Anna wiped laughter from the corners of her eyes. "That makes sense. She's either wholeheartedly for you or set against you."

"I can't say we are friends again, but I think we are on the same side—Zechariah's side."

Plants watered and trimmed, the women rested on the stone bench. Anna leaned close to Elizabeth so her words would not be overheard.

"While the men are still inside and before Mary returns, will you tell me—if not, I understand—do you know what the vision was about? Would Zechariah mind if you shared it with me? I ask out of love for you and Zechariah. If you're uncomfortable…"

"I am glad to tell you. I've told no one." She smiled. "You are my heart-sister, and there's no one else I'd dare share this with, but I don't want to burden you with the strangeness of it. Whatever you think I'm going to say, this will be stranger. I'm still trying to grasp it."

Anna's chin trembled. "Are you dying? Is Zechariah dying?"

"No. It's the opposite."

"You're living?" Anna squinted as she tried to make sense of Elizabeth's words. "You were dead and now you're alive?"

"Almost." She leaned close and whispered the news in Anna's ear.

Anna's eyes rounded. She gasped. "You're—"

"Shhh. No. Not yet. It is the vision Zechariah was given."

"It's impossible! Elizabeth, you're so old! So is Zechariah."

"Thank you for reminding me I am well stricken in years. If you remember your scriptures, Abraham and Sarah were older."

"But they were Abraham and Sarah. You're just…Elizabeth, my dearest friend." Anna pursed her lips. "You're telling me you are going to be in the middle of a miracle?"

Elizabeth pulled back. "I should not have told you. It is too unbelievable to fathom."

"I want to believe you."

"But you don't." Elizabeth laced her hands so she wouldn't fold her arms and appear defensive. "Truthfully, I didn't believe it at first either."

"You've both wanted this, prayed for a child for so long. Zechariah is certain of this vision? He is confident it is from Elohim?"

Joy rose in Elizabeth. "Think, Anna. Could anyone, anything other than our Adonai have changed him so much?"

Anna lifted her gaze to meet Elizabeth's. "If you believe it, I believe it." She grinned mischievously. "When it happens, wait until our family returns for the next festival to tell Myrah. I want to see her skunk face when she hears you're expecting."

"Anna!"

Joachim appeared in the doorway. "Elizabeth, why does my wife have tears running down her face while she's laughing?"

"You'd never believe me."

Elizabeth hurt to see Zechariah sit behind the other men at the synagogue. Myrah might be able to curb the women's tongues, but the men shunned him with a subtlety no one could fight.

Unable to speak, he could not be invited to read the Torah portion. A younger rabbi taught the children. The men's section in the synagogue suddenly became too crowded for him to sit in the front bench as he had for years. A space in front of and behind him remained oddly vacant. Only Jesse and Caleb greeted him on the Shabbat and sat beside him. No one else risked being seen as befriending the man stricken silent in the Temple.

Elizabeth too sat alone except for Libi and Myrah, who begrudgingly plunked herself next to her sister-in-law. Nila waved from across the room, but she seemed ill at ease when they met at the well or in the market. The older women at the well, those she'd often helped with heavy water jugs, developed unexpected strength and no longer accepted her help.

Lepers must feel this way. She half expected for them both to be named as outcasts and given an order to ring a bell and cry out a warning of "unclean, unclean." She'd become accustomed to sideways glances during the long years of childlessness. Zechariah had not. She hurt for him.

She did not speak as they returned home. He took her arm when her foot slid on a rock and continued to hold her once she righted. She leaned into him. He did not pull away.

After removing the cloth from a tray of fruits and bread and cheese, they ate in comfortable silence. She recovered the tray. Cleanup would wait until the Shabbat was over. She opened the balm for his hands and massaged it into his fingers.

"It is hard to feel so alone. I know. I've felt this way for many years." She gave a wry smile. "I never told you that the first time I was reprimanded for not conceiving was by Matthias's imma the day of Myrah and Jesse's betrothal. That is why I became so angry when you mentioned it."

She gouged balm from the jar without looking at him.

"The pity was worse than the ridicule. Being childless cast me as less than the other women, a failure."

He shook his head.

She spoke sharply. "I heard it said, Zechariah. It is not my imagination. Why do you not believe me? You thought the same, that I was less than Myrah and Nila and Anna and every other woman in the town, that something was wrong with me—a secret sin that Adonai punished by closing my womb. Do not deny it. I felt your judgment. I saw your face. I heard your prayers."

She rose from kneeling and replaced the jar on the mantel beside the amphora.

"I know what you thought of me. I've lived with it for years." She turned. Zechariah stood too close, reaching for her.

"Do not touch me."

Panicking, she staggered back, her arms raised to push him away. Her elbow jarred the blue glass. The amphora wobbled. Toppled. She stretched out her arms. Gasp intersected crash.

Elizabeth stared at the stone floor. Imma's wedding gift lay cracked and chipped—one handle splintered, the other a jagged hook.

"See what you've done? We will never have a child. We are broken, unusable, like this is now. Maybe once… But now it is too late."

She knelt. Picked up the fractured pieces. Unexpectedly, Zechariah did the same. Stunned, she offered no protest.

He stood. Brought a broom. Swept the splinters into a pile.

He knew how to use a broom?

He returned the handleless amphora to the mantel. Walked out of the house. Returned with flowers from their courtyard. Placed them inside.

Open-mouthed she looked at this man she'd married years ago and did not know.

He held out his hand. Smiled.

She placed her hand in his and let him lead her to their room.

Progress. Zechariah grinned. She'd let him hold her all night. There would be no baby in nine months, but hope lit both their eyes. She'd confided more as he cradled her head against his shoulder. Now he understood why she drank so much milk when it made her cough and risked eating mandrake stew from the market, even knowing its roots or leaves would poison her. At times she'd hesitated, broken off her words, and he knew there was hurt she might never share.

Again, he thanked Almighty for removing his ability to talk. When the gift of speech returned to him, he'd tell her daily that she was precious to him. When he could talk, he'd be more to her than her abba had been to her imma. When he was an abba, he'd teach his son to honor his imma.

When he could… Hillel's words slipped into his thoughts. *"If I am not for others, what am I? And if not now, when?"* Loving his wife might not be what Hillel was speaking of, although he had been married, so perhaps… He shrugged. Hillel would take no offense if his former student borrowed the wisdom for marriage.

Tomorrow, they'd join Myrah and Jesse for the Shabbat meal. Tomorrow, he'd find a way to honor her in front of them.

Elizabeth realized she was snailing again. It happened every time a visit to Myrah's was imminent. Her steps slowed. Her stride shortened. Contrary to the outward lagging, her heart raced and her hands trembled.

Zechariah didn't seem to notice her hesitation as he strolled along the way to his sister's house. If he ever had—or could—she'd say he wanted to whistle.

She was disappointed he did not notice she tarried—not that he had ever noticed before—but he'd been so different that she hoped he was more aware of her now. She shifted the basket of food she'd chosen to share for the meal. Myrah could not complain that she'd ruined dates, nuts, raisins, and figs. She'd be pleased at the gift and not critical of Elizabeth's cooking.

Enough. She silently scolded herself. *Stop acting like a beaten dog. You have done nothing to deserve Myrah's long harshness. Stand tall. You are the daughter of one chosen to serve Adonai, the wife of one chosen to serve Him and, maybe, if the vision was right, you'll be the imma of one chosen to serve Adonai, a priest like Abba.*

The realization stopped her midstep. It had been easy to be Abba's daughter and to obey, even when he refused to be cajoled. She'd been the adored only child, and if Abba had been busy, Imma was a comforting presence. People loved Abba and welcomed her with love because she was his child.

Being the wife of Adonai's servant was much harder since Adonai always came first and she always came last. She'd been tolerated as Zechariah's wife even when she remained childless, because his knowledge was respected in the community. Now, with both of them shadowed with doubt and suspicion, nothing was certain.

If she became the imma of Adonai's servant? Her insides turned to jelly. How did one teach a child to faithfully serve Almighty, Creator, the Everlasting God? To follow Him with confidence? To listen for His voice above all others—and obey?

The truth terrified her.

The child would look to her, Elizabeth bat Joseph, to see if she listened and obeyed. Arms shaking, she clutched the basket tighter. "I can't do this."

Zechariah had returned and stood a few steps away. He pried the basket from her arms and tugged her forward.

She balked. "I can't."

He tilted his head and gestured to where Jesse stood at the open door.

She shook her head. Zechariah studied her then walked away and motioned for Jesse to go to her.

"Turnip? What's upset you?"

"I can't, Jesse."

"Can't cope with Myrah? This thing with Zechariah has changed her. I'll send her out. Maybe you two can make peace."

She shook her head, but he'd already started down the path calling for his wife.

Myrah marched forward. "You are making a scene. If you don't want to be here, hurry home before sunset."

She hunched her shoulders and tucked her chin to her chest. "I can't do this."

"What are you talking about?"

"I can't have a baby."

Myrah raised her hands heavenward. "Everyone knows that. What is wrong with you?" She moved closer and sniffed. "Are you drunk?"

"I tried and prayed and thought I heard His voice and could carve a path, and I've failed, and I'll never raise a child to be a faithful, obedient servant because I'm not one." Elizabeth covered her mouth, appalled she'd revealed her fears. Tomorrow at the spring, her words would be repeated, the remnant of her reputation shredded.

Myrah grabbed her shoulders. Shook her hard. "I'll say this once and deny I said it. Understand me?"

Elizabeth sniffled.

"You are as godly as my brother. We'll never again be friends, but I see how you try to honor Adonai." Myrah turned her and pushed her back up the path. "Now go home. Eat something. Sleep. Don't upset Zechariah anymore."

***

Elizabeth stirred in her sleep, woke, sat up—confused. She did not recall walking home last night or removing her headwear or footwear. Her eyes, gritty and swollen, told of a long cry. She groaned, remembering her words to Myrah. If she ever learned to curb her tongue, she'd stop making trouble for herself.

Hearing no snores, she realized that Zechariah's side had not been slept in. She murmured the morning prayer—"Hear O Israel, the Lord our God is One"—then swung her feet onto the floor and padded to the outer room. His tallit, no longer covering his head but draped over his shoulders, told her he had finished praying.

She'd always loved the look in his prayer-eyes when he'd communed with Adonai. Now he beckoned her to sit beside him. She refused, embarrassed by night breath, puffy eyes, and sleep-rumpled clothes. He stood, laid aside his prayer shawl, and crossed to where she stood with her arms folded—shamed and regretful of her outburst.

At least he couldn't question her about last night.

Unless Myrah told him.

Her eyes darted to his face. He knew. Myrah had told him and probably half the world by now.

She waited his unspoken rebuke, the frown of censure—or worse, his agreement with all she'd blurted out last night. Silence grew long. Her heart dropped further with each shallow breath. Unable to endure her unknown fate, she lifted her head.

Such love glistened in his eyes that her mouth opened, and she poured out her heart.

"I am so afraid, Zechariah. I am afraid we never conceived because I am unworthy." She clutched the sides of her tunic. "Nothing has changed. I pray and commit my life to seeking and serving Him, and then disappointment and disbelief tangle my faith. Not disbelief in Adonai, but disbelief that He'd use one so fickle, one whose promise of obedience wavers and fails."

He stepped forward. She retreated.

"No." Tears raced down her face. "There's more."

Jagged sobs tore from her throat. "I cannot bear to hope for what I've already grieved. If Adonai reconsiders, if the angel spoke falsely or—forgive me—if you misunderstood and there will be no child, I cannot survive another hope that ends in disappointment. It will destroy me."

He opened his arms.

Myrah's voice announced her imminent intrusion.

Elizabeth tensed and hiccupped a sob. A sleeve served to wipe wetness from her face before, head down, she headed toward the door. Zechariah caught her arm and raised a finger to his lips. Turning her around, he nudged her to their room and hurried into the courtyard.

Myrah's voice hovered between disbelief and concern. "She wasn't at the spring this morning, and you just shrug? Did she leave with a water jug? Did you see her leave?"

Zechariah must have pointed to his lips and shaken his head.

"After last night, when she was so distraught—over nothing, I might add—what are you thinking letting her wander alone? How can I help her if she's not here?"

Help her? Elizabeth choked on Myrah's words. She covered her mouth with both hands. Myrah must not discover she was here.

"I'll begin searching and asking others if they've seen her. Where should I look—maybe a back trail? She's too old to climb trees and hide like she did as a child. Maybe she went to Nila's house. You stay here in case she returns. Here, take this lentil stew I made for you. You've always preferred the way I cook. You're so thin, I wonder if you eat her meals at all."

The return of bird trills confirmed Myrah's departure and the clunking of the bar to secure the door assured her she'd not soon be discovered.

Zechariah entered their room, eyes twinkling, lentil stew in hand. A laugh escaped her as he made a face and set it on a table.

He reached out a hand. Touched her skin. The warmth of his touch sent chills up her arms.

She walked into his embrace.

The night was long and sweet.

CHAPTER FOURTEEN

Zechariah loved that she blushed every time she looked at him. Once, she'd giggled, like the young girl he'd fallen in love with and hoped to marry. Blushes and giggles looked good on her. They were going to happen frequently for the remainder of their lives. He refused to return to silence and loneliness.

The years of lost joy and harmony haunted him. He, a mere man, could never redeem that time, but the prophet Joel had written that when Adonai intervened, He restored the wasted years, those the locusts had eaten. Had he been a locust, damaging their marriage?

He'd seen the devastation of a swarm of locusts. The swath of destruction left behind meant hunger and poverty for those whose lands were decimated. Who besides Elizabeth had suffered from his actions?

Zechariah covered his head with his tallit, wrapping himself in prayer.

Before You, O Adonai, I am shamed by my sin, by the brokenness I brought to the marriage You blessed.

Resentment slithered in.

His jaw tightened. Elizabeth was not blameless. He listed her sins. The chasm in his family was her doing. He'd never failed to provide for her or fulfill his marital duties. She was the one who withdrew. She was the one who moved to sleep in another room. The reluctance to fulfill the prophecy by Gabriel rested on her alone. She too had failed.

The tallit suffocated him. Approval from Almighty ceased. Conviction weighed heavily. He stood alone before the Lord for his disobedience.

Almighty, I cannot even repent without Your help and mercy. Forgive me for judging her. Teach me to love as You love, to honor You by honoring her. Hear my prayer, O Adonai.

Zechariah rocked back and forth, meditating in gratitude on Adonai's greatness. He lowered the prayer shawl, assured of forgiveness, sensing he remained wrapped in peace.

If he failed again, he'd try again, like the children who learned their alphabet. Over and over, they scratched the lines too large or too small or in the wrong place, rubbed the wrongness out and tried again. The pride on their faces when they succeeded showed that perseverance was worth the effort. He'd be relentless in learning to honor his wife. Somehow, he'd show her that he'd choose her every day.

Elizabeth entered the room. She blushed. He grinned.

***

Elizabeth yawned. The fire's sweet warmth and soft crackle coaxed her to close her eyes and nap. She sat straighter and tightened her grip on her spindle. Yesterday and the day before had been the same. Sleeping midmorning and again in the afternoon kept her from finishing her work. She listed her incomplete chores until the listing made her sleepy—and tired.

The need to sleep was either a snare of age or not sleeping enough at night. A third possibility tickled her mind. She resisted the thought of Zechariah's vision and the name he'd written on the tablet. It refused to leave. Even if the prophecy was already coming true, it was too soon to tell, wasn't it?

Scrunching her face, she searched her memory for overheard whisper-scraps, the signs other women mentioned to a friend when first carrying a child. Avoiding their conversations for so many years left her in ignorance. If Imma still lived or Anna was close by, she'd confide in them. Maybe Nila? Libi was pregnant again. She'd like to talk about her first signs, but if Libi mentioned the conversation to Myrah… Asking Libi was not a safe plan.

She remembered more than once hearing Nila insist she knew almost the first week of being with child because she was so tired and her breasts became fuller and sensitive. Myrah scoffed, but Nila had proven the prediction six times out of eight. Two little ones miscarried before she could claim pregnancy and the blessings began to show.

She pressed an arm against her breast. Was it sensitive? Fuller? Or was that her imagination?

Elizabeth laid the spindle aside. Fresh air would awaken her, and the birds' seeds needed replenishing. She swung the door open and squealed. Snow! Clean, white, beautiful snow. While lazing by the fire she'd missed watching gentle flakes transform the earth. Enough had fallen to almost cover her feet. She made a footprint before stepping back in to the house.

When she was a child, snow meant a day of baking sweets, extra cuddles, and fewer outside chores. Now that she was an adult, it meant that and more.

She could watch snow fall for hours, mesmerized by its beauty and power. One tiny flake did not affect the land's appearance, but it began imperceptible changes. Enough of the tiny flakes and the world was transformed. Each tree branch emerged from a blur of browns and grays to glisten in delicate outline.

Could enough small flakes of kindness transform her world? Could it change a relationship? A town? Snow came only once or twice a year. Did Adonai send it to remind His people of the difference it could create or of the multitude of His mercies covering them?

Not caring that her hem brushed the snow and would chill her ankles, she stepped outside, lifted her head to the gray-white sky, and caught snowflakes on her tongue. She spun around at Zechariah's chuckle. He must think her a silly girl. Tears welled in her eyes. What was wrong with her?

He urged her inside, closed the door, and tugged her hand until she sat by the fire. She sniffled and, maybe, lied. "I'm sorry to be so foolish. I've no idea what the matter is with me." *I think I know, but I'm afraid to say the words aloud.*

"Maybe I'm sick. My head hurts." Thankfully, he could not barrage her with questions. There were good things about having a husband who could not speak for a season.

She saw him smile. Oddly vexed, she realized he suspected. Fine. She'd hold her guess close until she knew for sure and certain. He'd have to wait to hear it from her.

He smiled through the evening meal. He smiled when she went to bed early.

She awoke while it was still dark. If a lamp were lit and she could see his face, she'd guess he was still smiling.

She groaned. *Almighty, forgive me. You have—I think—given us a most precious gift and answered prayers of a lifetime, and I steal the joy with my pettiness.*

This time, she knew the reason for her tears. Shame.

This is Zechariah's child as much as mine. Forgive me for withholding any moment of this from him.

She rolled over to see if he slept, the bright whiteness of the snow lighting the room. A low rumble told her what her eyes could not.

Adonai, there's more I ask You to forgive. My fear. If these signs reveal truth, I'm scared. Anna nearly died, and I'm older than she was. Walking up the hill from the spring tires me. Laboring to birth a child, sleepless nights, a two-year-old, a ten-year-old—I want this with all my being, but it terrifies me. I'm so old to do this. Why did You not allow it to happen sooner?

If these signs are my imagination, I'm scared. Too many times I've been ridiculed for being barren. Declaring I'm with child and being proved false... She groaned. *I cannot bear more pity and scorn. Please do not ask it of me.*

She curled into a ball. "I can't do this."

Trust Me.

She'd heard the words before, accepted them, stored them deep within, a hidden treasure. This time she questioned, pushed back against the Presence.

"Trust You. Abba and Imma trusted You. Is that why I trust?" Yes, partly, she acknowledged. The two people she wholly trusted never doubted Adonai. She'd trusted them because they provided for and protected her, always spoke truth, delighted in her, comforted her when she hurt.

"You protect and provide like they did. Your Word speaks truth, and I have known Your approval."

She raised her head and uncurled a bit. "You comforted me when they died." She curled up again. "But You have not protected me from Myrah." She dared sling the accusation.

Truth swung around and confronted her. She surrendered. "I brought that on myself. You never promised to protect me from my wrongdoing.

"But You did not shield me from the words and looks of scorn." She sighed and stretched out. Those wounds too, her doing. She'd allowed the opinions of others to scar her heart instead of seeking His face only.

Before her lay a choice. Trust Him or...herself? Right. She was so wise she couldn't tell if she was with child, struggled to control her tongue, and hadn't realized it was snowing.

Snow—the mystery of a multitude of tiny flakes. She trusted Adonai with each flake of life—breathing, swallowing, walking; trusted Him with the earth quaking—the deaths of her imma and abba; and the thunderstorms—Zechariah's former coldness, his family's disapproval of her. Choosing to trust Adonai whether He knit a child within her womb or not, she wondered if trust was like snowfall, altering all it touched.

She rolled to face Zechariah. The night had lightened. He smiled in his sleep.

Even aware her husband knew what she was going to say, she was awkward, a stranger in her skin, her movements clumsy. If she'd had this news to share when it was summer, she might have packed his favorite foods and coaxed him into walking with her to a place where the tree branches arched over a shadow-speckled path, and she could share her news in Adonai's sun. If they were much younger and it was cold, like now, she'd have placed a blanket in front of the fire and told him as they sipped hot tea. If she'd been full of mischief, she'd tell him he was to be an abba as soon as he took a bite of chewy bread. Today, she was mostly full of nervousness, wanting only to say the words and erase last night's evasion.

Zechariah rubbed sleep from his eyes and swiped tufts of hair into submission. He smiled at her. It was a good-morning smile, not the knowing smile of yesterday. He slathered honey on warm bread and propped his elbows on the table.

Since he was no longer able to teach because of his muteness, and some still suspected him of hidden misdeeds, he remained home except for short walks through the woods. Being in the snow made his joints ache. He'd be inside all day. The sooner she told him, the better. She hesitated from fear, but which fear? And what words did she use? "Honey, I'm with child." "Husband, your vision was correct." "Zechariah, you are an abba."

After opening the jar of balm, she took his hand and rubbed the ointment into his knuckles. He nodded and flexed his fingers as the medicine soothed his pain.

Elizabeth found her voice after several tries. "Zechariah." Her voice was a croak.

He gazed up at her.

"Zechariah…"

He cocked his head forward and raised his eyebrows.

She cleared her throat. "Zechariah…"

This time, a slow smile eased across his face. He patted the space beside him, coaxing her to sit. He took her hands, his eyes full of tenderness, healing—a flower budding in the promise of new life.

"Zechariah…"

He chuckled, gathering her into his arms.

Shyly, she took his hand and placed it on her belly. "We might… It's possible… I think… John." She twisted and buried her face in his shoulder, riding a crest of hope so high she dared not risk sharing it.

His shoulders shook. She lifted her head and gazed into his eyes that glinted with tears and a tremulous smile she'd hold close to her heart. They rested in each other's arms, savoring joy they'd never expected to experience.

She drew back and curled a hand around his bearded jaw. "Zechariah, let's keep this to ourselves for now. I'm not ready to tell others."

His smile dimmed. A frown shadowed his face. He pushed away, shook his head, and lifted his hands in disagreement and confusion. Minutes later, he left the room.

The beauty of the telling shattered.

Elizabeth broached the subject that night and again in the morning. He refused to understand. Snowmelt would happen soon, and Myrah or Nila and Caleb or Libi would be by to check on her. If she and Zechariah were not in agreement—meaning, he did not see it her way—he'd find a way to share, and the entire town would hear before sunset.

Frustrated, she stopped trying to explain. That night, they slept beneath a silence colder than a blanket of snow. She woke chilled and shivering during the night but did not tuck her toes next to his.

Rhythmically turning the quern the next morning warmed her and calmed her. She would have her say today. Blessedly, he could not argue with her, and short of covering his ears, he'd hear her words even if he pretended he did not. Seldom had she crossed him. He had no idea how stubborn and persuasive she could be.

When he ventured from the bedroom, she placed fruit and bread before him and returned to her work, ignoring his scathing glare.

Keeping her hands busy, she began to talk, her voice calm, matter-of-fact. "Zechariah, our news is a gift from Adonai, a gift that can't be explained fully because you can't speak."

She heard no huff or snort. "We are already regarded with suspicion. You because of the Temple incident and me because, well, we know why. If suddenly we announce that I carry your child, will people rejoice with us or doubt us more?" He shifted on the bench.

"When I'm more certain, we will tell the world, and no one can doubt the proof of our words."

Zechariah shoved the bench back. This is where she'd lost him yesterday. Again, he left the room and stormed into their bedroom. She followed and blocked the door so she did not need to trail him around the house. He glowered and turned his back.

"Many women, my own imma, Nila, Myrah, have lost a little one in the beginning of pregnancy. If I do not carry John, if this pregnancy is"—she gestured helplessly—"to prepare the way for John, then let us grieve in silence, invisible, not in public amid clamors of falseness."

Zechariah turned, his eyes softening. She held up her hand.

"Beloved, I am not doubting you nor the vision nor Adonai. I long to sing a lullaby to our child. This miracle happened to only one other couple I can recall—Abraham and Sarah. Let me become accustomed to the wonder of our miracle before the world intrudes. These first few weeks, may we hold it close? For so many years, there has been distance between us. Let this weave us together like warp and weft."

She clasped her hands over her belly. "Zechariah…" It was a plea.

His disappointment evident in the slump of his shoulders, he nodded, his agreement another bridge connecting them between hope and hurt.

Not wanting him to be sad, she made a quick decision. "Dearest, I have an idea. What if I tell one person—Nila—and from her reaction we decide how soon to share with others? Nila knows us and loves us. She will want to believe and celebrate with us."

His agreement was reserved, but it was agreement. If Myrah or Caleb knocked on the door, she'd remain calm and unflustered.

Elizabeth picked her way through slush and mud puddles to Nila's house. This time of day, Caleb would be at the synagogue. She and Nila could visit without being overheard.

A loud voice from behind startled her. "Turnip!"

"Jesse!" Laughter warmed her words. "Your regular voice can be heard in Jerusalem. Must you sneak up on me and yell?"

"Are you well? Myrah said one day you went wandering around upset and unsupervised. I fear for us all if no one is restraining you."

Elizabeth's pleasure at seeing her friend shifted to caution. "I'm quite well and need no supervision. I never have."

"She said..." His voice trailed away as she glared at him. "I'm sorry, Turnip. I worry about you—always have. If you ever need anything..."

"Shalom, Jesse."

CHAPTER FIFTEEN

She quickened her pace to Nila's. If Jesse returned home and told his wife he'd seen her, Myrah would trace her to Nila's and ask annoying questions. She did not want questions today. She wanted answers.

Nila welcomed her in from the cold and seated her close to the fire. Her toes thawed, and the hem of her tunic began to dry. Warmth began its mysterious soothing. Elizabeth gathered her wits before she became too drowsy.

"Nila. I have something to share with you—only you. Promise it will stay between us."

"You need to ask? Of course. I will hide it in the depths of my heart, and no one will know. If you weren't so old, I'd be waiting to hear you're expecting."

Suppressing a smile, Elizabeth inhaled the deepest breath she could manage and slowly let it out. "I am so tired. All the time. No matter how much I sleep at night, I need to sleep in the morning and again in the afternoon."

Nila paled. "No, Elizabeth, oh no. I'm so sorry. How can I help? How long have you been sick?" She covered her mouth with both hands. Tears filled her eyes.

"No, you don't understand." She gestured to her breasts. "They are fuller, tender."

"My aunt had that sickness. That's how it began. Oh, Elizabeth."

"Nila, no. I'm not sick. I'm with child."

Nila gasped. Her eyes widened larger than Elizabeth had ever seen. Her hands dropped from her mouth to her lap. "Oh no! After all these years it's finally happened."

Elizabeth's voice remained calm. "Nila, Zechariah and I are delighted. We thought you'd be happy for us."

An umph burst from Elizabeth as Nila flung her arms around her and held her close.

"I worried this might happen someday. I'll stay with you. I'll still be your friend."

Elizabeth pulled back, bewildered. "Well, I hope so."

Nila slid her hands down Elizabeth's arms and clasped her hands. "Dear one, we've always been truthful with each other. Trust that I'm speaking truth to you. You are not really with child. You are lying to yourself."

Elizabeth recoiled. "What?"

"Not really lying. Wishing too hard. Maybe hoping too much. Or imagining how it would be. Myrah mentioned that you were acting strangely, but I didn't believe her. You have wanted a child for so long and so intensely that you've convinced yourself it's finally happened. I've been afraid of this. Dear one, you are too old. It's impossible."

"But I am. I'm constantly tired, and I've cried more in the last few weeks than I have my entire life. And certain smells are unbearable. Besides, Sarah was pregnant when she was older than I am."

Nila scrutinized her. "You cannot mean to compare yourself to Abraham's Sarah. You've heard others complain of those symptoms. Believe me, you are not expecting."

"Yes. I. Am."

Nila patted her hand. "Don't worry. No one will ever hear from me what you said. It's between us. I would never shame you."

Frustration showed on both their faces. Elizabeth looked away first. Time would prove her right. She had no one to trust with her news, no one to ask questions. If this was Nila's response, she dared not share with anyone else.

Weary and defeated, Elizabeth's head drooped. She made no protest when Nila embraced her, no response to Nila's assurances, and ignored her looks of concern. She wanted only to escape to safety, where she and Zechariah could delight in John, their secret miracle.

She dragged herself home, not acknowledging those who greeted her and avoiding any who started to speak. Brisk wind seeped through her clothes. Mud slowed steps already heavy with disappointment and fatigue. The door opened as she approached. He'd been watching for her. Another hurt sifted away in the wind.

"She didn't believe me."

Zechariah tugged her into their warm home and gathered her close. His lean strength comforted as no words could have. Woven together, frayed, but with a strength beyond their own.

"All these years I've waited to be able to share in this part of being a woman, and now that it's happening, I am so alone. Yes, I have you and I'm grateful, but you're not a woman and you've never carried a child. And I don't know what to do or expect or what's right, and there's no one I can ask. I was right about not telling anyone, and now I don't want to be right. And Jesse said Myrah said I needed supervision, and I'm hungry." Her voice rose in a wail.

Would she weep the entire nine months? Fresh tears flooded past old tearstains at the possibility.

"I'm a mess, and I'm not sure how to not be a mess." She swiped her hand across her face. "I want my imma."

Another time she might have laughed at the bewilderment on Zechariah's face, but today she welcomed him snuggling her closer.

<hr>

Libi brought a basket of broccoli, artichokes, and cabbage from her garden along with rumors of Elizabeth's strange behavior.

"Aunt Elizabeth, you and Uncle are talked about everywhere—in the market, at the spring, on the streets."

Elizabeth shrugged. "It never stops. What is it this time?"

"Two days ago, when you went into town, you seemed upset. Imma hasn't helped by telling everyone you disappeared from home one day, but it's so unusual for you not to speak to everyone in town. People care about you, Aunt Elizabeth, even if they sometimes judge you for being barren. They are afraid."

"Of me?"

"Of you. You seem like a godly woman, but you're childless. I think they are afraid something awful like that could happen to them too, like leprosy."

"Libi-girl, are you saying I'm a leper?"

"Aunt Elizabeth!"

"Teasing, dear. I'm developing deeper compassion for lepers, but I don't think childlessness can spread from one person to another." She rubbed her eyes and hid a yawn behind her hand. "I'm sorry. I didn't realize it would offend. I could think only how tired and cold I was, not how rude I appeared."

"Auntie, forgive me, but are you ill? You told my abba you were well, but I've never heard you sound this tired. Are you sleeping?"

Elizabeth chuckled. "I'm sleeping. I'm well. Tired? Yes. Maybe it's my age."

Libi bit her nail. "I have an idea. Until something new happens for people to pick apart and complain about, let me do your marketing for you. Your house is on my way to market. You tell me what you need, and I'll bring it by on my way home."

"You are a dear, but I don't need help marketing. Not doing my own marketing makes me feel ancient."

"You said you were tired. This gives you a chance to rest. Maybe just for a few weeks?"

Elizabeth slanted her eyes at Libi. "Or nine months?"

Libi did not blink at the subtle reference to a pregnancy. "However long you will let me help or until you are no longer so tired."

"Twelve years?"

Confusion furrowed Libi's forehead. "If that's what you need, but I don't think I can bring up the water. Try to go when no one else is there or to the little spring."

Elizabeth phrased a refusal, but when her mouth opened, words of acceptance came out. "You're right. It would be wise for me to stay away these first few months."

"First months of what?" Libi moved closer, peering at her.

Elizabeth fidgeted under her scrutiny. "Winter. These first months I become easily chilled, and with the roads slippery, I worry about falling. At my age, falling can lead to a long recovery." She smiled brightly. "When it's not so cold and muddy, I'll resume my trips to the market." She coughed and managed a realistic sneeze. "I might need to miss Shabbat services too."

"You're not well. I knew it. Stay home. I'll mention to Imma that you are suffering from the cold weather and coughing. She'll stay away and tell enough of the others that everyone will assume you're too sick to be out. You are so old. They'll understand."

Elizabeth resisted the urge to pinch her niece. Instead, she listed the items she needed and counted out the necessary coins.

She latched the door behind Libi. This was a perfect solution. In three months, her appearance would have changed enough that no one would question her claim of pregnancy. Zechariah's vision could be made known and celebrated, and he'd regain his place of respect.

During these first months when so many women miscarried, she'd remain secluded, keeping John as safe as in her power to do so. She'd soften cloths for swaddling and begin sewing clothes for when her little boy outgrew swaddling. Her little boy. She hummed a lullaby she remembered—one she'd sung to soothe Libi as an infant.

Libi, Adonai help her, chose flawless fruits and vegetables but could not see an arm's length in front of her nose. If she kept her distance, Libi wouldn't notice as her aunt's body thickened, and her movements became slower and awkward. Too, Libi was one person Myrah would never doubt. When Elizabeth's pregnancy became evident, Myrah would not accuse Libi of deceiving her.

It was all perfect. Except, for the next few months, she still had no one to talk to who knew more than she did about carrying a child. She was still alone. She still wanted her imma.

Zechariah returned from the synagogue, scroll in hand. Reading the Law of Moses served to distract and comfort him during this time of isolation. He'd complete one scroll, and when he knew the synagogue was empty, exchange it for another one.

His countenance warned her that he'd been subjected to another tirade or snub. He sat, stiff shouldered, and held his hands to the fire's warmth.

The jar stood beside the broken amphora. She opened it and rubbed the newest balm between her hands to soften it. Massaging it into his fingers, she told him of Libi's visit. He did not protest her decision to remain secluded.

Silence rested between them, both as broken as the beautiful blue jar, both comforted and healed in each other's presence. Contentment welled up in Elizabeth. This is what her parents knew. This is what she'd longed for.

She returned to preparing a meal. She peeled an artichoke, wrapped the curl around pomegranate seeds, and popped it in her mouth. So good. Eight curls later, she glanced at Zechariah. Horror-stricken, he stared at her.

Flustered, she pushed the ninth curl away. Had she eaten something that endangered baby John? It sounded so good when the combination occurred to her. The sting of hot tears increased her frustration. How could she survive these next months alone?

Elizabeth caressed her belly and the unnoticeable place where John rested. Was it supposed to be hard? Was it too small or too big? Should she eat more or was she eating too much? Could he hear her? Why wasn't he moving? Was there a way to be sure it was a boy before he was born?

If only Imma were here. Tears—her constant companion— blurred her eyes.

How was she to be an imma if she didn't know anything? Pretend until it became reality? Imma told her, when she doubted Adonai, to act as if she had faith and faith would return. If she acted as if she knew how to mother, would that come too?

Once, she'd loved to pretend to cook with Imma. She'd copy whatever Imma did even if she didn't understand what was happening. As she grew up, she learned that a lot of cooking was thinking, being sensible.

For now, secluded while their precious secret remained unspoken, she had only herself and what seemed sensible to rely on. But a long time ago, when the expectancy of pregnancy still lived within her, she'd watched other women who were with child.

It had been many years since Myrah and Nila had been pregnant, but she remembered Zechariah commenting that Myrah drank a lot of milk. Both had eaten cheese and fresh vegetables and fish. Nila propped up her feet when sitting. She'd seen a lot of belly scratching and listened to numerous complaints of aching backs.

There must be other things she needed to know. If just before she fell asleep, she thought of pregnant women she'd seen at the spring and in the market and at synagogue, perhaps she'd remember more and know what to expect. There was a time it seemed that expectant mothers were all she'd seen.

She pushed against the tautness of her belly. It wasn't painful, so maybe it was supposed to be this way. The artichokes and pomegranates she nibbled when Zechariah wasn't looking hadn't made her sick. She didn't want to do anything to harm this unborn child they'd been promised.

Promised. Tension eased from Elizabeth. She closed her eyes and lifted praise to the Lord, the Merciful One who calmed her deepest fears.

A promised child. Already named. The angel hadn't stopped at merely a prophecy of pregnancy. The Almighty had formed plans for this little one inside of her. He was to be set apart for Adonai's service as a priest.

He would live despite her ignorance and mistakes. He would survive birth and childhood and grow to be a man. It was prophesied. It was promised. Adonai kept His promises.

Into her garden of praise slithered a new fear. Not promised was her survival of childbirth, her chance to be an imma.

Tears burned her eyes. She wanted to coax out tiny burps to ease his tummy and tell him the stories of his great-grandparents. She wanted to teach him to obey Adonai and recite the Shema. Zechariah could teach John to read, and he'd learn to sing from her.

Her fingers would brush the hair from his eyes and bandage skinned knees. She'd hold him on her lap and make the stories of Noah and David come alive in his mind. She'd bathe him and clip his little nails. He'd climb trees and run fast and be all that brought joy.

Impatient, she counted the months until he'd arrive, the months she knew she'd still be alive. Seven more months. She'd carry him through the heat of summer. He'd be safe and cool inside her. He'd be born just as the leaves turned to bold reds and sunshine yellows and before the cold winter rains began.

If her only task, her only privilege, was to carry him, to cradle him in her body as Adonai knit him together, then she'd glory in every single moment of it. She'd nurture him as best she could and provide for his infant needs whether she was allowed to raise him or not.

Would he be crawling while it was still winter? She shrugged, not remembering when children crawled. Winter or spring, the stone floor looked hard and cold. She'd weave rugs for him to crawl on.

CHAPTER SIXTEEN

If she wove one more rug, her fingers would fall off. Every scrap of cloth she'd saved for the last twenty years lay woven into a rug. Fun in the beginning, weaving helped pass the quiet hours between Libi's weekly visits and Zechariah's nightly snores.

Elizabeth patted the almost imperceptible rounding of her belly. "Six more months before I see your sweet face, little John." She held her breath and focused on feeling something, anything. Nothing. John must still be too small or his kicks too gentle to feel.

Now what could she do? She stood. Circled the room. Counted the rugs. Poked the fire.

Listened to the rain. Sat down.

"What shall we do next, baby boy?"

Zechariah looked up from his studies. The frown warned she'd interrupted his concentration. The smile that followed assured her he was not perturbed. Nevertheless, she needed to be quiet.

She inhaled. Stretched her back. Exhaled. Wiggled her toes. Sighed.

She stuck her belly out as far as possible. She'd stopped wearing a sash, not wanting any restriction hindering John's growth, but no rounding curved her tunic. When would her pregnancy be visible enough to share their news and be believed?

It was almost impossible for her to grasp, and she was the one experiencing the changes of her body. What would she tell others?

"Yes, I am with child. The Lord has done this for me."

For her, Elizabeth, He opened her womb and would take away her reproach. Because she was the daughter of a priest and of the house of David? As important as that was to her, it did not seem true. Why bless her in this way?

She smoothed a hand over her belly. She would do anything for John. He was her child, created in her body, part of her and the man she loved, part of Imma and Abba and all the way back beyond Aaron and David.

She was Adonai's creation. He did this for her because He loved her. Yes, that held truth but… She chewed her bottom lip. Not every woman was rescued from the scorn of barrenness.

Why her? Many—even Myrah—might name her righteous, but Almighty God saw her heart and heard every word she never spoke. She and Adonai both knew she was undeserving of His mercy.

She unwrapped a round of bread from the morning's baking and stirred the fire under the simmering pot. From the top shelf she chose two bowls and filled them with soup.

Placing the brimming bowls on the table, she giggled. She was a soup bowl. Adonai allowed her to be the vessel, to carry a child because of a plan He had for this particular child, her child.

She sobered. There was no one to share her odd humor with. The comparison of her womb to a soup bowl would not amuse Zechariah. He'd shake his head and return to studying.

Years ago, when they were young girls, Myrah would have cackled, and Nila would have laughed until she cried. Someday she'd tell Libi. No, the sweet girl did not have Myrah's sense of the ridiculous.

Steam rose from the soup bowls, but she was no longer hungry. Loneliness shrank the walls inward, lowered the ceiling, thickened the air. Overhead, thunder rolled past and rain battered the house. Three months pregnant and confined by mud and rain, gossip and rumors, her husband mute, her friends busy with children and grandchildren.

Tears teased her eyes. Did this drippy part of pregnancy last the entire nine months? Between the time she ladled soup into bowls and placed them on the table she'd crested hilltops of awe and humility to be so valued by the Creator and tumbled headfirst into a ravine of isolation. Pregnancy hid more dangers than she'd ever guessed.

Elizabeth propped her chin on her hands. When it was time to tell Myrah, would it mend the hurt between them, or would Myrah be jealous that Adonai ordained Elizabeth's son as a prophet? Would Nila be embarrassed that she'd refused to believe? Would Jesse think it odd she carried a child so late in life? Had Zechariah told Caleb of the vision? Did he already suspect she was with child?

"Stop it!" she demanded, her voice too loud in the quiet room. "Stop right now. Comparison does no good. Fretting about reactions to my condition isn't good for the baby.

You are a woman grown, expecting a child. So stop it, Elizabeth."

Zechariah raised his head and frowned.

Though she covered her lips in apology for disturbing him, inwardly she fumed. If he couldn't talk to her, she'd talk to herself. Hearing a voice once a week when Libi came was not enough to keep her from needing to scream at the silence. She was beginning to understand what birds said, since that was the only chatter she heard.

She tore off a large chunk of bread, slathered it with honey, and stuffed it in her mouth. If she ate more food, she'd show more and sooner be around someone who'd talk to her.

Zechariah understood why warriors married and immediately left for months or years at a time. It might be too late for him to become a warrior, but it was a great dream of escape.

A woman with child did not talk about anything other than her pregnancy and her plans for the coming child. She ate foods no sane person would consider allowing past their lips. She cried if he frowned or smiled or hugged her or didn't hug her long enough. She snapped at him. She sulked. And she rubbed her belly all the time like she was polishing a lamp. He'd never realized babies needed to be polished.

He owed the men of the town a humble apology for judgmental thoughts when their wives had been expecting. Many had hidden in the synagogue for hours until he insisted they return home. Now he knew their prayers had been genuine pleas for mercy and deliverance.

I'm not complaning, Lord. He rubbed the ache in his hands. *This child is the greatest blessing of my life. It's only that I didn't understand what I was asking.*

He owed the men of the town a compliment for their courage and endurance. Most of them had survived a pregnant woman multiple times. His stomach flipped.

Lord, You know the depths of my being. Thank You for not giving me a quiverful of children.

Their confinement might be worsening Elizabeth's behavior, but if she was free to move about the community and did something his sister thought an expectant mother should not do—he cringed—he'd be found hiding in the synagogue three towns away.

Myrah. There was a challenge.

How were they—or Elizabeth—going to explain this late-life blessing to her? Myrah would need to be one of the first to hear of John or she'd be livid. If Myrah stood beside Elizabeth during this time, the other women and men would also. It could be a time of healing and reconciliation between the two women. Myrah would become protective, and Elizabeth would be relieved to have someone experienced to share concerns with, someone other than him to talk to about her pregnancy questions.

Pleased with himself, he set to addressing the details.

They'd invite Jesse and Myrah for Shabbat dinner when Elizabeth was looking more pregnant. She was still not very big. Libi could give her parents a message. He'd suggest they plan it for…

How? As a flame jumped, the polished candlesticks glowed. There! Direction from the Lord, an affirmation of his plan. He'd point to the candles. She'd understand he meant Shabbat dinner. Four fingers and she'd realize he meant in a month—maybe she'd look more pregnant by then. Jesse was tall and Myrah short. If he indicated the different heights, maybe she'd understand.

***

The storm on her face showed that she understood.

"What are you thinking? Wait! Let me guess. You are thinking of yourself. You're tired of being with just me and want someone else to be here."

Explaining his reasoning was difficult without words. He smiled. That was a mistake.

"You think asking me to do extra work is amusing?"

He stopped smiling, lifted his hands to placate her.

"You sit in comfort and read all day while I carry your child and cook and make unguents for your hands and clean and, so no one will realize I'm pregnant, lug water in the heat of the day or before sunrise from the spring farther away while everyone else is inside resting, and you think nothing of inviting your sister who hates me to come and criticize everything I do and cook?"

Myrah didn't hate her, so he shook his head in denial. Her growl and the slammed door meant he'd made another mistake.

Irked, he snatched his bag of scrolls, strode across the floor, jerked the door open and slammed it closed as he left. Let her experience what it felt like to be misunderstood. This was not easy for him either. Bitter, he'd like to remind her he literally had no one to talk to. She visited weekly with their niece and soon would have all the town women clucking around her with their stories and advice.

Hers was not the only life impacted. Hers was not the only one whose sleep was disrupted when she got up three or four times a night. He was forced to watch her eat disgusting food and hear details of bodily changes he didn't need to know.

He stomped to the synagogue. If others were there and snubbed him, so be it. He wasn't staying in the house to be scolded for another minute.

Lord, I made a vow—three times now—to honor this woman who is my wife, but I don't recognize this person she's become. Will she return to being the Elizabeth I knew before she was expecting?

As he entered the synagogue, he raised his right hand to touch the mezuzah, kissed his fingers then paused, contemplating the blessing. *I enter Your house to worship with awe in Your sacred place...* The sacredness of the scripture inside the small box brought his thoughts to reverence, to the blessing he'd been given.

Again, Almighty, forgive my grumbling and irritability. Elizabeth bears the burden of Your gift and my doubt of Gabriel's message. If I had not doubted, she'd not be alone. He walked slowly to a bench and sat, head bowed.

I'm at a loss as to how to honor her in this or ease her burden. She's afraid of something she hasn't told me, but I don't know what it is or how to coax it from her. And if I did, I couldn't speak to it.

Zechariah leaned forward until his head touched his knees. *You see her unspoken fears. Please, Adonai, ease her distress.* Frustrated, he clenched his teeth. *All my fears are unspoken except to You. Maybe that's why You struck me mute, to prevent me from infecting Elizabeth with my worries.*

I am afraid of being too old to raise a son, too accustomed to quiet study and not the sounds and activity of a child. I am afraid of failing to teach this child to faithfully serve and obey You because so often I fail. I'm not good enough or strong enough or young enough. I'm afraid I will shame my family.

• • •

Elizabeth jumped when he slammed the door. Fine! Let him go sulk somewhere else.

He must think bread made itself each morning, an extra trip for additional water was an easy stroll, and if she blew it a kiss, the house began to sparkle. She yanked the bed covers tighter, daring a rumple to show its face or a pummeled pillow to protest abuse.

Arms crossed, she thumped down on the wisely uncomplaining bed. Her heart slowed, her mind cooled. Reason returned with a basketful of regret. Would she ever guard the gate of her mouth?

Zechariah's request was sensible. In another four weeks she'd appear more pregnant. Family should hear their news before others learned of it, and sharing it was safest here in their home. Someone might see her if she went to Myrah's, and then the rumors would begin. Myrah's faultfinding of her cooking and housekeeping would be nothing she hadn't heard before.

She bit her lower lip. Myrah had not been a critical person when they were girls. She'd admired her friend's unfailing acceptance and encouragement of others, tried to be more like her and speak with gentleness. She'd failed then, and now, years later, still struggled.

"Almighty, curb my tongue. Train it to speak in kindness and truth, not in censure." It'd be easier on them both if she just slept until the baby arrived. Falling backward onto the bed, she fell asleep dreading Zechariah's return.

⁂

Libi pushed open the door and entered without knocking. "Shalom. You buy the same items every week, so I didn't stop to ask this time—just bought them. Same cost as usual."

Elizabeth frowned. Libi's voice was strained. Did she tire of this weekly errand for them?

She looked closely at her niece. Dark circles shadowed her eyes. She was pale, and her mouth pinched tight as if unwell. She'd lost weight too.

"Libi, you've been so kind to us, but I can go to market now that winter has ended. The roads are dry, and I'm not afraid of slipping in the mud."

"No. I'll still go, but Aunt Elizabeth, I have something I need to tell you. Imma guessed and of course my husband knows, but I wanted you to hear it before anyone else. I'm expecting again." Libi lifted the market items out of the basket and placed them on the table.

"Libi, that's wonderful." Elizabeth leaned forward. "Tell me how you're feeling. When is the baby due?"

"I'm tired and queasy and crying a lot. You wouldn't understand. Aren't you going to hug me?"

"Of course." She leaned across the table and squeezed Libi's arms. Libi would guess her secret if she really hugged her.

"You used to give the best hugs. Have you forgotten how?" Libi's lower lip quivered.

"I'm sorry, dear. Let's try again." If Libi guessed she too carried a child, Elizabeth would ask for it to remain their secret, but the forlornness on her niece's face made the possibility of discovery worth the risk.

"You don't feel like my aunt. Something is different." Libi drew back. "You've always been so slender, and you've grown rather round."

Elizabeth laughed, relieved. "I'm sitting in the house, not walking as much, and I have a new way to make sweets with dates."

Libi's eyes widened. "Oh, I have other news. Eli and Matthias, Abba's little brothers—I never met them—sent word they are remaining with the Essenes in a place called Quinrsun, no, Qumran. Abba said you knew both his brothers and would want to know what became of them."

"Matthias was a scholar even as a child. The life suits him, although I'd like to see him again."

"Abba is already making plans to visit them. He wants to make sure peace is between them." Libi chewed her nail. "Truthfully, do you think you and my imma will ever be at peace? Abba said the three of you used to be good friends. I wish it was still that way."

Elizabeth's eyes twinkled. "Truthfully, I have learned that miracles happen."

"Not for you and Uncle."

"Libi, your uncle and I have received miracles we choose not to share yet. The Almighty brings healing and answers others may not see until much later, not when they happen. When the time is right, I'll share one of our miracles with you."

"We needed a miracle, but there wasn't one for us. If this baby dies too…" Libi pressed her knuckles against her lips. "I'm supposed to be happy—and I am—but so scared. All I can think of are the last times. I pray and ask Adonai if this one will live but there's no answer." Her eyes watched a private memory unfold. "I still dream of our first child, watching him turn blue and cold in my arms."

"Pray, Libi-girl. Not in the hope of being answered—continue to pray for comfort. Pray to draw close to Adonai even in loss."

"Did you ever have a miscarriage, even a very early one?"

"No."

"Then you really can't understand, can you?"

Though sadness and not disdain colored her words, Libi's words scraped raw a wound not healed.

Five more months and decades of the intangible barrier separating her from other women would be lifted. She'd no longer stand outside the invisible gate, barred from understanding nods and secret smiles. She'd be a member of the sisterhood of mothers, and more, part of the elite tribe whose sons were priests.

Elizabeth raised her face to bask in the soft spring sun. This, her favorite time of year, a fleeting respite between the winter cold and the summer heat. Plants watered, herbs trimmed, and crumbs scattered, she sat down to rest.

Drowsy, she leaned back against the stone wall and soaked in the hoarded warmth. Light weighed her eyelids closed. She was weary. She'd been working before dawn, grinding grain for flour, setting beans to soak and bread to bake. The walk to the far spring took longer these days.

She did not resist sleep's lure.

A butterfly kiss, unexpected but welcome. She smiled. Imma's special way of saying I love you.

Except…

It was inside her—the butterfly kiss. Her eyes flew open. All thoughts of sleep vanished.

This is what the women felt as they glowed with life. The miracle of life moving inside. A person lived inside her. She'd known she carried a child. Known he lived because of the vision. Known but never understood. She carried life.

The delicate flutter returned. She placed a hand over the movement, the quickening a sweet assurance of the prophecy—this person inside her suddenly real, banishing any doubt of his existence, any illusion she'd only imagined him.

She breathed as lightly as possible waiting for another butterfly kiss. When it came, she laughed aloud. Speech became impossible as her throat thickened and tears gathered in her eyes. She'd heard of the quickening, never imagining that the silent miracle resounding through her body would ignite such deep emotion.

Pain, physical and intense, slammed into her. The longing to share this with her parents tightened her chest until it ached. Imma would be a bundle of smiles, and Abba's beam would light the sky. She was a bridge between them and John, the past and the future.

She would be the one to guide his little heart to the Lord as Imma and Abba had guided her. Doubt crept in on little mouse feet. Could she do this? What if she failed?

Fail when her heart's prayer was answered? Impossible. She wanted to run—or waddle—through the town proclaiming her news to everyone she saw and send a message requesting Anna's presence and loop her arms around Myrah insisting she release the past and celebrate with her. She wanted to bar the door, hide in her house, hold incredulity close to her heart and tell no one, not even Zechariah. She wanted to race to the synagogue and drag Zechariah outside to hear the news and feel the movement of their son. She wanted to serenely enter the synagogue on Shabbat, her reproach removed by the Lord.

She wanted to prance through the market and laugh when people turned to stare at the old pregnant woman.

Children and youth ran races. Pregnant women and ancient women did not. She was both pregnant and rather old, and the darting back and forth between emotions exhausted her.

She imagined rocking her child to sleep and pacing with him in her arms all night as he teethed. She'd dress him in soft linens she'd sewn and—she scrunched her nose—scrub the cloths he'd soil. He'd nurse at her breast and throw up in her arms. She gagged.

Motherhood was a mix of contradictions.

CHAPTER SEVENTEEN

Elizabeth stopped scratching her belly when Zechariah frowned at her. If he itched, he scratched, and she didn't glare at him. Deep breath. Not worth upsetting John, who kicked her insides whenever she tensed. Her son would be a good player in children's ball games.

Distracting herself from the itchies, she sampled the vegetable soup she'd serve Myrah and Jesse tonight. Pickled watermelon rind and chickpea cakes were ready to set on the table.

With a covert glance at Zechariah, she sneaked a cake into her mouth. Embarrassed to be constantly eating, she hid it when possible, but she was always hungry. Whether it was the baby or the food, there was no longer any mistaking her condition.

She could grow no more before the seams of her tunics needed to be let out—the material neared tautness across her belly and breasts.

Elizabeth changed into a clean tunic, her largest one, and washed her hands and face. She scanned the room for everything Myrah would criticize. Her heart quickened. Her stomach clenched. Her shoulders tensed, tremors shook her hands, and a dull headache began to throb. John delivered a sharp kick.

An invisible force compelled her to look at the fire. Watching the flames, she was gripped by a conviction of wrongness. This anxiety, the critical spirit of herself, the expectation of condemnation from others, was not good for her or for John.

Each Shabbat, she gathered in the promise of the flames, believing Adonai's light dwelled within her. Tonight, she'd not extinguish His light by expecting tension between herself and Myrah. She'd hold close God's light that lived inside her.

Breath came easier. Her six-month-pregnant body felt lighter. She straightened and smiled. Inside, John flipped over. He must approve of her choice.

Jesse hailed the house, and Zechariah opened the door, inviting them inside. They were early. She'd expected it.

"Shalom."

"Shalom." Elizabeth stepped from a shadowed corner into the light. There could be no mistaking her changed shape.

Jesse noticed immediately and stared at her as if she'd become a strange creature from a foreign land. "Turnip?"

Myrah, busy scrutinizing the house, had not glanced in her direction. "Can I hem your curtains for you, Elizabeth? They do not fall straight. Your eyesight is failing."

"Thank you, Myrah. That would be kind of you. Sewing is not my favorite task, and you're much better at it than I am."

Myrah's head swiveled. Seeing Elizabeth, her eyes widened.

Elizabeth had seen fish open and close their mouths exactly as Myrah was doing.

Except for the crackle of the fire, silence framed the room into a vignette she'd always remember.

Hold close God's light that lives inside of me.

Zechariah's nod of approval bolstered her confidence. A shared smile of amusement at Myrah and Jesse's reaction encouraged her to move forward.

"Thank you for joining us tonight for Shabbat meal. We have news we wished to share with you as our family before any others heard of it."

Jesse's swallow sounded loud. He reached for a chair and sat heavily. Zechariah moved close and squeezed his shoulder.

Myrah stared first at her belly and then at her face as if suspecting deceit and ridicule.

Elizabeth stepped closer and whispered. "It's true, Myrah. I am blessed to be with child."

"Libi didn't… I never guessed… How far…? Is it true?"

"The sixth month has begun."

"I don't think so. It's impossible." Myrah backed away. "You are too old to conceive a child. You told me yourself it was too late."

Elizabeth did not argue. She carried the proof. She went to stand by the fire and turned so Myrah saw her profile.

"It's a girl. I can tell by how you carry her."

Elizabeth smiled.

Myrah crossed her arms. "You're too old to live through the delivery."

Her smile faltered. Myrah spoke too close to her own fears.

Jesse found his voice. "Myrah, stop. Do not fill her with fear. Zechariah, Elizabeth, we rejoice with you in God's blessing."

Her husband gestured to the table, inviting them to sit for the Shabbat meal. Elizabeth lit a taper from the fire, dismayed that her hands trembled at Myrah's words and annoyed that she'd let her inward light dwindle.

Elizabeth lit the two candles, shielded her eyes from the light, and recited the blessing. "Blessed are You, Lord our God." She offered her private prayer, folded the light into herself.

Opening her eyes, she offered Shabbat Shalom to Zechariah and her guests.

No one spoke during the meal. Zechariah could not, and neither, it seemed, could their guests. Jesse avoided looking at her, blocking her from view by twisting his body toward Zechariah. Myrah nibbled a piece of bread, never looking away from Elizabeth.

The meal complete, Myrah lingered as the men strolled outside. "Did you use a potion? An amulet?"

Elizabeth recoiled. "No! Never. This is a blessing from Adonai."

"So you say."

Myrah slanted her eyes at Elizabeth's belly. "Or it could be a demon inhabiting your womb."

"Stop!" Elizabeth's face contorted. "How can you say this to me? I thought it would bring us closer, that you'd stand with me when we tell others."

Myrah sneered. "I don't stand by those consorting with the evil one. And do your own shopping. Libi will no longer help you." She scurried out the door as the men returned.

Zechariah tilted Elizabeth's face up, scowled at his sister's back, and wrapped an arm around his wife's shoulders.

Desolate, she leaned against him. Myrah would share her suspicions with others.

Shabbat was beautiful with a clear blue sky and enough breeze to refresh the air as the keeping of the day refreshed the spirit. For the first time in five months, Zechariah and Elizabeth walked side by side to the morning service. Her heart thudded harder with each step. Glancing at his face, she guessed his did too.

She'd dressed with special care this morning. Zechariah had trimmed his beard and wore his best tunic. Another few steps and they'd be in sight of the synagogue. Would this be a day of celebration or skepticism with friends and neighbors?

Greetings dropped to murmurs. The milling of the people shifted to one direction—theirs.

Gasps became silence. No one looked at them—only at her belly. Maybe she should draw a face on it. Whether old and pregnant or young and not, everyone seemed to find her belly quite interesting.

If she could run, she would have. Really fast. Straight back home. Without stopping. But Zechariah's grip on her arm propelled her forward. He abandoned her next to Nila.

This was not the way it was supposed to be. Where was the sisterhood of women, of mothers who surrounded each other with loving support? Even wolves protected their pack. Where was the rejoicing of her people that Adonai had blessed a woman with new life?

Elizabeth raised her chin. She was the daughter of a priest and a descendant of royalty, and even greater than that, she was valued by the Creator. She carried a miracle.

A gracious nod. A serene smile. Iron determination like Abba's smile. She entered the synagogue and sat on the front bench in the women's section. She was here to praise her Lord, not to explain or apologize for His doings.

Wordlessly, Nila sat beside her. Libi sat to her other side. Someone touched her shoulder. A voice whispered, "Blessed."

But it was Myrah's hiss of "Cursed" that everyone could hear.

Elizabeth curbed her retort. *Cursed if she was with child. Cursed if she wasn't.*

* * *

Elizabeth wondered why she'd ever thought it would be exciting to walk through the market and have people stare at the "old pregnant woman." It was not. Awkward, uncomfortable, frightening, embarrassing, yes. Exciting? No.

Being invisible had been easier—those years when she was confirmed and labeled barren. No one expected much of her. She was an oddity but an accepted part of the view, like the crumbling edge of the stone wall lining the road. Everyone knew it was there, but no one saw it. Since the last time she walked through the market five months ago, she'd become the center of speculation.

She ran her hands through the peppercorns and sprinkled a few on a white cloth to search for tiny black bugs. Seeing none, she paid for a bag full and nestled it in with her other purchases.

A voice from behind her spoke clearly. "It's not right, a woman that age expecting a baby."

"M-might n-not be r-real."

"False as Menahem claiming he was messiah."

If she turned around, moved very close, and John kicked one of them would they still think it was false? A false pregnancy? Who would choose the stares and sneers she was receiving?

The next vendor was a woman she'd not seen before, a newcomer to their town.

"Shalom. Cinnamon, please, and if you have cloves, that as well."

The woman did not move. "You're pregnant."

Elizabeth smiled. "Yes, I am."

"Foolish woman. Don't you understand you're too old? Neither you nor the child can survive the birth. That's unfair to your other children."

Her smile wavered. "This is my first child."

"More the fool. Go. I'll not sell my goods to one such as you." The vendor shooed her away. "Go, now."

Elizabeth backed away, her face flaming.

"She's flaunting it."

"Do you think old Zechariah is really the father or…?"

Did people not realize she heard their words when standing beside them?

"No one has seen her since winter, and then she saunters into town looking like that."

"Should've stayed hidden. She's disgusting."

"It must be sorcery."

Reeling, she pressed forward to escape the comments and condemnation. This was her blessing, and she refused to allow sneering or questions to ruin it. She shifted the basket in front of her to take up less room and wove in and out of the milling shoppers, searching for vendors who did not know her and might hesitate to comment, although the last one had shown no reluctance. Stalked prey must feel like she did, unsure which way was safer, which way led to certain capture.

She'd gladly return home and stay there until John was born, but marketing was her responsibility, and certain foods could only be obtained from the market. Herbs and small vegetables grew plentifully in the courtyard, but their supply of grains and spices was low. Libi would not defy her imma's orders not to help, and Zechariah would be embarrassed for others to see how unusable his fingers were most days. Nila befriended her at synagogue but seemed so uncomfortable that Elizabeth hesitated to ask for help as she grew bulkier in these last months.

If Anna were here, would she stand beside her or shun her? She'd ask Zechariah to send a message to Anna and Joachim. If Anna was able to travel, maybe she'd attend the birth.

Elizabeth worked her way through the market until her back and feet ached as much as her bitten tongue did from refusing to snap back at the gawkers and gossips. Next week might be easier. If not, they would be eating a lot of tomatoes and basil or rosemary-flavored bread.

Ahead of her, Myrah too walked home from shopping. She moved slowly, head down.

"Myrah!"

She turned. Surprised her sister-in-law waited for her, Elizabeth sped up to walk beside her.

"Shalom."

Myrah raised both eyebrows in question. "What do you want?"

"To walk together. To talk. To answer any questions."

Myrah's stride shortened. "Why you and my brother? Do you think you're favored like Sarah and Abraham?"

Elizabeth wished she'd not called out to her. Myrah's question sounded accusatory, not curious. "Seems that way, but I don't know."

"Or won't say." Myrah halted.

"Can't say," Elizabeth said over her shoulder and continued on the path. "Can't say if I don't know."

Myrah caught up with her. "Does my brother?"

"He might, but he has no way of telling me. His hands hurt too much to write anything."

"Would you tell me if you knew?"

"Myrah, you call me cursed, suggest I carry a demon, and accuse me of consorting with the evil one. If I knew more and risked confiding in you, would you believe me?" She walked faster, not waiting for an answer.

Zechariah realized as soon as she opened the door that Elizabeth was upset. The basket hit the table with a thud. She jerked the scarf from her hair with an impatient twist and poked the fire with more energy than he'd seen in her for months. She made no comment when she carelessly splashed precious water from a jug into a cup and then did not wipe it clean.

She must have seen Myrah.

He set aside his reading and rubbed the ache in his fingers as he waited for her to acknowledge him. Temper spent, she leaned against the table then crumpled onto the bench. He stood and moved behind her to rub the tightness from her shoulders.

"Myrah."

He kissed the top of her head.

"And the market. I'm foolish and flaunting and faking and you're not the father." She slapped the table. "What do you think about eating tomatoes and basil for the next three months? Zechariah, it was terrible. I sympathize with how caged animals feel when everyone points and stares at them."

He sat beside her, tilted his head, and raised his eyebrows.

"Yes. It was that bad. And afterward, Myrah was walking alone so I called out to her. She actually spoke to me. She thinks I'm keeping information from her. After what she said, why would I tell her if I did know something?"

Zechariah shrugged.

"Exactly."

Elizabeth scrutinized his face. "Did more happen in the vision? Do you know more than you've told me?"

He nodded and lifted both arms in a helpless shrug. There was so much more to share with her. The prophecies of John's life he'd save for later. In the beginning he'd tell her he'd loved her since he first saw her, and he'd tell her… He scratched his head. There was something else he'd planned to say when speech returned.

He closed his eyes and pressed his temples attempting to remember. Futile. What else had slipped away? Uncertainty gripped him. Gabriel had promised he'd be allowed to speak again, hadn't he? He was no longer sure he recalled all of it correctly. *See, Lord? My memory is failing.*

Unable to speak, unable to write—no end in sight—powerless to communicate. Condemned to silence by his doubt—the thief that robbed him of speech and left him bound on the side of life—slivers of self-loathing overtook him. *Lord, I am unworthy to raise this son to be a godly man. I'm too tired, too old to play with a child. I'm too…me.*

"Zechariah, you're not listening to me. Since you can't speak, at least listen."

Desperate with fear, he looked up, riveted his gaze on hers. *Lord, let my face reveal what I cannot say.*

"What's wrong? Are you ill? Is there another vision? You look terrified."

Closing his eyes, he nodded. She'd seen him. Given him what often he'd failed to give her—understanding. Tears filled the lines around his eyes and trickled down his face.

"You're afraid?" She wound her arm around his and rested her head on his shoulder. "I am too."

He lifted her beautiful face, gestured to his ear, needing to hear what she feared, hoping she'd understand that he'd listen this time.

"I'm afraid with all these fears, I seem ungrateful to the Lord."

He tapped his head and heart.

"I am grateful, and you're trying to assure me the Lord sees my head and heart, and I'm telling you, in both places, He sees I'm terribly scared." She sniffled. "We're not ancient like Abraham and Sarah, but we are well along in years. Abraham was like royalty. They had servants and slaves to help. I doubt they were snubbed, or anyone dared sneer at Sarah when she was expecting. She didn't have to market either."

Wryly, he agreed. He tapped an ear indicating he wanted to hear more.

"Childbirth—I dread it—but it does not frighten me as much as what comes after the birth." She twisted in his direction but lowered her head and averted her eyes. "Zechariah, it shames me, but after all these years of His faithfulness, I still struggle to trust Adonai wholeheartedly, to obey Him without faltering or balking."

Panic strained her voice. "How can I teach John to do what I cannot do?" She pressed her fingers against her eyes and whispered, "I am not good enough. I will fail, and our son will bear the consequences."

Lord, how do I negate her words? How do I remind her that this is Your doing? Just as my muteness. Gabriel had no authority unless it came from You.

He held her close, tears wetting her hair.

CHAPTER EIGHTEEN

Elizabeth could not think of a time she'd felt so alone. Confident the community would rejoice with them, she'd bided her time until there'd be no doubt she was with child. Not many people doubted—she carried unmistakable proof before her—but no one seemed excited that she'd been blessed.

It baffled her. She'd been happy for the other women's blessings even as she grieved her own lack of children. Could they not return joy to her?

Either way, a shadow of disapproval hung over her. Inadvertently, she'd broken tradition and did things backward—pregnant at the wrong time, not pregnant at the right time—as if she'd chosen this way to defy and confound.

She poured a measure of grain into a bowl and added water to soften it.

Those women she knew to be true friends had dwindled. She knew some friendly greetings turned to gossip when they assumed she could not hear them. Not all older people lost their hearing. Both she and Zechariah still heard most of what was said and much that others didn't think they'd heard.

Some friends had died, some moved away, some no longer left their homes, some remained locked in their memories, isolated from the present. Some became so enthralled with Myrah's every word, they'd long ceased to pretend friendship.

Elizabeth sprinkled salt over the grain·mixture and drizzled oil over the top. She'd chop dates and almonds for the cake. It would be a nice surprise for Zechariah when he returned from his walk. Dinner's pot of fava beans simmered over the fire. A watermelon lay on the table ready to be sliced.

She chose a knife to slice and pit the dates. If the community did not rejoice in her pregnancy, would they embrace her son or exclude him? She knew the heartache of being the outsider. Zechariah indicated that the vision told him more. Maybe he knew if John's future had been prophesied.

Cramps gripped her belly. Dates scattered across the table and onto the floor as she slammed the knife down and hung on to the table. What was happening? It was too early for John to be born—three months too early. The pain peaked and subsided.

Frightened, she sat down and reached for a cup of water. As her heart slowed, she remembered Nila and Anna having what they called practice contractions. Practice was good for making breads and learning to write, but she didn't want to practice that again.

Clumsily she bent to retrieve the dates from where they'd landed. They were too sticky to roll far. She washed them, chopped them into small pieces and added them to the cake mixture along with a handful of almonds. She poured the batter into a pan and snugged it into the embers.

Tired now, she sat in the shade in her courtyard. John rested quietly, safe in her womb. The buzzing bees and chirps of birds lulled her to sleep.

"Shalom. Cousin? Zechariah? Are you home?"

The voice came from a distance. A familiar voice. A beautiful, musical voice she'd not heard in too long.

Waking refreshed, she stood and hurried toward the entrance as Mary entered.

"Elizabeth!"

Elizabeth caught her breath as Truth, sharp and pure, jolted through her being. John leaped within her womb, and joy surged in an absolute knowing that Mary's strong young body cradled Messiah.

As John rejoiced, Elizabeth's arms encircled her belly, sharing her unborn child's exultation as the Holy Spirit came upon her.

In a clear voice, she exclaimed, "Blessed are you among women and blessed is the child you will bear! But why am I so favored, that the mother of my Lord should come to me? As soon as the sound of your greeting reached my ears, the baby in my womb leaped for joy. Blessed is she who has believed that what the Lord has said to her will be accomplished!"

Holy light filled Mary. She lifted her hands and began to sing.

"My soul glorifies the Lord and my spirit rejoices in
    God my Savior,
for He has been mindful of the humble state of His
    servant.

From now on all generations will call me blessed,
for the Mighty One has done great things for me—
holy is His name.
His mercy extends to those who fear Him, from generation to generation.
He has performed mighty deeds with His arm; He has scattered those who are proud in their inmost thoughts.
He has brought down rulers from their thrones but has lifted up the humble.
He has filled the hungry with good things but has sent the rich away empty.
He has helped his servant Israel, remembering to be merciful to Abraham and his descendants forever, just as He promised our ancestors."

Elizabeth opened her arms, enfolding Mary within. "I am so honored you are here and so happy to see you."

"The angel Gabriel told me you were expecting a child. He said you are in your sixth month, and I think you look beautiful. I've never seen you so radiant. Imma will be overjoyed when I tell her."

"Your visit, my dear, is a gift from our Lord. Come sit down. Are you thirsty? Hungry?" Elizabeth sniffed. Something was burning. "Oh, the cakes!" She scurried to where Zechariah's surprise was filling the house with smoke.

"Mary, he will be so glad to see you, maybe he won't notice the burned smell."

Zechariah chose that moment to return home. He pointed to the charred cakes, saw their guest, and opened his arms to embrace her.

"Dear, you'd better sit down. Mary and I have a lot to tell you."

Mary's voice was soft and low. "Elizabeth, there's more I need to tell you."

Elizabeth laughed. "We too have a story to share."

Mary washed travel dust and dirt from her hands and face while Elizabeth baked another batch of date nut cakes. Zechariah stood watch over the fire. Baking complete, the three took their cakes and cups of water to the courtyard and settled on pillows placed against the benches.

"Will you tell us, Mary?"

She nibbled the cake and set it to one side. "I was alone, and then I was not." She sketched a figure in the air. "A light pulsing with life in the shape of a tall man was suddenly with me, speaking to me."

Zechariah leaned forward, nodding and pointing to himself.

Elizabeth turned to her young cousin. "That's what Zechariah saw in the Temple. What did he say to you?"

"He said I was highly favored, and 'the Lord is with you.'"

"It terrified me. Not as in a sense of danger but of confusion. I could hardly think. Why would the Lord be with me?

Yes, I'm of David's line, but our family is poor, and our town is full of Gentiles and Roman soldiers, not priests and important people."

"Did you ask?"

"I was so scared I couldn't speak. He must have realized this because he told me not to be afraid." Mary shook her head and chuckled. "But his next words were more frightening. That's why I'm here, Elizabeth, to talk with someone who is living the impossible."

Elizabeth reached over and squeezed Zechariah's hand. "It hasn't been easy, but we have survived with Adonai's mercy."

Mary inhaled a deep breath and blushed. "You both have known me since I was an infant. On all that is sacred and holy and as I stand before the Lord, I vow I am a virgin. Joseph and I are never alone. No one has touched me."

Zechariah and Elizabeth nodded.

"Gabriel said I would be with child and give birth to a son and to name Him Jesus." She paused, studying their eyes. Reassured, she continued. "My son, my little Jesus, will be great and will be called the Son of the Most High."

"God's child."

Words tumbled from Mary's mouth. "The Lord God will give Him the throne of His father David, and He will reign over the house of Jacob forever; His kingdom will never end."

"Could you speak? Yes? What did you say?"

"'How will this be? I'm a virgin.'" She shrugged. "It was all I could think to ask, although now I have more questions than my mind can hold."

Elizabeth tsked. "I'm impressed you could think of anything to ask." She pinched off a piece of cake rich with dates and popped it in her mouth.

"Gabriel said the Holy Spirit would come upon me and the Most High would overshadow me so Jesus would be called Son of Man." She stroked her belly.

"Mary, you are the imma of the Son of God and Son of Man."

The three sat in silence, cakes forgotten.

Sunset lit the sky silhouetting tree branches, summoning gnats and a cooler breeze.

"Is there more, Mary?"

"He told me of your miracle, said nothing is impossible with Adonai." Mary's hands tightened across her lap. "I told him I was the Lord's servant and to let it be as he had said. And then I came here without telling my imma or abba or Joseph what happened." She studied her clasped hands. "Will they believe me?"

Elizabeth noticed Zechariah avert his eyes and knew his thoughts. Disbelief was a more common reaction to the miraculous than belief.

"You have shown great faith without doubt." She considered her words, not wanting to offer false hope. "I hope—I think—your parents will believe you. Your birth was uncommon, so it's not the first time they've experienced Adonai's unexpected blessings. Joseph...?" She shrugged. "I've never met him."

Mary's eyes moistened. "We are betrothed. He is a good man."

"Even a good man doubts the impossible when it touches his life." She glanced at her husband, who acknowledged her words with a dispirited nod.

"This is what I do know. It seems impossible that a child, the Messiah, is within you by the power of the Most High, and yet it has become a reality—truth. I wonder if Gabriel was reassuring you when he said nothing is impossible with the Lord. Leave Joseph to God. He will reveal Truth to him. Your parents too, and someday, all of Nazareth, all of Judea."

Relief shone from Mary's eyes.

"This is your next act of faith. Believe that the Almighty will guide your words with your parents and Joseph. Of all the women in the world, you have been chosen to mother Jesus. Since Adonai is His Father, He will provide for you, whether it is friends or food or a shoulder to cry on."

"Elizabeth, our sons are both miracles who will know each other."

Zechariah abruptly stood and spread his arms wide.

"Are you saying there's more than that?" Elizabeth waited for his nod. "The Lord has caused them to be born close together for His purpose?" Another emphatic nod. "Mary, did Gabriel tell you more?"

Mary glanced at Zechariah. "No, and I'm not learned like you." She fidgeted with her headdress. "But I love to listen to the Torah, especially the prophet Isaiah. There's a verse—I may not say it right—'Prepare the way of the Lord.'"

Zechariah nodded and raised his hands heavenward.

"I wonder if your son will in some way minister with my Jesus."

Elizabeth startled when Zechariah grabbed her arm and pointed to Mary. "Mary, Zechariah knows more of John's—that's the name Gabriel gave our son—path than I do. It seems your words are truth.

"Dear ones…" Elizabeth's voice shook. "We are surrounded by miracles!" She grasped Zechariah's and Mary's hands. "I cannot go another breath without praising Adonai. Will you join me?"

Hunger drove them inside. Elizabeth set out fresh bread from the morning and a bowl of hummus along with the last of the date nut cakes. That would suffice until she completed the evening meal.

Mary's words and Zechariah's reaction ran through her mind as she prepared tomatoes. She stopped midslice. Years ago, she'd pledged almost as Isaiah did, "Here am I, send me." Many years passed, but He'd heard and included her in His plan.

Isaiah had lived close by—in Jerusalem—known its rare snow and rainy season, walked its rumpled hills, and felt the heat in its sunbaked walls. Isaiah had been a true prophet, a messenger from the Lord. He'd stood against Ahaz until…

She gripped the knife. Until he was condemned to death. She quaked, faced a truth she longed to deny. Adonai did not offer His chosen a life of ease but of service, hard service and often death. Someday would her little one be condemned for speaking God's truth? Hands trembling, she released the knife. Seized it again. She'd run. Hide John where no one could find him. He'd be safe.

Holding the knife, she gazed around the room, planning what to pack for their survival. If Adonai would not protect him, she would.

Mary returned from drawing water. She paused at the doorway, the last flicker of sun behind her.

Memories of Mary's song of praise intertwined with Isaiah's words—"Here am I... May it be to me... Send me... As You have said."—their messages a celebration of life and tragedy, hardship and honor, sacrifice and service.

She'd lived through sacrifice—years of standing excluded on the outside of the circle, looking in, hungry to be included. Mary faced hardship as an unwed mother. What would their sweet chosen babes endure?

Angry tears blurring her vision, she shoved the uncut tomato away. Their choices, not her choice. They'd be grown men having shrugged off an imma's care. She'd never seen her child, never held him in her arms, yet her heart wept at the thought of his future.

"Mary, what will become of our boys?"

"You too thought of the prophets' hardships."

"I don't want that for my son or yours."

"Nor do I, but it's not our choice, is it, Elizabeth?"

Elizabeth reached for the tomato and twirled it on the table. "We had a choice. When you and I each decided to be servants of the Lord, we placed our lives in His hands. Now we trust. That's the harder part—trusting His plan and living in trust."

Mary lifted tear-rimmed eyes. "What if I can't do this? I believe and I doubt at the same time—not doubt He can do this, doubt of myself. What if it's too hard to keep going?"

"It won't be. Tomorrow, I'll tell you a story. Tonight, let's eat and rest."

"It was His voice that spoke to me—once, a long time ago—that sustains me. He started with 'Don't be afraid.'" Elizabeth closed her eyes, remembering its timbre.

"And so, I wasn't afraid though I was almost still a child. I didn't know grown men tremble when hearing His voice. Rather, I was comforted, certain of who spoke to me. Nothing like that has ever happened since." Her gaze drifted beyond Mary. "I wish it had happened again and again, but this one time…" She searched for the right word. "Sustained. It sustained me no matter how dark or fearful I became over my life. Somehow, in some way, it happened, and I knew. Not like 'belief.' Beyond belief. Deeper than belief." She looked back at Mary. "I *knew* Adonai saw me. He spoke to me."

Mary leaned forward. "What did He say?"

"Trust Me."

Echoing her words, Mary whispered, "Trust Me."

Elizabeth's eyes widened. "And yet I've spent so much of life worried and fearful."

She brushed a tendril from Mary's face and tucked it behind her ear. "I told my abba when it happened. Since then, I've never confided it to anyone—never dared—but after what you shared, I knew you'd understand."

Mary clasped her cousin's hands. "You're trembling, Elizabeth. What you shared is safe with me." Her brow furrowed. "But how can you be so certain and still be fearful? It's like walking in opposite directions—impossible."

Elizabeth hesitated. "Remember David's psalm when he calls out 'My Adonai, why have You forsaken me?'"

At Mary's nod, she continued. "Yet at the end of the song, he says 'I trust You.' When I doubted Adonai heard me, still I claimed Him as my Lord. No matter what happened or did not happen, no matter if I understood or did not, Adonai is my God.

"I longed for Him to turn His favor upon me, to remember me with a child. I never doubted He could, just that He would. My wish may not be His will."

"And this time it was. You carry a child, Elizabeth!"

She caressed the curve no longer hidden. "An old woman like me, expecting a child!"

"Like Sarah."

Elizabeth shook her finger at Mary. "Stop! I'm not *that* old. Did you know I almost copied Sarah in another way? When I was ten years childless, Zechariah's family urged him to divorce me. In mercy, he did not. Finally he will have his son."

Mary plucked a mint leaf and rubbed it between her fingers. "When Gabriel appeared, I couldn't decide whether to run for my abba or fall to my knees in awe or hide. His voice was the most beautiful sound I've ever heard. The music, the rhythm, even his words flowed more like a song than simply words strung together into a sentence. At first, I feared losing the music if I spoke aloud. I wonder if I'll ever hear Gabriel's voice again."

"Either way, what you heard will dwell in you forever."

"Elizabeth, may I ask what He told you to trust Him with?"

For a time, she was silent. "At the time, my imma was dying of a wasting disease. The sickness weakened her until she slept most of the time, could not eat, and became so frail she no longer looked like my imma. Abba never left her side. I was convinced if I lost one, I'd lose both."

"How old were you?"

"Not a child, not a woman—that in-between time a girl needs her imma to guide her into womanhood."

"You prayed."

"For hours. Earnestly. Desperately. Wholeheartedly. Confidently. And when He answered…I have never forgotten the certainty I felt, the peace."

"Certain of…?"

"That it was His voice speaking to me. Elizabeth bat Joseph." She patted a bulge that might have been John's elbow or foot. "Mary, hold tightly Gabriel's words. It is hard to be highly favored by the Lord."

Mary dipped her head. "Yes. Praising and crying jumble together. Hiding in a cave sounds appealing, as does announcing the news in the market." She lifted her hands. "I don't feel pregnant, but I know I am. Do I sound crazy?"

"You sound pregnant."

CHAPTER NINETEEN

It was inevitable that Elizabeth must return to the market. This time she did not venture there alone. Mary walked beside her carrying the basket. The midmorning sun weighed heavy, but an early start had been delayed by Mary's queasiness.

"How long will this last, Elizabeth?"

"Probably three months. Some suffer the entire nine months, others not at all or only in the mornings. Ginger root makes a tea that will ease your nausea."

Elizabeth debated telling Mary of last week's marketing fiasco. As if she read her cousin's thoughts, Mary wrapped her arm around Elizabeth's waist.

"This is hard for you, cousin."

At Elizabeth's look of surprise, Mary continued. "The closer we are to the market, the shorter your steps. We will do this together until it's too difficult for you to walk this far, and then I'll do the shopping. Show me the vendors who are honest and grateful for our business."

A friend—another gift from the Almighty.

Despite Mary's assurances, Elizabeth dragged her feet. *Hold me together, Lord, and guard my tongue.*

Another experience like last week and she'd resort to eating leaves. Mary and Zechariah could go eat with his sister. She whispered "artichokes and pomegranates" to Mary, then stuck the tip of her tongue between her teeth, prepared to clamp down at the first derogatory comment about herself or Zechariah.

The purchase safely stored in Mary's basket, Elizabeth motioned toward the stand of exotic spices from the islands of Hellas. She risked releasing her tongue from its captivity.

"Ginger root, please. A large one."

"You're the old priest's old wife." The man cackled at his own humor.

She took a deep breath as Mary placed a cautionary hand on her arm. Should she leave now so Mary didn't witness how cruel people could become?

"I am."

"Glad to see Adonai blesses His own."

Breath whooshed out. "Thank you. Two ginger roots, please."

Ahead of them, three women watched their progress, sneering and murmuring among themselves. Elizabeth's teeth recaptured her tongue. She veered in the opposite direction, but Mary tugged her arm away and continued straight ahead.

"Shalom. It's a beautiful morning to market. I'm Mary of Nazareth visiting my cousin, Elizabeth. Are you her friends?"

"Oh, we've heard of her."

Mary beamed at them. "I'm so happy for you. Everyone tells me what a godly woman she is. Truly, you are blessed by Adonai. Have a day of peace."

It was unclear who was more befuddled, Elizabeth or the women. Mary looped arms with Elizabeth and guided her to the next vendor. Something was added to the basket. Elizabeth was unsure what they purchased or how much they paid.

The spice vendor refused to look up or speak. Two women swished their tunics away to keep from brushing against Elizabeth. Myrah nodded curtly, then turned her back to them. Nila waved from a distance. Whispers of "cursed" were twice heard.

It had been better than last week. Buoyed with hope, at first Elizabeth did not realize Mary was drooping and dragging her feet. She understood without asking.

"Yes, it is possible you too will be shunned and shamed. Adonai didn't offer anyone on earth an easy journey." Imma's words came back to her. "He gave us a greater promise, a wonderful mercy. He promised He'd always be with us."

Mary raised stricken eyes to hers. "Will Adonai be with me when I tell Imma and Abba or when my little Jesus is born? If Joseph divorces me, will Adonai comfort my fatherless son?"

"Yes."

"You sound so sure of this."

"I am. Look backward. No, not toward town. Think back over your life. It's full of tender mercies, more than you can name or know. Those mercies were our Lord being with you. No matter the circumstances, He's not going to abandon you no matter who else might pull away or not believe you."

The tightness around Mary's face eased.

"Eat and sleep. When you are hungry and tired, doubt wedges its way in and makes itself at home."

***

Zechariah listened to Elizabeth and Mary share information when they forgot he could hear them. Never had he dreamed he'd live with two expectant women and their constant exchange of information: swollen feet, stretch marks, cravings—she still ate artichokes and pomegranates—sleeping woes and indigestion. Remember to walk. Remember to laugh. Drink ginger tea. Carry water in smaller jars. Sleep. Walk. Sit.

Talk about the birth itself brought him quickly to his feet and propelled him out the door for a long walk. He'd heard the pain was excruciating. He knew many women died. If he lost his Elizabeth… The thought was too painful to complete.

The survival of his wife became his prayer focus. Over the years, the multitude of prayers for a child became a mere fraction of those he prayed for Elizabeth's life to be spared.

In secret, he'd sent a painfully written message to Hillel requesting the name of Jerusalem's best midwife. The woman recommended was a descendant of Shiphrah, one of the Hebrew midwives who'd defied Pharaoh to save little Moses. She'd arrive when Elizabeth's time was near. Although Myrah often acted as a midwife, Elizabeth would be more comfortable with someone else—anyone else.

He'd set in motion all he knew to do to assure Elizabeth's safety. Content, he watched the women, their heads close together, one silver, one deep brown, stitching a blanket for little John. Though Elizabeth was old enough to be Mary's grandmother, their roles appeared fluid—one day, Elizabeth the encourager and the next day, Mary the comforter.

He and Elizabeth had grown to be like that. If he lost her, he'd lose himself.

Their voices brought him back to the present. They had again forgotten he could hear.

Mary dropped the sewing in her lap and rubbed her shoulders with both hands. "I am unworthy to carry this child, this gift to our people."

"Our worthiness does not determine Adonai's gifts to us."

Pride raced through Zechariah at his wife's wisdom.

"Elizabeth, forgive me. I hear your words and will think on them, but I just noticed your imma's amphora.… It's broken. What happened?"

Guessing she'd glance toward him, he frowned at his reading as if engrossed.

"I startled, backed into the mantel, and it fell."

He felt her pleasure as she reminisced.

"Zechariah helped me pick up the pieces and then filled it with flowers. I still see the flowers and not the brokenness."

He glanced at her, and they shared a smile.

"Even broken it would be beautiful with flowers." Mary set aside her sewing. "I'll fill it again."

Elizabeth nodded. With Mary out of earshot, she smiled at Zechariah. "It's like what our Lord did for us. We were broken, and He filled us with beauty."

Tears blurred his eyes. *Adonai, spare her life. John and I need this woman. She's full of wisdom and grace. Mercy, Lord, mercy.*

Elizabeth wiped tears from her face as she packed food for Mary's return. Three months had passed since Mary's arrival. It was time for her to return home to Nazareth.

Deeply spiritual, Anna would believe Mary's story and shield her from the curious and condemning. Joachim's response was less assured. Joseph? Elizabeth shook her head. Not knowing him, she couldn't guess his reaction.

"Elizabeth, I folded the coverlet and left it on the bed." Mary's red-rimmed eyes revealed that she'd been teary too. She clutched her small pack of clothes in front of her belly like a shield.

"Dear, you are not showing yet. No one will realize you carry a child."

"I feel different. Heavier. How can others not guess?"

Elizabeth studied her. Mary was right. Her face was rounder, her figure a little softer, fuller. "Your imma will know, but no one else. They will think I'm a very good cook who stuffed you full of date cakes."

"You are and you did. How long can I use that as an excuse?"

"Not long."

"That's why I need to return now and tell Joseph." Mary's eyes filled. "It would be terrible if someone guessed and asked him about it. He'd be humiliated."

Elizabeth folded a piece of cloth over the food and handed it to Mary. "Have you thought how you will tell him about Jesus and about Gabriel's visit?"

"I've thought of almost nothing else." Mary untied her pack to add Elizabeth's offerings. "Backwards. I'll tell him the story back to front. First, I'll say an angel told me you were six months pregnant."

"He won't understand that's a miracle. Be sure to tell him how old we are and that this is our first child." Elizabeth chuckled. "Only child too."

Zechariah looked up from his studies and nodded.

"You're right. It will help him understand why I left home so quickly to visit you. Then…" Mary knotted and unknotted the pack strings.

"Then?"

"Then I'm not sure." She shrugged and sat down hard on Elizabeth's bench. "That's as far as I've gotten. I can tell Imma the whole story front to back. Even if she's shocked—and who wouldn't be—she will listen and ask questions if she's confused, but how do I tell my betrothed that I'm with child? He knows it's not his child. An angel informing me I'm going to have a baby and Adonai is His abba sounds a little peculiar."

Elizabeth laughed. "It does, doesn't it?"

"And stranger, that of all the Hebrew women in Judea, the Most High chose me, a young, poor, Galilean girl to carry His Son."

"You are of the line of David, but yes, it sounds a bit unlikely."

"Joseph will back away from me like I was a viper and then turn and run as fast as possible. I would if I were him."

It hurt to see the uncertainty on Mary's face. "And if he does?"

"He will divorce me, I could be stoned, my family will be shamed. I cannot imagine dishonoring my parents." She raised hopeful eyes. "Maybe I could live here and we'd raise the boys together."

"You are always welcome here." Elizabeth sat beside her young cousin. "Yes, shamed and divorced are possible, but leave Joseph and your abba to our Lord. You need not fear being stoned, just as I need not fear miscarrying or John not surviving the birth. Your Jesus and my John have been promised and named by Adonai. They each have an ordained role. They are safe as children and youth."

Elizabeth pleated the towel draped on the table. "It is for their lives as men that I fear. Prophets are not loved. Will the Son of God be accepted?" She wadded the towel. "Do not listen to me. I've spent too much time fretting instead of faithing. Do you like my new word?"

Mary giggled like the young girl she was. "I'm going to practice faithing all the way home."

From the corner of her eye, she saw her husband cringe.

"I miss you already. Dear one, you have been an answer to prayers I didn't think to pray. It's been pure joy to have you here, to have someone to talk to, and it's been an honor to have the imma of my Lord with me these three months. I wish you could stay another three months."

Tears washed down Mary's face. "I'm crying again. You'll send word when John arrives?"

"Give your parents my deepest love. Tell them I am convinced you speak truth."

Mary nodded, picked up her pack, and followed Zechariah out the door. He'd walk with her until she found a group of families to walk with.

Elizabeth followed them to the head of the path, waved, and blew kisses. Once out of sight, she walked slowly home.

The house that had been so lively with Mary's laugh and their chatter was too big, too quiet, too dull. She wandered to the courtyard, back into the house, and into Mary's room. Her scent remained. On the bed lay a gift, a bracelet of slender reeds. She recognized the design as one she'd taught Anna to make so many years ago. Sliding it on her wrist, she prayed from her heart that Joseph would believe Mary, that he'd be a kind and loving abba to little Jesus, a faithful husband to Mary.

Zechariah's shuffling steps told her he'd easily found a family for Mary to travel with. She saw him standing in the middle of the house looking around as if he too missed her laughter. She went to him and rested her head against his shoulder, grateful for his presence, grateful he believed Mary, grateful they'd shared this pregnancy from the beginning.

"Lord, have mercy on our Mary."

His arms encircled her, and though he could not speak, she felt his amen and echoed it.

Elizabeth heaved herself to her feet. She hoped they were still there. She hadn't seen them in several weeks. Were they clean? Had her toenails grown into claws? The list of little indignities of pregnancy grew each day. Seeing other women heavy with child, she'd thought them serene and beautiful, never guessing the constant need for a chamber pot or that they'd not slept well for a month.

Zechariah watched her as if any moment their child would burst out and he'd need to catch him and swaddle him. Nila visited every few days with the message from Caleb that the midwife had neither arrived nor sent word. Zechariah paced more with each message. She alternated between wanting to assure him and dismissing the panic in his eyes. Many women gave birth alone. She'd be fine.

Myrah did not visit.

Leaves changing color warned that winter approached. With the cooler days came visitors, townspeople who happened to be walking past, mothers with children who chose this path by chance, men concerned over Zechariah's absence. Some brought small gifts for the baby. Older women brought pots of cooked food, insisting they accidentally made too much.

Elizabeth smiled graciously, accepting their offerings gratefully.

"Zechariah, are they concerned or curious?"

She guessed his nod meant both.

Lacing her fingers over her belly, she interrupted his reading. "I wish Myrah would come by."

Zechariah looked at her in shock.

"John's birth could be a new beginning for all of us, and he needs to grow up knowing his family." She rubbed her lower back. "I mostly want this to be over, but in one way I hope it never ends. Life inside of life is…beyond words."

His look said she sounded ludicrous. She supposed other women would agree with him.

She was eager to meet this little boy. Elizabeth caressed the mountain that was her belly. Yet, as uncomfortable as she was, she didn't want this time to end. He was safe inside her.

Would John have Abba's green eyes? Imma's broad smile? Zechariah's deep voice?

"I think Nila will attend the birth while you wait in the synagogue. Most men will be wondering if they've had a boy or a girl. You can relax and not worry about anything."

He gazed at her for so long she snapped at him. "What? Oh, I forget you can't speak." With his concern so evident on his face, she softened her voice. "I'm sorry, dear. I will be fine. I'm no longer afraid. If I do not survive…" She stopped when he held up his hand and turned away.

She awoke one morning more energetic than she'd been in a long time. Grinding grain and making bread went quickly. She swept the house and courtyard pavers, watered those plants that would survive the winter and covered the ones needing protection with a thick layer of dirt.

A pot of legumes soon hung over the fire. She chopped dates for the cakes Zechariah enjoyed and set out honey and warm bread for his meal when he awoke.

Pain tightened her back. Today, it hurt more than usual.

Her water supply low, she took a small jug and walked slowly to the spring. She'd ask someone to fill it and carry it uphill.

The only "someone" there was Myrah.

Suddenly, she was tired. Back aching, feet swelling, and thirsty, she was weary of trying to make peace when peace wasn't wanted.

Lord, how do I obey You with this woman who dislikes me? I've tried to believe You could heal this relationship, but she wants nothing to do with me. I don't think I can keep believing it will be healed.

His voice broke through her thoughts.

Trust Me.

He'd healed Imma and Elizabeth's marriages and opened her closed womb. Faith included trusting His timing. Maybe today was the day.

"My brother married a fool. Why are you here alone? You could fall and lose the baby."

Maybe today was not the day. "Shalom, Myrah."

"Why are you here?"

To annoy you. She averted her eyes before Myrah perceived her thought. *Lord. My tongue! I need a gatekeeper for my mouth.*

"We're almost out of water."

Myrah snatched the jug from Elizabeth's hand and knelt to fill it. "Here. That little bit won't do you much good."

Imma's words wafted through her mind. *"Act as if you have faith, and faith will come."* If she trusted the Lord to heal this fractured friendship, was that acting in faith? *Help me, Lord.*

She relaxed her face into a smile she'd have given Anna or Nila. "Thank you, Myrah. Our baby is blessed to have you as family."

"Am I family? Is it Zechariah's?"

Elizabeth kept her voice soft and warm. "You are and yes, there is no doubt between us that your brother is the baby's father."

Elizabeth hoisted the jug to her shoulder and turned laboriously to climb the hill.

Myrah did not offer to help, but neither did she sling another caustic comment.

Thank You, Lord, for little mercies.

Zechariah met her on the way home. He took the water jug from her with one hand and with the other hand hauled her forward. This was how an errant child must feel. She tucked away the indignant feeling for when she needed to correct John's behavior. There must be a better way.

"Myrah was at the spring and helped me with the water. Wasn't that kind of her? We had a little chat. I think it went well." Maybe she could distract him. At least he could not scold her with his voice, only with disapproval on his face. She peeked at his expression. He was very disapproving.

"We needed water." A band tightened around her belly and released. "I don't know when he'll be born, so I can't sit and wait until someone offers to help."

Zechariah scowled at her.

"I'm fine. Walking is good for women at this time, and I took our smallest jug. I need more water, though." She rubbed the ache in her back. "There's a lot of cleaning to do before the baby comes."

They arrived at home. Elizabeth dropped to the courtyard bench. "I admit I'm tired." The band tightened. Released.

Zechariah brusquely pushed past her, leaving her outside and alone. She leaned her head against the wall, the day's earlier energy evaporating. She'd placate him later after she rested.

Thirsty but too weary from the long walk to enter the house for a drink of water, she closed her eyes and dozed. The band tightened. Released. She moaned as her sleep was broken.

Sunlight stretching through the surrounding trees warmed her face, waking her. A tightening. She sat up uncomfortable and confused. Why did she hurt? The pain eased. She'd been sitting too long.

Elizabeth maneuvered off the bench and into the house. A tightening. She groaned and bent over. Release. Her breath caught in realization.

"Zechariah?" Her voice came thin and breathy. "Zechariah?" No answer.

Water trickled down her legs. Embarrassed, she yanked her headdress off and lowered herself to the floor. Using the headdress as a rag, she soaked up the puddle. The band tightened. She clawed the floor. When the easing came, she hung her head and panted.

Unable to stand, she crawled to a chair and heaved herself upward. Pain returned. She doubled over. *Dear Lord. Help me.*

Oily sweat and salty tears covered her face. The bed was too far away. She knelt, pain driving her head to the cold stone floor.

Thin, wiry arms encircled her, helped her to stand. She leaned against someone's body, clutching her belly. Guided to the bed, she fell backward and looked up. She'd never been so glad to see Myrah's scowling face.

"I told Jesse you were a fool, and I was right. I knew this would happen when I saw you this morning at the spring. You never did have any sense."

As she fussed, Myrah untied Elizabeth's sandals and slid her tunic over her head. With the practiced ease of years of helping others, she raised Elizabeth's legs and covered the bed with a thick cloth.

"I don't want to be here. You and the baby are both going to die, and I'll not have Zechariah blaming me for your death. I'm here only until Nila comes and as a favor to my brother. Do you understand? I'm not here as a friend."

Elizabeth's nod became a grimace as pain engulfed her.

Myrah's voice softened. "You're too old, Elizabeth. It's hard on even young women."

"Zechariah?"

"He doesn't realize it's your time. He was worried and sent me to stay with you while he goes for Nila. The midwife from

Jerusalem was ordered to attend a Roman official's wife. She's not coming."

Elizabeth clutched the bedding at another bolt of pain. Jaws clamped shut, she refused to scream.

"Did you prepare a basket for the birthing?"

Elizabeth nodded and pointed, her eyes squinched closed as pain came and lingered.

A voice called from the outer room.

"You stay out there." Myrah's tone was firm. "Send Nila in."

"Myrah, come out here."

"Jesse?" Myrah mumbled under her breath as she left the room. She returned subdued and shaken. "Nila fell and broke her foot."

⁂

Between Elizabeth's labor pains, the two women stared at each other. Elizabeth looked away first.

"I'm sorry, Myrah." Elizabeth gasped as another contraction began. "I know you don't l-like me and don't want to be h-here."

"I don't want you to die."

"Because Zechariah will blame you." Elizabeth gripped the bed covers. "Ohhhhhhhh."

"Breathe, Elizabeth. When it starts, breathe in and then a long breath out. In, now out, long out. Good. Again."

"Is it almost over?"

Myrah snorted. "This is the beginning."

Tears seeped from the corners of Elizabeth's eyes and trickled into her hairline. "I never knew."

"You can do this. You'll be fine."

"You said I was going to die," Elizabeth wailed. "I don't want to die."

For a long time, Myrah said nothing except to remind her to breathe in and out. "I'm afraid, Elizabeth."

"Zechariah won't blame you."

"No, I'm afraid you're going to die and we're still… Breathe, Elizabeth. It will hurt less. Trust me."

"I'm sorry. I broke your trust as a friend…" She panted. "Talking about Zec… Ohhhhhhhh."

Myrah wiped the sweat from Elizabeth's face. "Stop talking. Rest when you can."

"But I…"

"You've said enough. It's my turn to talk." She held a cup to Elizabeth's lips. "Drink."

When the next contraction eased, Myrah straightened the damp covers. "I don't understand why I've been so hateful to you, why I've held a grudge." She shrugged. "It got hold of me, and I didn't want to let go of it. You've tried…. Breathe. Squeeze my hands. Good. The pains are coming closer together."

"That's good?"

"Trust me."

Elizabeth managed a weak smile.

Myrah reached out a tentative hand. "Peace?"

"Peace." Elizabeth gasped at the powerful tightening. "Now I can die."

"Don't you dare. I can't lose you. Listen to me. When you feel the need to push, I'm going to help you…."

Elizabeth heard no more. Pain existed. Nothing else. No words, no emotions, no comprehension. Day turned to night turned to day.

At last, instinct guided her to push until her body surrendered the child and she heard a lion cub's roar of displeasure at leaving the warmth of her womb and Myrah's cry, "A boy!"

Exhausted, she slept as the infant was rubbed with salt and oil and wrapped snuggly in swaddling cloths. Myrah cleaned her and changed the fouled towels on the bed before nestling her son in her arms.

His squashed old-man's face was beautiful, his body perfect, his damp hair curled in tiny knots. She could not look away from this tiny person who'd lived inside her. Miniscule lashes surrounded his eyes. He yawned and squinted at her.

"He lives." Myrah's relief was clear. "He's beautiful, Bethy. You have a son. *Mazel tov.*"

"A son and a friend."

Myrah echoed her words. "A son and a friend."

Zechariah watched his wife and child sleep. He'd never imagined how precious the sight would be or how he wanted to etch it in his memory. If it was the last thing he ever saw, he'd die contented.

He hoped she'd seen the joy in his eyes when he'd first held their son. More, he hoped she recognized the love in his eyes when he looked at her. If only he could speak the words.

His voice had not returned at the child's birth as he expected. Maybe Adonai forgot or decided not to lift His penalty. He'd not argue nor plead for it, his gratitude for Elizabeth's survival too great. This incredible blessing, another mercy. He'd ask for nothing more.

Untrue.

His mind and heart staggered at the enormity of what lay ahead.

More than ever, he must have Adonai's guidance. He was just a man, an old man, tasked with raising this son in the way of the Lord that he might be a prophet like Elijah.

Overwhelmed, Zechariah stared at the child who would turn their people to the Lord. Doubt shoved its way past gratitude.

Lord, I can't do this. How could You ask it of me? John needs someone younger or someone wiser.

He rubbed the ache in his knuckles. *You expect too much of us. I prayed for a son to carry on my line, not to be a prophet.* He backed away from the bed. *These fears—are they why I still can't speak?*

John stirred and opened his eyes.

I don't know how to be an abba, little one. John yawned. *I don't even have a voice to tell you I love you, and my hands… I can't throw a ball with you or teach you to write. Oh, son, what good am I as your abba?*

Elizabeth awakened and held out her hand to him. "You're troubled."

He stretched his mouth into a smile and shook his head.

"Your speech has not returned. Is that it? We've been married a long time, Zechariah. It's useless to try and hide it. I can tell when something bothers you."

Unable to convey his fears and doubts, he nodded. *I begin my life as an abba by lying. Lord, is this who You want to raise Your prophet?*

CHAPTER TWENTY

Elizabeth greeted Myrah with a smile and burst into tears. "What?" Myrah asked. "Is he sick? Not eating? What's wrong? Are you bleeding a lot?"

"I'm sore and still crying, and I don't know how to be an imma. He cries, and I don't know why, and then I cry. I'm so tired. What's wrong with me?"

Myrah laughed. "Nothing is wrong with you. Most new mothers go through the same thing."

"It's nothing like I expected." She held the unhappy infant against her shoulder and patted his back.

"This is motherhood. Nothing will go as expected. He will throw up as you walk out the door late to synagogue. He will cry at the top of his lungs when you take him to market, and every time you sit, he will need something that requires you to stand."

"Will I ever sleep through the night again?"

"In a few months or a year—depends. Libi didn't sleep through the night for almost two years."

Elizabeth groaned.

Myrah took the fussy infant from Elizabeth's arms. Sitting, she placed him on her lap, face down, and jiggled her knees gently. An indelicate burp and the fussing stopped. She handed him back to Elizabeth.

"Myrah, I know nothing about being an imma. How am I going to do this?"

"You tell me, Bethy. You learned to be a priest's wife. How?"

"I watched my imma."

"Then watch the other mothers, but I think it's more than watching. You changed from a girl who thought only of herself to a woman who thinks of others, is kind when they are cruel and caring when they are indifferent. How did you do that?" Myrah hunched her shoulders. "I think that's why I stayed angry with you. You were becoming someone I admired, and I didn't understand how. You left me behind."

Incredulous, Elizabeth stared at her. "I've spent years thinking you hated me."

"Oh, I did. I wanted what you had."

"What I had? The scorn of not doing my sacred duty?"

"Not that! You have a…a serenity."

"I have a flock of fears and doubts—I release them to the Lord and then herd them back to me."

"Exactly."

"Myrah, I am lost. What are we talking about?"

She locked eyes with Elizabeth. "You talk to Adonai, don't you? Really talk as if He hears when you speak and sees you and cares."

"Yes."

"Why?"

Elizabeth frowned, puzzled. "Because He does."

Myrah pushed harder. "How can you be so sure?"

She looked down at her lap and traced the curve of John's chin with her finger. "When I am afraid, I tell Him, and He brings to mind a scripture, and then I see things differently. Or sometimes He uses a tree or making bread or washing dishes to show His care."

"Bread?" Myrah's confusion prompted her to explain.

"Grinding grain reminds me that He might need to break the hard kernel inside me, like a bad attitude that keeps me from being kind. Bread… Myrah, I'm still hungry all the time."

John began to whimper. "And he's always hungry." She nestled him closer to feed.

"That's good. Eat to make milk for the baby. Do you ever doubt?"

"Doubt I'm hungry? Never." She blinked. "Oh, you mean doubt God. Yes. My faith wavers too often."

"And then what do you do?"

Elizabeth narrowed her eyes. "Why these questions?"

Annoyed, Myrah shrugged. "Just tell me."

"Two things. First, I recount the blessings and mercies He's already given me. It might take a long time."

Myrah brightened. "Easy. I can do that."

"The other one is harder. Imma told me that when I doubt Adonai sees or hears or cares, I need to do what He requires—obey—and my faith will return." Elizabeth's brow furrowed. "This might offend you, but it is not a game. Scripture teaches that God sees your heart. You must desire faith more than you desire water after walking uphill in the middle of a summer day, not like you desire another bite of sweet cake."

"I do what He requires." Myrah's chin jutted out. "I obey the commandments."

"Try to remember the Shema prayer…love the Lord your God with all your heart and soul and mind…. It's not thinking 'I didn't kill anyone today so I'm pleasing God,' it's, 'How do I show God's love?'"

Myrah crossed her arms. "So what if—"

"No. I'm not giving you answers. I don't have them. This is between you and the Lord." She switched John to the other side and flinched as he latched on to her breast. "Ouch. No one warned me this hurts."

"I'm not sure I understand."

"Or you don't want to." Elizabeth clapped a hand over her mouth. "I'm so sorry. I shouldn't have said that or thought it. Please, Myrah don't pull away from me again. We've finally found peace and already I've ruined it."

Myrah studied her thoughtfully. "Are you sorry because you hurt me or because you disobeyed God?"

"Because my disobedience hurt you… And if you pull back, it hurts me too."

"I never thought like that. It's…different."

"Myrah, please…"

"I've lost too many years being angry with you, while you tried to restore peace. I'm not sure about having faith and not doubting Him, but I don't doubt you."

So many possibilities lay before this child in her arms. So much love surrounded him. She'd wanted him all her life and loved him the second she knew he existed.

Elizabeth looked into his face and saw her chin, Zechariah's arched brows, Abba's nose—thankfully not Zechariah's—Imma's crinkled ears. In her arms she held those she most loved—all except Anna and Mary. Had they received the message of John's birth?

She unwrapped his binding cloths. He stretched, revealing delicate creases beneath his arms. After she wiped his bottom clean, she left his legs free to curl and kick. Myrah insisted swaddling comforted an infant like the snugness of the womb, but John seemed happy without the restriction. She hummed the soft lullaby she'd waited years to share.

The door opened. Zechariah entered and sat on the bed, John snuggled safely between them. The three of them, a family sharing a moment's peace, swelled her heart with gratitude.

"Our Lord promised him, and he's here and kicking, and it's still more than I can fathom. Is he real or am I dreaming?"

Zechariah's beautiful smile shone through his beard. They gazed at their infant, the miracle they'd never expected.

"Do you wonder what he'll be like when he's grown? Will he have green eyes like my abba? Will he be loved and respected? Will Adonai bless him?"

Zechariah's smile dimmed. Disappeared.

"What do you know that you haven't told me? He is healthy. He is well formed. Tell me Adonai will protect him." She swept John into her arms, cradling him. Fear like she'd never known, grief beyond the death of her parents and losses greater than unmet desires bound her until she struggled to breathe.

She kissed her son's head, his face, caressed the rounded shoulders. She'd fill him with so much love it would be a shield against all harm. If no one else protected him, she'd defend him unto death. She'd wrap unending prayers and the strength of her arms…

Her wrinkly skin, old woman arms, raised-vein hands, and gray-haired self could raise an infant to a child and perhaps a child to a youth. Protect an adult man? Imma's words surfaced. *Speak truth to yourself.* She'd pray for him as long as she had breath, but her arms would someday fail. She'd fail him. He needed someone stronger to guide and defend him as a man.

Faith fought to surface. Fear won.

Easier to surrender herself to Adonai than to surrender her child.

Speak truth to yourself.

Faith rose triumphant, gave her the words: "Adonai is faithful."

Zechariah rested his hand on John's fragile back. Approval shone in his eyes.

John too belonged to One who'd love and guide him beyond her return to the earth as dust. Adonai had a plan for this little life. His cousin, Jesus, would be the Son of God. Nothing could keep John from Adonai.

Zechariah stroked the tiny neck.

Elizabeth woke alone on the eighth day of her son's life. Zechariah's unrumpled side of the bed showed that he had spent the night in prayer at the synagogue. If he'd stayed home and heard baby cries during the night, he'd have brought water to her and sat with her during the feedings. She'd never expected he would be such an attentive abba.

Covering her face, she said the morning prayer. "I am thankful before You, living and enduring King, for You have mercifully restored my soul within me. Great is Your faithfulness."

Pressing her hands against her eyes, she added a personal plea. "I need Your faithfulness, especially today. So many people are coming to witness his circumcision and I'm still tired and sore and not ready for people. Please guard my mouth. And Lord, if they don't believe me when I give his name, give me courage."

Something—maybe a jar of water—thunked on the table in the other room. A broom scratched on the hard floors. Myrah had arrived early to help her prepare. She heard a voice and grinned. Myrah was talking to herself.

John whimpered in his sleep. In a minute the whimper would become a wail.

"Shhhh, baby, shhhh."

She lifted him from the cradle and positioned him to nurse when he fully woke. If Myrah didn't hear him, she'd have a few precious moments of solitude with her son before this monumental day began.

"Breathe. Breathe. The Lord is with me."

The rabbi would perform the task of a *mohel* for the rite of circumcision. Soon, the men of the town would arrive as witnesses. Their wives would accompany them to celebrate and to see the baby, see her as an imma, offer advice and warnings—the rite of welcoming her into their circle. Today his name would be announced. She had not dared break tradition and speak it other than with Zechariah and Mary until he'd been circumcised. Would the people believe her when she told them his name?

Myrah tapped on the door before entering. "When you're ready, I have a surprise for you."

"I hope it's something you made. Your sewing is better than mine."

"Because you have no patience."

"Myrah, I need to ask—there's been doubt about your brother's righteousness since he became mute."

"Yes. It spilled on to us too," Myrah agreed grimly.

"And there've been questions about me for years, and now, even who is the father of my baby."

Myrah reddened. "I'm sorry. You'd never be unfaithful to Zechariah."

"No." Elizabeth brushed away the apology. "I'm asking will Joh—the baby suffer? Will our people acknowledge he's Zechariah's son?"

"If Zechariah accepts him, they will. When he names the child after himself there will be no doubt."

Elizabeth looked away and busied herself preparing his bath.

Together they bathed the baby and wrapped him in fresh cloths. Elizabeth cleaned herself and covered her hair.

Someone coughed in the other room.

"Are they already arriving?"

"Just one person. She's been here a while. Come see, Bethy. I'll carry the baby."

"Nila! How did you manage this?" Tears puddled in Elizabeth's eyes as she reached down and hugged her. "I never imagined you'd be here."

"Two of my sons carried me in this chair. It was too far to walk with a crutch, but I couldn't miss this or let you go through it without friends. Stop crying and let me see your son."

Myrah brought the baby.

"He has your imma's dimple. Elizabeth, he's beautiful." Nila reached for her hand. "Forgive me for doubting when you told me you were with child."

"I could hardly believe it myself." Elizabeth wiped her eyes. "I still struggle to believe it." She sniffled. "Are my eyes ever going to stop leaking all the time?"

"Yes." They chorused.

Myrah left to sweep the courtyard and prepare for the circumcision. Nila held John as Elizabeth slowly set out foods she'd prepared and stored for the celebration.

Voices multiplied outside. Women entered and clustered around Nila, exclaiming over the baby. Myrah returned, looked at Elizabeth's face, and whispered her to sit.

"No. I'm fine."

"You are the color of a sheep. Go sit."

"They will stare at me."

Myrah pursed her lips. "You should be used to that. Sit." She guided Elizabeth to a chair, took the baby from Nila, and nestled him in his mother's arms. "It's almost time. I'll pull a chair to the door, and you can nurse him when he cries."

"It hurts him?"

One of the women shrugged. "Maybe, but this rite is part of who we are."

"Mine screamed the entire time," added another.

"My son cried as soon as his swaddles were removed," said a woman she'd not met.

Elizabeth held him tighter. "He'll cry?"

"You will too," Myrah said.

Zechariah opened the door for Jesse to announce they were ready to begin. Elizabeth's chair was moved to the door. Zechariah paused beside her.

"Elizabeth, I forgot to ask. Who will carry him in?" Myrah searched the room to discern who was so honored. Hearing no answer, she turned and saw both her brother and her sister-in-law smiling at her.

"You, Myrah. You and Jesse."

Speechless, Myrah buried her face against the baby's head.

"Turnip? Really? After all that's happened?"

"After all that's happened, we are still family and again friends."

Amid the hugs and smiles and sniffles, John raised his voice in protest. More laughter followed, and then they sobered. This day marked the baby's entrance into the covenant with Adonai.

Myrah carried him outside where the mohel waited to pronounce the blessing and perform the ritual. She handed him to Zechariah as Jesse repeated the father's blessing. The mohel's sharply honed knife sliced quick and clean. John released a bloodcurdling scream.

The witnesses responded: "Even as this child has entered into the covenant, so may he enter into the Torah, and the nuptial canopy, and into good deeds."

The mohel accepted a cup of wine from Caleb. The naming ceremony came next.

Elizabeth's heart began to thud. Would she be believed, or her words challenged? She wiped sweat from her hands beneath a fold in her clothes. Years of taunts and shame surged forward to disable her. Long ago, she'd learned to make herself small in the presence of others.

The mohel murmured a question to Caleb. Caleb nodded his head and turned to Jesse. Jesse shrugged.

"Zechariah will be the name of the child before me." The mohel reached for the cup of wine to perform the naming blessing.

"No. Wait." Her whispered voice was not heard. "His name…" She cleared her throat. "He is to be called John."

Whispers like wind in a field of wheat surrounded her.

Caleb moved closer. "Elizabeth, there's no one in your family or your husband's whose name is John. He should be named after his abba." He grasped Zechariah's elbow. "Surely you agree, my friend."

The whispers grew. Snatches came to her, wounding her with their words.

"It must not be her husband's child."

Beside her, Zechariah shook his head.

A gasp. "Look, he denies the child his name."

Impatiently, the mohel waited. "He must be named at this time. Zechariah, what will you have him called? Do you claim the child as yours?"

Zechariah motioned for a writing tablet then stared at his knobby hands, panic freezing his features.

Elizabeth stood up, brushed away the hands that sought to calm and restrain her. "The Lord has done this for me. In these days He has shown His favor and taken away my disgrace among the people. This child will be called John."

No longer, never again would she be the rabbit fleeing a hawk's shadow, a mouse beneath an owl's watch, a caged animal ridiculed and mocked.

"Myrah, please find a tablet and stylus."

She stood before her husband and reached for his hands. "Beloved, I understand it is excruciating for you to grasp a marker and write. Here, try. Please. You, alone, understand how important it is that he be named John."

Zechariah took the tablet. Painstakingly, the letters uneven and clumsy as a seven-year-old's first attempt, he wrote, *His name is John.*

Then—a sound she'd longed to hear for over nine months, its music warm and rich and manna to her ears—Zechariah's beautiful deep voice rose in praise and thanksgiving.

The Lord had loosed his tongue, restored his speech, kept His promise. Zechariah's words soared above all other voices.

"Praise be to the Lord, the God of Israel,
    because He has come to his people and redeemed them.
He has raised up a horn of salvation for us
    in the house of His servant David
(as He said through His holy prophets of long ago),
salvation from our enemies
    and from the hand of all who hate us—
to show mercy to our ancestors
    and to remember His holy covenant,
    the oath He swore to our father Abraham:
to rescue us from the hand of our enemies,
    and to enable us to serve Him without fear
    in holiness and righteousness before Him all our days."

Elizabeth watched through blurred eyes as Zechariah cradled and prophesied over this long-awaited child. His tears anointed John's face. The infant stared up at his abba as if he understood the importance of the words.

Silence replaced the earlier whispers and murmurings. Word of this happening would spread throughout the hills, reaching Jerusalem and Nazareth. The crowd leaned forward to hear Zechariah's every word, watching the joy and awe on his face.

"And you, my child, will be called a prophet of the Most High;
for you will go on before the Lord to prepare the way
for Him,
to give His people the knowledge of salvation
through the forgiveness of their sins,
because of the tender mercy of our God,
by which the rising sun will come to us from heaven
to shine on those living in darkness
and in the shadow of death,
to guide our feet into the path of peace."

Elizabeth covered her mouth with both hands. Her son—a prophet. John would prepare the way for his cousin Jesus, the Lord. That is why he'd leaped in her womb. Even before birth he'd recognized his Lord in Mary's womb. The wonder of it too amazing to grasp.

The mohel recited a prayer over the cup of wine and announced the infant's name as "John." He handed the cup to Zechariah. Zechariah sipped and gave the cup to Elizabeth.

"John bar Zechariah. A fine name," Myrah said. Nila hugged her.

Jesse, Caleb, the rabbi who'd served as the mohel, and a dozen other men surrounded Zechariah, intent on hearing the story of his vision. Finally, so all could hear, they agreed to meet in the synagogue.

As they walked away, Zechariah turned back, caught Elizabeth's attention.

And winked.

Letter from

THE AUTHOR

Dear Reader,

I've always admired Elizabeth. I think of her as a female Job—anchored in faith no matter the circumstances.

Her culture's expectation was for women to have children. Period. End of Sentence. No discussion.

Yet she remained childless.

If you live in a community with an HOA, you know communication is sent to homeowners not living up to expectations.

"Weed your yard."

"Water (or don't water) your grass."

"Trash cans may not be visible from the street."

Imagine what was communicated to those who did not or could not conform to bearing children! Yet, despite negative comments, disappointments, and heartbreak, Elizabeth is called "righteous."

In the Old Testament, "righteous" means being right with God. Being right with God meant having faith—no matter the circumstances.

Elizabeth has several milestones in which she makes a choice about faith. I'd love to hear from you about what draws you to deep reflection and then to wholeheartedly commit your way to our Lord.

Just for fun, the following fascinated me:

A year after a woman's cycle stopped, she was considered "old" in Bible times.

Menahem was a false messiah who lived just before our Lord Jesus.

Zechariah was the only man to inform his wife she was about to "be with child."

Blessings,

Texie Susan Gregory

A SCHOLAR'S VIEW
OF PRIESTLY CUSTOMS

Zechariah and Elizabeth's story is one that is steeped in ancient Jewish customs and history. As a member of the priesthood, Zechariah would have been able to trace his lineage back to the priestly order of Abijah, the division that began with King David and his desire to build the Temple. However, the priests' origin reached even further back to the Levites, the tribe named for Jacob's son Levi. After the exodus, at the foot of Mt. Sinai, they received an important distinction by being the only tribe that came to Moses's side to punish the tribes who worshiped the golden calf. The Levites were set apart and blessed for service to the Lord.

As the exodus unfolded, the descendants of Gershon, Kehot, and Merari, the three sons of Levi, had special assignments to carry the Ark and religious articles. Their descendants became the priests in the Temple. Along with these ceremonial tasks came special regulations. Levites were forbidden from drinking intoxicating beverages while serving in the tabernacle, having any contact with the dead, and marrying certain women. They also wore special vestments, turbans, and colorful sashes.

Another significant group may have been tied to John the Baptist's story. Some contemporary scholars suggest that John the Baptist may have been a member of the Essenes, who set themselves apart to pursue holiness and righteousness.

The Essenes are not mentioned in the New Testament. The first mention we have of them comes from the Roman scribe Pliny the Elder who described them as not having money, creating their own priestly class, existing for thousands of generations, and not marrying. He placed their location next to the Dead Sea. However, the only detailed account of the Essenes comes from Josephus in his singular history of the Romans conquering Israel. Only from his writings do we learn any details of Essene existence and their strict observance. Josephus tells us that they took a *mikveh* bath every morning, forbade any expression of anger, would not practice slavery, and were attentive to the names of angels kept in their sacred writings.

From Josephus's writings, we discover that the Essenes numbered in the thousands and lived across Judea. While fewer in number than the Sadducees and Pharisees, they shared in a common life in various cities. Their influence was undoubtedly felt by a priest like Zechariah.

I have walked through the ancient stone remains of their buildings and stood in the shadow of the towering cliffs overlooking the Dead Sea. The barren land was properly called the wilderness, with its treeless cascading cliffs and hidden wadis. If they wanted to escape civilization and the political turmoil plaguing Israel, the Essenes could not have found a more remote landscape. As I looked at the sheer steep bluffs where the Dead Sea Scrolls were found, I could see how devoted they must have been to maintain and keep safe the sacred writings.

Essenes began each day by facing the rising sun shining down on the Dead Sea. As I stood there and watched the red and orange reflections spread over the blue water, I could feel the inspiration they must have received.

A number of years ago, I met an antique dealer, Kando, the man who had first bought the Dead Sea Scrolls from a Bedouin. As we talked, he wanted me to see the clay jar the scrolls came in. Touching the vessel was like reaching across eons of time.

The connection to John the Baptist is mainly built on their similarities. John and the Essenes both practiced a baptism that required a change of heart and saw themselves as voices in the wilderness. The Essene leader called the "Teacher of Righteousness" was believed to be the messiah, while John proclaimed Jesus to be the Messiah. John had disciples, and the Essene community had many followers. Though there are undeniable commonalities, it cannot be decisively concluded if John the Baptist was, in fact, an Essene.

John the Baptist's life greatly resembled the life of a Nazarite. The name means "holy unto God." Two of the most notable Nazarites were Samuel and Samson. Their vows imparted extraordinary capacities, giving Samson physical strength and Samuel spiritual strength.

To become a Nazarite, a person took a vow to abstain from grapes or anything made from grapes. While they might drink other beverages containing alcohol, the *kashrut* law prohibited any consumption of wine. They could not trim their hair and allowed it to grow extremely long. In addition, they maintained ritual purity by having no contact with the dead, even within their own family.

A person became a Nazarite by verbally proclaiming their vow. Women as well as men could make the declaration. They proclaimed how long they wanted to be bound by the vow from a few days to a lifetime. In the days of John the Baptist, the person concluded the vow with a sacrificial offering at the Temple in Jerusalem.

Another aspect of Jewish identity we see in Elizabeth's story is the appearance of angels. Often described as "burning," meaning they had a fiery countenance, we can determine that angels must have been overwhelming when they appeared in that form. When Zechariah was confronted at the temple altar, he was gripped by fear.

Throughout the Old Testament angels brought messages and direction that God had for His people. In these stories, angels generally appear as humans surrounded by an aura of light. They are referred to as "sons of God," as well as "holy ones." Because angels are mysterious and often not understood in the Old Testament stories, they may leave us confounded just as Zechariah was. In the contemporary world, many people either have no idea that angels exist or doubt their existence. Nevertheless, the ancient stories stand as a testament to their importance.

Finally, and perhaps most centrally, we see the theme of a barren woman giving birth in her later years, only for that child to grow up to be greatly used by God to bring about His purposes. Elizabeth, being well past the time of childbearing, could not have found it easy to believe it when she found herself pregnant. But, like many women before her, she yielded her life—body, soul, and spirit—to God's greater purposes, and became the mother to the forerunner of the Messiah.

Zechariah and Elizabeth were surrounded by the hallmarks of time and eternity.

Fiction Author

TEXIE SUSAN GREGORY

Every night when Texie Susan Gregory was a little girl, her mother, with an expressive voice and face, brought life to a Bible story. The stories became so familiar that sometimes the people seemed like distant relatives—Grandfather Abraham, Uncle Paul, Cousin Esther.

After discovering Elizabeth Speare's book *The Bronze Bow,* she realized people other than those she "knew" had lived and loved and laughed during Bible times. Astonishing!

Thus began her quest to write the stories of both the unknown and well-known people of biblical times.

Studying why people act and respond the way they do fascinates her. She has a master's degree in School Counseling as well as in Religious Education.

North Carolina born and bred, she and her husband are now empty nesters living in Michigan.

Nonfiction Author
ROBERT L. WISE, Ph.D.

The Rev. Robert L. Wise, Ph.D., is the author of thirty-five books and numerous articles published in English, Spanish, Dutch, Chinese, Japanese, and German. On the internet he weekly publishes *Miracles Never Cease* and monthly presents live interviews on YouTube with people who have experienced divine interventions.

Read on for a sneak peek of another exciting story in the Extraordinary Women of the Bible series!

WOMAN OF REDEMPTION: BATHSHEBA'S STORY

BY GINGER GARRETT

Tell me a story, Abba," Bathsheba said, sitting on her father's knee, her head cradled against his chest. He smelled of balsam today, which was rare. He usually smelled of his donkey, but Imma had prepared a bath for him to celebrate his return. The outlaw king Abba served, David, had gone to seek counsel from Samuel, and so his Mighty Men had dispersed to their homes. Those who had homes nearby, that is. Some men were rogues and loners, strays who lived in the shadows. Other men, like her grandfather Ahithophel, one of David's military advisers, stayed close no matter what, always whispering in David's ear.

Bathsheba did not like her grandfather. Betel seeds always stained his teeth, and his breath stank of onions. His eyes darted around the room when he talked, and he never looked at her.

"Your abba needs to rest," Imma scolded Bathsheba, extending her arms, urging Bathsheba to abandon Abba's lap.

Bathsheba turned away, refusing to see. Although eleven years old and practically an adult, she could still pretend she was a little child.

"It's all right, my love. One story before bed." Bathsheba felt Abba's laugh resonate throughout his chest.

She loved the evenings of his homecomings. Imma made such good food, the fires burned late, and she didn't have to go to bed when the sky was still pale. She could wait until all the world was dark, and the stars roamed overhead. Abba said the great God, Yahweh, called each star by name. They had names and answered to His call! What did Yahweh feed them, that flock in the sky?

"Let's see, my little one…," Abba murmured. "It's been four years now since that day."

Bathsheba loved her little stone-and-mud home in Giloh, a sleepy town near Bethlehem, just south of Jerusalem. Her abba was gone from it too often, fighting with David and all his men. Although Bathsheba had only seen this outlaw king David from a distance, she knew he was a fierce, wild man.

Because of that man, Imma was often alone. Because of him, Imma worried.

Why didn't Grandfather Ahithophel give David counsel that would bring peace, and not endless fights? Bathsheba blamed him, even if she knew the situation was complicated. But she saw the hard glint in Grandfather's darting eyes whenever he visited. He desired power above peace. When Bathsheba was busy preparing food, she felt his eyes upon her, like a man who wants to turn a stone over and see what hides underneath. He wanted to know if she had secrets. She could feel it. He wanted to know if she might have anything of value.

Grandfather Ahithophel stayed with David wherever he went. Many people said he had the gift of military wisdom. He was a strategist, they said. Bathsheba knew that wisdom was different than goodness, however. Grandfather was a cold man with no smiles for children.

Imma was too busy running the household to worry about her father-in-law and his ambition. Imma just worked and worried. King Saul's men always hoped to capture David and put an end to his claim to the throne. Raiding parties from the East worried her too, but Sea Peoples might attack from the West. That would be worse, Bathsheba thought. No one knew much about the Sea Peoples, only that they were cruel and lived on the water, attacking villages for supplies and slaves. There could be no worse fate than to be carried away to serve as a slave to a pagan tribe.

The village of Giloh was quiet whenever Abba and the fighting men left. That was what troubled Imma most, Bathsheba knew. The men who remained in the village were tradesman, craftsmen, farmers. None were warriors, and these were lawless times. King Saul had hunted David, and her abba, for years.

It made little sense. David was once Saul's armor-bearer and court musician. He was also his son's closest friend. Why did Saul choose David, love David, then mark him for death? What had Saul seen in him?

Bathsheba was grateful that Abba had never attracted the attention of an inconstant king like Saul. He had a good life here at home with Imma, Bathsheba, her older brothers and younger sisters.

She nestled further in, waiting for the story.

Imma frowned at them both. "Not one of the scary tales, Eliam. It is too close to bed." She walked to the front door, cracked it open, and then looked out in either direction before withdrawing the oil lamp from its perch near the door.

Even now, with Abba at home, she worried.

Abba laughed, and Bathsheba felt the vibration in his chest, the booming sound of his laughter as an echo. No one was stronger than her abba. The king had never wanted to kill the Mighty Men, anyway. Truthfully, Saul needed them desperately to fight the Philistines. Saul's only desire was to kill David. It was a strange obsession, a hunt for a prize that eluded him year after year. Bathsheba had seen Saul only last year when he passed through Giloh seeking supplies after another battle with the Philistines. Dark circles had shaded the skin under his eyes, and his lips were a thin line, with no gratitude for his people, even as they came out from their houses bearing gifts. He didn't even seem to see them, though his eyes scanned the crowds, running back and forth. Perhaps he hoped to see David, but the look in his eyes scared Bathsheba. This kind of hope had a bitter, dreadful edge to it. Bathsheba hoped she never felt that.

"And so it was that King Saul was chasing us through the desert of En Gedi," Abba began the tale.

"Why was he chasing you?" she asked.

He tapped her lightly on the head. "No interruptions."

She giggled. She'd heard the story before and knew when he had left out an important detail.

"King Saul wants to kill David, of course. The prophet Samuel anointed David as the next king many years ago, when David was a boy of no more than twelve. Just about your age, in fact. Saul heard the report and was displeased. He likes being king."

Bathsheba giggled.

"But David's men can climb the crags as well as any ibex or goat, so we climbed and hid in a cave, waiting for Saul and his men to pass by. Did you know how many men were with Saul? Three thousand! We could see the dust their animals kicked up from miles away! How did he plan to sneak up on us?"

"But you only had six hundred men," Bathsheba prompted.

Abba clicked his teeth, reprimanding her for the interruption.

"Six hundred were loyal to David, but have you ever tried to fit six hundred men in a cave? No, most of the men separated from us and traveled on, hoping to lead Saul away. David and a few remaining warriors hid in the cave. But the strangest thing happened. Saul had to relieve himself."

"Ew!" Bathsheba could not resist adding her commentary. She did not like the details at this part of the story.

"Guess what cave he chose? Ours! The very cave we hid in." Abba pretended to slap himself in the forehead, and Bathsheba giggled again. "He had his back to us, and the sun coming in from the mouth of the cave illuminated his outline like he was a golden calf. We could not see each other's expressions in the darkness, which is a blessing from Yahweh, I am sure, because we might have burst out laughing. When he lifted his robe and squatted down, we all saw his bare bottom. I have never fought a harder battle than I did that day, restraining myself from laughter. But David crept forward, like a lizard, silent, stealthy, and lifted his knife. Saul had no idea he was about to die."

Bathsheba held her breath, waiting.

"Yet David crawled back to us in the darkness, a tassel in his hand."

"He had Saul's *tzitzit?*" she gasped. What an insult, to cut away one of the tassels Yahweh commanded men to wear at the four corners of their robes. The tassel was a visible reminder of the power and majesty of the Lord and the glory of His commandments. David had stripped Saul of his obligation, and now the king wore a damaged robe. She wondered what Saul did with the robe. He probably burned it in fury, but he deserved to wear it just as it was.

"David refused to act in dishonor," Abba continued, and told of David confronting Saul outside the cave. "To kill a king appointed by Yahweh, to take the throne before it is given? No. David contents himself to wait for the proper time."

Bathsheba's eyelids were getting heavy. "David waits too long, Abba. I don't want you to be gone so much."

"It can't last forever, darling girl. Saul knows we spared his life and that his reign is ending. David is, and always has been, the more honorable man. That is why I follow him. That is why he will be our greatest king."

"When he is king, will we be rich?" she asked.

He laughed and stood, lifting her in his arms as he did. "Rich? I am a man who has everything in the world already."

"But I would like a doll from the traders," Bathsheba said. "One with embroidered eyes and a linen robe."

Abba kissed her forehead. Her eyelids were heavy. Bathsheba smiled as she drifted into sleep, safe in Abba's arms. Tonight, she would dream of a day when Imma did not worry and the right man wore the crown.

"Samuel is dead."

The words were like burning cinders floating in the air, terrifying Bathsheba as they fell.

Abba had returned home, looking despondent when he made the proclamation to the family. It was the following year, and Bathsheba had been hoping for news that David was now king.

"Was it Saul?" Bathsheba asked. Since Samuel had been the prophet to anoint David as the next king, Saul must have wanted revenge. In her heart, secretly, she wondered if her grandfather had betrayed the old man. Samuel had anointed David years ago, but David hadn't gotten the throne yet. Maybe Grandfather tired of waiting and thought killing Samuel would hasten things along.

"No." Abba's stern look silenced her. "Not even Saul would dare touch a prophet of Yahweh."

Bathsheba cast her eyes to the floor, shamed that she had harbored such thoughts about her own flesh and bone. But she knew the truth about men in power, even if Abba did not want to remember. King Saul had killed priests of Yahweh years ago, in a fit of rage after they hid David and helped him and his men escape. Abba owed his life to those dead priests, and he never spoke of it. The debt, he worried, was simply too great, and he feared it would fall on his sons to repay the Lord. But who could repay the Lord for a murder of one of His servants? Bathsheba reasoned easily that if Saul could kill a priest, he could kill a prophet. Especially a prophet that anointed another man king in his place.

"It was time that killed Samuel," Abba replied wearily. "He lived to see ninety years of age." Abba sat back on the reclining couch, and Imma ran to fetch him a cup of wine. Bathsheba noticed how her hands shook. Death was never comforting news, no matter the age it arrived.

Abba crooked a finger to motion Bathsheba to come near. She did, and he reached into the sack at his waist and retrieved a cloth doll made from linens dyed blue and red. The craftsman had embroidered the eyes with delicate stitches. She gasped with delight and hugged him, forgetting the somber occasion for his return home. Abba always had a gift for her, whether it was a kind word or a present he brought home from his travels. And she'd never had a doll as lovely as this. She kissed Abba on the cheek and settled on the floor to play, listening to her parents and their concerns. Although she was twelve, and probably on the verge of betrothal, no girl could resist a doll as lovely as this.

"What will become of us?" Imma asked. What would become of the Hebrew people without a prophet, a man who stood between them to speak for God?

Why had the people begged for a king? Samuel had never wanted to anoint Saul, but anointing David had caused no end of strife. The family of Saul hated the family of David.

Bathsheba did not understand. If Yahweh wanted David to be king, why was Saul still on the throne? Now they had no prophet. And with the conflict between Saul and David, there was not one king, but two.

Abba's rich voice filled the room. "The Lord is my shepherd. I shall not want."

Bathsheba loved this song of David's! She stood next to Abba, her voice joining his. Her older brothers joined after a moment's hesitation.

"He maketh me to lie down in green pastures. He leadeth me beside the still waters. He restoreth my soul. He leadeth me in the paths of righteousness for His name's sake."

Imma watched them all with a tender smile, then gave in and sang the last verses with them.

"Yea, though I walk through the valley of the shadow of death, I will fear no evil, for Thou art with me. Thy rod and Thy staff they comfort me. Thou preparest a table before me in the presence of mine enemies. Thou anointest my head with oil. My cup runneth over."

Bathsheba quieted her voice on the final line, wanting to hear her abba's deep voice resonating against the mud-and-stone walls of her home.

"Surely goodness and mercy shall follow me all the days of my life, and I will dwell in the house of the Lord forever."

Breathing deeply, she felt the peace of the Lord in these words, and in this home. How did David capture the very essence of petitioning prayer and put it into words? That was how his songs seemed to her, and to everyone who sang them. He did so much more than just lead men into battle. He led souls to worship, and knees to bow before the highest throne. That was why her abba trusted David. That was why Imma could know the family would be secure, even after the death of Samuel. Bathsheba felt her heart glowing like a coal from the oven, thinking of the goodness of this outlaw king. One day David would wear the crown with the blessing of all the tribes of Israel, and she would rejoice.

Find inspiration, find faith, find Guideposts.

Shop our best sellers and favorites at
guideposts.org/shop

Or scan the QR code to go directly
to our Shop

Printed in the United States
by Baker & Taylor Publisher Services